The Shots at Iron Mountain

A Story of Two Men – Tom Horn and Geronimo

By

Jiri Cernik

DORRANCE
PUBLISHING CO
EST. 1920
PITTSBURGH, PENNSYLVANIA 15238

Dorrance Publishing Co
585 Alpha Drive
Suite 103
Pittsburgh, PA 15238
Visit our website at *www.dorrancebookstore.com*

ISBN: 978-1-4809-3503-7
eISBN: 978-1-4809-3526-6

To all those who believed he was not guilty.

Riding hard, drinking hard, fighting hard - so he passed his days, until he was crushed between the grindstones of two civilizations.

Glendolene Myrtle Kimmell

Table of Contents

PREFACE

The history of crime is replete with cases when culprits were never apprehended or if he or she was, the results of the investigation were not always received by the public as fully satisfactory. Just offhand we can mention the famous murders committed in England in 1888 by so called "Jack the Ripper", only a nickname for the perpetrator who was never caught. Here in the U.S. we can mention the death of John Peters Ringo, or perhaps Ringgold in 1882. Ringo was one of the leaders of the infamous "cowboy gang" in the vicinity of Tombstone which was eventually dispersed by the Earp brothers and John H. Holliday. On July 14th, 1882 his body was found in an oak grove near Smith's ranch house. It was believed that he had committed suicide, but his cartridge belt was upside down, his pistol was stuck in the watch chain, his foot-wraps were clean even though it had rained the previous night and the head wound did not bear any signs of burned gunpowder. The more realistic conclusion would be that he was shot from a distance and then the body was carried and leaned against a tree fork not far from his campfire. From the more recent history we can mention the assassination of President John. F. Kennedy. The questions of whether it was solely an act of a loner Lee H. Oswald or whether it was a matter of a larger conspiracy still linger.

From the legalistic point of view the story of Tom Horn has all three essential elements - the murder, the arrest of the killer and the trial. What numerous historians, legal minds and authors do not agree about, however, is the question whether Tom Horn had actually committed this crime. The book I am presenting to the readers is not an accurate historical narrative but a novel based on historical facts, in another words creative non-fiction written as a mystery. Even though most of the characters are real and most episodes actually took place, their sequence and description were modified to fit better into the literary format of the story. For example, the original trial lasted two weeks and not three days as mentioned in the book and many more witnesses were called in. To maintain the flow of the narration and not to overtax the reader's memory, only the most essential testimonies are introduced.

The book is based on two biographic works, namely *The Saga of Tom Horn* by Dean F. Krakel (University of Nebraska Press, 1954) and *Tom Horn* by Chip Carlson (Beartooth Corral, 1991), and the autobiographic work *Life of Tom Horn, Government Scout and Interpreter* written by Tom Horn when in prison and published for the first time in 1904 by John C. Coble. As additional sources I used the court records, correspondence between Tom Horn and his friends, letters written to his lawyers and an extensive statement of Glendolene M. Kimmell.

The Denver Post reporter Rick Jackson is a fictitious character and his articles "Chatting with the Chief of Indian Scouts" are modified excerpts from Horn's own book in order to give the reader some idea about his background. Here we can say that the lives of both men - Horn and Geronimo - were closely connected and it is a sad irony that in the end they both became the victims of a rapid societal change to which they could not or perhaps did not want to adjust.

The description of the landscape and places where individual episodes took place is relatively accurate and is based on many available materials including my own visit of this area. On this occasion I would like to thank James McGuire, a rancher from Chugwater and his wife who kindly took me to the top of Iron Mountain and showed me the spots where Miller's and Nickell's ranches and Miss Kimmell's school used to stand and to a small monument which up to the present days marks the site where two shots prematurely ended the life of a fourteen year old boy, Willie Nickell.

Special thanks go also to Angela Adams who proofread the original manuscript.

The Author, December 7, 2015

1

A stocky youngster walked out of a log cabin, looked around at the overcast morning sky and carefully studied the low lying clouds. In a short while the drizzling rain made his face wet, so he turned around and stepped back inside. Several minutes later the door opened again and the same boy appeared in the doorframe. This time, however, his body was wrapped in a long slicker and his head was covered by a large felt hat. The raincoat as well as the hat apparently belonged to an older person because the raincoat reached to his feet and from under the hat one could see only his freckled nose.

The boy who could not be fifteen years old yet, jumped over several puddles and ran down a long, gentle slope toward a large enclosure. There he opened a little gate and as soon as he slipped inside, bleating from about hundred sheep which demanded the morning feeding, filled the corral. The boy pushed his way through the avalanche of white furs to a small shanty and using a metal bucket he began to carry out ground corn mixed with oats and dumped it into long wooden troughs. The sheep submerged their pink muzzles in the feed and after a while the entire enclosure fell silent.

The youngster threw the bucket in the shanty, climbed onto the fence and tried to count all the sheep. Yesterday evening he shot a coyote near the creek. It was probably attracted by the bleating of the young lambs and if he did not have his dog Shepp with him, he would not have known that it was stalking the herd.

"...fifty-two, fifty-three, fifty-four, fifty-five..." The boy's lips were slowly moving and his index finger kept rhythmically pointing toward the furry animals.

The moment he started to count the sheep at the second trough, a silhouette of a man flashed on the opposite hill and all of a sudden a rifle barrel emerged behind a large boulder. It slanted toward the corral, once or twice it moved to the left and to the right as if the man holding it were not sure where to aim and then it became motionless.

"...seventy-six, seventy-seven, seventy-eight..." Suddenly it occurred to the boy that he had counted the sheep with black ears twice. "Seventy-seven, seventy..."

A shot cracked from on the hill. The youngster spread his arms and as if swept by some giant hand then fell among the sheep. He lay there for several seconds stunned by pain and then he slowly moved to the fence, carefully crawled under the lower board and tried to get up. His right shoulder burned as if it were on fire and the bloodied arm hung limp along his torso. He finally erected himself and took a few steps toward the cabin when another shot rang out. The boy felt a sharp pain in his chest, his knees gave out and he collapsed again on the ground. He could not see anything, only the bleating of frightened sheep kept ringing in his ears, but it got gradually weaker and weaker as if coming from a far distance… and then it stopped.

2

Rick Jackson leaned back in his chair which dangerously creaked, looked at a corpulent guy on the other side of the room, and mumbled rather to himself than to him, "Damn work. Jeff stays at home and I am supposed to take care of it."

Now a few words of explanation are needed. The fat guy in an unbuttoned vest was Pete Swain, the editor-in-chief of the popular Denver daily *The Denver Post* and Jeff was Rick's colleague who covered events in the whole territory of Colorado. The past two or three days he had been fighting the flu, but today it really knocked him down and he had stayed at home. Rick had to substitute because a newspaper does not stop appearing just because of one sick guy. It sure did not make him happy. Rick's job was to inform the readers primarily about events in the neighboring states and there could not be any doubt that within a single day more than enough things happened to report. Then around noon came a report about a mining disaster in Telluride. He had never been in a mine and now he was supposed to come up with a story about collapsed tunnels and decide from whose point of view to present it. Should he report it from the miners' view that they did not timber enough because they were paid only for the extracted ore or from the point of view of the mine owners who could care less about the lives of a bunch of people working for them? He had been sweating over this article since lunch but he still did not like it.

Rick got up, stepped up to the window and looked at the blinding glare of the gilded dome of the state capitol. The setting sun turned it literally into a giant burning ball which now shone over the whole town. Then he watched with envy about a dozen of boys who with yelling and screaming conducted a major snowball battle near the entrance to the city park. He just wondered what Pete would say if, without saying a word, he would run down to join them. Rick enjoyed for several minutes the idea of pressing wet snow in his hand and trying to hit some of those unkempt heads but then turned around and went back to his desk. When he was about to sit down, the door flew suddenly open and the messenger from the telegraph room on the first floor ran in. He was waving a piece of paper in his hand and seeing the asking stares of both men, he exclaimed, "They arrested Tom Horn today in Cheyenne! Look, right here. It's the cable from the sheriff's office."

Rick grabbed the cable and scanned several lines which dryly announced that Tom Horn had been arrested that afternoon in Cheyenne due to suspicion that he was the murderer of William Nickell who was killed on his father's ranch in June last year. On the bottom of the cable there was the name of the Cheyenne sheriff and the day's date - January 13, 1902.

Pete's surprised eyes, hidden behind glasses with a wire rim, travelled from the messenger to Rick and back to the messenger, but then he could not resist the curiosity and extricated himself from behind his desk and shuffled over to both men. Rick, without saying a word, handed him the cable and stepped up to a tall file cabinet storing hundreds of folders with newspaper articles and other printed materials collected within the past ten years. While Pete studied the cable, Rick kept pulling out one drawer after another, went through neatly filed folders and eventually pulled two of them out. The first one, pretty worn out due to frequent use, carried the typed title "Cattle Rustling in Wyoming", and on the other one there were just two handwritten words – "Tom Horn".

Rick sat down, opened the folder dealing with the cattle rustling and began to rummage in the clippings from the local, as well as out of state dailies, that were primarily from Cheyenne and Casper.

Pete signaled the messenger that he may leave and then bent over Rick.

"Here it is," interrupted the silence as Rick pointed at two articles.

One read "Fourteen-year-old William Nickell murdered. His neighbor J. Miller is the prime suspect. Due to the lack of evidence, the further investigation was stopped." The other one offered follow-up information: "Kels Nickell seriously wounded and taken to the Cheyenne hospital. While gone, his herd of sheep was destroyed. The perpetrator or perpetrators are unknown."

"Both articles are from the *Cheyenne Examiner* and based on them I prepared a report for us."

Pete scratched his bald head and then while hesitating a little asked, "And what has Tom Horn to do with all that?"

Rick smiled, opened the other folder and spread a pile of old yellowing newspaper articles. Some came from local publications, others from Phoenix, Tombstone, Cheyenne, Oklahoma City and one even from Florida. One could smell the atmosphere of the Old West which the local old timers kept reminiscing about in the Denver saloons. The faded photos of cavalry troopers, Indian scouts and Apache chiefs, whose names once horrified all settlers south of Phoenix, were taken twenty or thirty years ago. Rick never met Tom Horn, but his personality interested him so much that for many years he kept collecting any information about him including even some insignificant tidbits. Based on these articles, readers could get a pretty good idea who this man actually was. As a sixteen year old he joined the U.S. Army, namely those units which oversaw the San Carlos and White Mountain reservations. His superior, Al Sieber, sent him to the village of Chief Pedro where he lived among the Indians and learned their language and customs. After a year's stay there he not only spoke fluent Apache but could spend weeks in the desert and come back in one piece. When Sieber retired, Horn took over his job as the chief of scouts. In 1886 he made himself quite popular by helping to track down Geronimo and mediated a meeting between him and General Miles. When the Apache war was over, Horn worked for the Pinkerton Detective Agency and successfully tracked down the McCoy Gang which specialized in train robberies. An article clipped from the Florida paper mentioned him as a commander of the supply units during the Spanish-American War in Cuba. The last article, from Cheyenne, brought the news that the big ranchers of Laramie County hired him as a stock detective whose job was to deal with cattle rustling.

"What has Tom Horn to do with all that?" repeated Rick.

"Maybe a lot or maybe nothing, but the fact is that the Miller's as well as Nickell's ranches are both located in the area where Horn was supposed to look for the rustlers. If he found stolen cow or cows at a place owned by some small rancher, it doesn't take a genius to figure out that the rustlers would try to put the blame for this murder on Horn. When would they get another opportunity like that?"

Pete kept flipping for while through the clippings and then he made a sort of a speculative remark. "Well, this chap has quite a reputation, that's for sure. I guess it wouldn't hurt to make an interview with him, would it? The only question is whether he would be willing to talk or not."

Rick happily grinned and readily responded, "Boss, leave it to me. When I show him this folder, he'll open up. You know how it is. We all have a hidden vanity streak. The Cheyenne train leaves every morning, but someone should call there to reserve a room for me because once the word gets around that

Horn is in jail, newspaper reporters like me will be swarming there by the dozen from all directions." Pete nodded his head, stepped up to the safe and placed on a table one hundred dollars in ten dollar bills. Rick put them in his pocket and sat down to his desk to finish the story about the mining disaster in Telluride before his departure for Cheyenne.

3

A locomotive with five Pullmans puffed into the Cheyenne depot around one o'clock in the afternoon. One could hear the screeching of the breaks, the hissing sound of released steam, and then the calling of the conductors announcing a fifteen-minute stop before the train continued to Casper. Rick carefully jumped from the foot board onto trampled snow, buttoned up his coat and holding a small suitcase in his hand walked to the depot building. He passed through a half empty lobby and was about to turn to the right when he couldn't believe his eyes. There were two cabs standing right at the wooden sidewalk. When he was in Cheyenne last summer no one would dream about such a novelty. Needless to say, instead of wading through snow on his way to the hotel, he readily climbed into one cab and called at the driver, "The Silver Horse Shoe Hotel!"

The driver clicked his tongue and the horse took off at a sharp clip toward the city center. Rick watched curiously the new brick buildings which had replaced the old clapboard stores and saloons and then he spotted the Cheyenne Club. The two-story, stone edifice built in the Victorian style was surrounded by numerous carriages and several sleighs upholstered with red velvet, indicating that their owners were quite well off. Some men in long fur coats and broad hats stood in small groups on the wooden terrace, and Rick could tell from the distance that they were engaged in a heated conversation. The others stood aside and read with great interest the day's issue of *The Cheyenne Examiner*. There was no doubt that the news about Horn's arrest had brought to the club most of the wealthy ranchers from Laramie County. As a matter of fact, most of them owed Horn a lot for bringing back many heads of stolen and rebranded cattle. A few of them also knew that when it was necessary, he stopped rustling once for all. His Winchester rarely missed.

The hotel was another surprise. The building was renovated, the black and white sign with the name of the hotel was brand new, and when Rick entered he thought for a moment that he had gotten the addresses mixed up. The old gas lamps dated back to the time of Wolcott's disastrous campaign against Buffalo were gone, and instead of them an electric and ostentatious chandelier, imported undoubtedly from the East, flooded the lobby with bright light.

Rick signed his name into the registration book, asked the bell boy to take his suitcase to his room, and stepped into the adjacent room serving as a saloon. The extensive renovation did not stop here either. A large color print of a naked woman which hung on the opposite wall for years was gone and it was replaced by a panorama of the snow covered Rocky Mountains. The eastern prudery obviously made it all the way here and so the rich buxom of an unknown model had to give way to morally unobjectionable natural scenery. The long wooden bar which wore the marks of many cowboys that used to stand there and wash down the dust after a long ride to town with cheap whisky was also gone. In its place stood a long, massive bar with a marble top decorated by rich, brass metalwork. Only the piano and the music teacher who was moonlighting here had not changed, however, his music did and instead of cowboy songs he played the latest Broadway hits. Needless to say, a cowboy covered with dust was nowhere to be seen.

Rick was about to step to the bar and order a glass of beer when he overheard an excited voice at its far end.

"Man, how can you claim something like that! I am Tom's friend. All the time he stayed in Wyoming he lived at my ranch. The crap you are telling me now is nothing but goddamn hearsay spread by this miserable paper."

A short man with mustache and dressed by the latest fashion waved his hand and angrily hit the bar top with the newspaper. It definitely caught Rick's attention. He remained at the door and waited to see how this debate would play out.

The other man, a tall, powerful guy with a tanned face giving the distinct impression that he was a rancher or a foreman, just looked at his cowboy boots and calmly remarked, "Tom Horn has a reputation of being a coldblooded killer. If I was you, I wouldn't stick up so much for him. 'Cause when the sheriff puts some heat to him and finds out who paid him, them big ranchers will be in pretty hot water." Then without waiting how the man with a mustache would respond, he threw a silver half dollar on the bar, put his hat on, and walked to the door.

Rick stepped aside, let him pass, and then focused on the other guy. The man had gotten red in the face, opened his mouth as if he wanted to say something, but then he waved his hand, took the paper and sat down at the next vacant table. There he opened the paper again and started to read an article which covered almost the whole page. Rick figured that now was the right time to start investigating. He walked to the table and politely asked if he could join him.

The gentleman with the mustache didn't even raise his eyes, just mumbled something like, "Yeah, help yourself."

Rick sat down and pulled out of his breast pocket a yellow envelope with the clippings about Tom Horn. He laid couple of them on the table, cleared his throat and addressed the unknown man. "Excuse me for interrupting, but I was quite unintentionally a witness to the conversation you had over there at the bar and, among other things, I heard that you are a friend of Tom Horn."

"So what?" came the growling response.

"Well, you know, I don't think that Tom is a coldblooded killer either. And as to the article here in this paper, I read it in the morning. It looks like he doesn't have too many friends among the local press corps, does he?"

The man with the mustache gave Rick a scrutinizing look and then glanced at the clippings on the table.

"Sorry for not introducing myself right away. My name is Rick Jackson and a while ago I arrived from Denver," added Rick and extended his hand across the table.

"John Coble," answered the stranger and hesitatingly shook Rick's hand.

"Why don't you look at this as it will certainly interest you," said Rick and pushed the clippings toward him.

Coble took several strips of yellow paper with his fingers and began to read. Gradually the sullen expression of his face disappeared and finally he asked quite excitedly, "Where did you get all this?"

Rick now struggled. Should he tell the guy that he was also a reporter or maybe wait until he was positively sure that he has gained his trust? He decided to start from the other end.

"Well, I have known Horn for almost twenty years." Coble, quite surprised, raised his eyebrows and so Rick quickly added, "Of course only distantly. Actually I have never met him in person, but I read about him for the first time in the paper when I was fifteen and from then on my interest in his life just grew. Then when I read in *The Denver Post* that he had gotten into a trouble, I decided to …"

"Wait," interrupted him Coble. "What trouble? According to this newspaper the sheriff arrested Tom under very strange circumstances. I am sure that when the judge looks at it, Tom will be set free right away. There is no trouble worth talking about."

"Exactly, but I think I could help Tom even before this whole affair gets to the judge."

Talking about help caught Coble's attention.

"Help? Of course we'll take anything that would help him, but how? You know a good lawyer or...?"

"Unfortunately not, but if this case goes to the jury, it will be necessary to change a little bit the opinion of the general public and that can be done only through the newspapers. In another words, if a paper published a series of articles which present Tom as a hero and a decent man, that would have definitely a positive effect, don't you think?"

"Yeah, but how do you want to do it? You have just read what they write about him."

Rick realized that he could not play this game any longer and that he had to reveal his true identity after all. "If you convince Tom to tell me something about his past, I do promise that unlike the local rags including *The Cheyenne Examiner, The Denver Post* will report about him only in an unbiased way and whenever possible it will highlight the positive information."

Coble put on again the sullen face, frowned and responded with sarcasm. "Why should I believe that you are any better than the others?"

Rick smiled and pointed at the clippings. "You really believe that I would hurt, without any reason, a person about whom I have collected this stuff on for twenty years? Didn't you say a minute ago that Tom could use any help he could get? I am pretty sure that you don't have too many offers like this, do you?"

It was obvious that Coble didn't want to act in haste. He thought a while about what he heard, then got up, paid the barkeep for the drinks and turned to Rick. "Okay. Let's go. The jail is not far away."

As soon as they left the hotel, they walked toward the railroad station and then they turned onto the Fourth Street. Along the way Coble talked freely where and how he met Tom Horn.

"It was in the spring of 1900. I was coming home to the ranch I own not far from Bosler in the neighboring county. I don't know if you are familiar with that area. It is about sixty miles from here going northwest. There was a cattle auction in Laramie and so I stayed there overnight. In the morning around nine, I stopped at the corral where the sale was going on. I figured I'd stay for a while, listen to the prices, and then keep on going home. First, they were selling individual cows and steers and I was just about to get up and leave when three cowboys drove in a whole herd of maybe ten heifers and four steers. The auctioneer looked at the bill of sale, nodded his head and started; however at that very moment a rider showed up at the corral, raised his hand and when the surprised auctioneer stopped calling the price, the man on horse announced that the herd was stolen. The auctioneer shrugged his shoulders saying that he was not aware of anything like that because the bill of sale seemed to be okay. The stranger stretched out his hand and the auctioneer handed over to him the paper. The whole place was so silent that you could hear a pin drop. Well, not to make the story too long, the man on horse was Tom Horn. He looked at the bill of sale and asked those three cowboys where they got that herd. They readily responded that the herd belonged to George Wrightman from the ranch Double O and that George had bought these cows last year from Jim Bowers. Horn frowned and what he said shocked all the present onlookers. He said, 'Jim Bowers died two years ago and his signature was falsified. These heifers and bulls belong to John Coble.'

"You can imagine that when I heard my name I almost fell off the bench. Horn then quoted the Wyoming law about stolen cattle and ordered the auctioneer to hold onto those cows until the original owners would claim them. Well, I didn't wait any longer and walked to the corral. All the cows were of the Hereford breed just like we have at our ranch. Some ranchers experimented with the black and white Angus because they are bigger, but I prefer Hereford. They are tougher and take better the cold weather. When I stepped into the corral and looked at the first cow, I had to admit that whoever re-branded 'J-C' to 'O-O' was pretty handy with the running iron; however, that first 'O' was not clean and one could still see a little bit of that upper bar from the letter J.

"Those three realized that the game was up. One tried to reach for his six shooter, but Tom pulled out his Winchester and the boys decided to hightail it for the mountains. So I introduced myself and invited Tom to my ranch. Along the way he told me that he was hired by the neighboring ranchers as a cattle detective to fight this lawlessness. Then he complained that these big ranches are quite far apart and sometimes it takes him several days to move from one to another. When I offered to let him stay at my place, because that would cut his travel time in half, he gladly accepted. Needless to say that from that time on my cattle stopped disappearing. On the other hand, it is also a fact that the small ranchers who didn't mind enlarging their herds on my account hated his guts. "

After about ten minutes of walking they stopped in front of a three-story brick building with a large sign over the main entrance: "The County Courthouse". Coble, however, took a few more steps toward the end of the building and opened the door next to which one small plaque bore a simple sign: "Sheriff and Deputy U.S. Marshal". Followed by Rick he walked in. The marshal's office was empty but in the adjacent room, thanks to the open door, one could hear a deep voice lecturing somebody.

"When food is being delivered to the prisoners, the man in the cell has to stand at least ten feet away from the bars and is not allowed to step any closer until the food is placed inside and the cell door is locked again." The voice further emphasized, "When the jailer has both hands full, he is defenseless like a baby, regardless of how many guns he has hanging on his belt. He must have his eyes glued to the prisoner until the moment when he steps out. Otherwise, it is only a question of time until some of the prisoners manage to grab the jailer's gun and pull it out of the holster. Then the jailer's life is not worth a pitcher of warm spit."

Both men were listening to his sermon for a while, but then Coble stepped to the door and looked inside. There he saw a tall, square-built guy with a tin star on his shirt as he was preaching to his new jailer on how to behave during his rounds among the prisoners.

When he finally paused, Coble cleaned his throat and said, "We are looking for the sheriff."

The hulk of man turned around and with appropriate importance announced that the sheriff was not currently present, that he was at the court and that he was his deputy. Then he quickly added, "While the sheriff is gone, I take care of all official business."

Coble recognized Leslie Snow as one of the cowboys from the neighboring ranch. "My friend and I came to see Tom Horn," he stated with a shaky voice.

Snow looked both men over and then coarsely laughed, "I'll be damned. This guy is really lucky. We locked him up yesterday and today he's already got visitors." Then he gestured them to step up to the desk and pushed in front of them a big green book to sign in. Coble took the pen-holder and wrote down his name and address and then handed it over to Rick. He signed his full name - Frederick Jackson - and in small letters added - *The Denver Post*, Denver. After the signing they were ready to follow the jailer upstairs, but Snow informed them that the official procedure was not yet over.

"Wait! First I have to search you. That's the regulations."

Coble was about to explode, but when he saw that Rick took it with enviable calm, shrugged it off and spread his arms, so the former cowboy turned lawman could make sure that they were not trying to smuggle any weapons into the jail. Once the body search was over, Joe, an older, friendly looking guy took the keys off the wall and all three headed for the staircase leading to the second floor. On the way up Rick looked around with great interest. When they were passing a small window, he noticed that the jail was actually a rectangular addition to the eastern wing of the courthouse. The cells were located only along the right side of the corridor and they looked more like cages for wild beasts than a place to house people. It also didn't escape his attention that the individual prisoners were not only separated by bars but that also the ceiling and the outside walls were covered with the lattice so that any attempt to dig one's way out was out of the question. To cut through the steel rods would require tremendous patience and also a significant amount of high quality files.

They stopped on the second floor at cell number ten. Joe pulled out his pocket watch, flipped the cover open and in an official voice announced, "The visit is allowed only for half an hour. During the visit neither of you nor the prisoner are allowed to approach the bars. If you have brought him something, you have to leave it downstairs in the office. You can sit here on the bench." Then he turned around, walked back to the staircase and sat down on a chair.

Rick leaned forward and looked inside the cell. There on a simple bed sat a dark-haired man. As soon as he heard somebody coming, he turned his head and looked into the corridor. He could be over forty. His handsome face was embellished by a thick mustache and his black eyes curiously watched the newcomers. Then he got up, took a few steps and stopped at a red line painted about three feet from the door.

He smiled a little and quietly said, "John, welcome to the Cheyenne jail. I bet you, that it has never crossed your mind that one day you would pay me a visit right here."

Coble, being quite excited, literally faltered but he got hold of himself and blurted out, "Tom, for God's sake, what are you doing here? Yesterday, Ora Haley stopped at my place, you know the one who hired you as a detective, and once he told me that you were in jail I dropped everything and rushed to Cheyenne. Then in the morning I bought the paper and I couldn't believe my eyes. You have allegedly confessed that you shot Willie Nickell? Is it true?"

Tom shook his head, "Far from it. It wasn't that way. Joe LeFors, you know, the Deputy U.S. Marshal, sent me a cable about a week ago saying that he would have a job for me in Montana. According to him, the rustlers were so brazen that they were stealing cattle during the daylight over there and he wanted to talk to me about it. And 'cause I have done a good job here, he would recommend me."

Tom wanted to continue but then he stopped, looked at Rick and asked Coble, "You forgot to introduce this gentleman to me. Is he my lawyer?"

"No, that's Rick Jackson," Coble quickly answered, then hesitantly added, "He is a reporter. He works for *The Denver Post*. You won't believe it but he has collected articles about you all the way back when you had worked in Arizona for Al Sieber. You can trust him. So what happened then?"

Tom set his black eyes on Rick as if he wanted to convince himself about the truthfulness of Coble's words, unnoticeably nodded and then continued. "Well, when I arrived here, we met at the Inter-Ocean Hotel in the morning. First, I ordered a shot of whisky, then Joe did the same and so it went like that for a while. Then he got up, told me that he had to take care of something but that he would come later to pick me up. 'Cause I felt sort of wobbly I moved to an empty room and took a nap. He showed up in the afternoon and wanted me to go with him to his office to talk about that job. So I went along and that was the mistake."

Horn paused for a moment, scratched his head and slightly embarrassed said, "It should have occurred to me that something was amiss. LeFors showed me that letter from Montana and wanted to know if those people could rely on me. I assured him that I would do a good job and whoever hired me wouldn't have a reason to complain. Then he turned the conversation to his job. He took his Winchester off the wall and began to brag about how many people he arranged an early funeral for with it. And that I should not be bashful and admit that there are plenty of notches on my Winchester as well, and that he knows what happened in Colorado when Dart and Rush were found with a hole in their heads. Well, everybody knows that LeFors in his entire life shot maybe a rabbit on the prairie, but since I was still a bit tipsy I let those remarks go and maybe embellished them a little. Then he started talking about young Nickell. I came up with a theory that somebody was waiting in the hollow for his father, old Nickell, and because the boy wore his hat and raincoat the killer just made a mistake. Then I said that it was a hell of shot to hit him at the distance of three hundred yards. It would have been my best shot but a pretty rotten thing to kill such a young boy. After that he wanted to know what kind of ammo I use and what scopes I have on my rifle. Finally, he asked me once more if I wanted that Montana job and if I would need any money for the trip. I told him I could leave the next day so he promised to write a letter and get me the train ticket. We parted and the next day in the morning, when I was about to pay, Leslie Snow appeared in the lobby and pulled out his gun on me saying that I was under arrest on account of the young Nickell's murder to which I had confessed. So that's the way it happened. But because of my own confession? No way. That's sheer nonsense."

Coble kept nodding his head and then interrupted Tom. "You should have watched out for LeFors. He is a corrupt character who would do anything for money. You know that there is a reward of one thousand dollars for any information leading to the arrest of the murderer, don't you? Was anybody else in the office? Any witnesses?"

"No, not a living soul. Just me and him."

"I don't think we'll get any rain from this cloud," commented Coble with an unusual certainty. "But I beg you, don't try to escape because any such an attempt will be viewed as a proof of your guilt. Now, Rick here would like to ask you about some stuff when you were in Arizona, write it down and then publish it. That's the only way we can head off all that dirt they spread about you here in Cheyenne. Before I go back to Bosler, I'll get you a good lawyer. I'll be damned if we don't get you out of this rat hole pretty quick."

Rick didn't say a word, just listened. At the bottom of his heart he had to wonder how this man more than six feet tall and built like Samson can speak so quietly. It was undoubtedly a habit from the days when hostile Indians were close and a loud talk could cost him his life.

As soon as Coble finished speaking, Rick pulled out a notebook from his pocket and began to ask Tom about his parents, how he got to Arizona and how he became an army scout. Tom again answered in low voice and the blank pages were slowly getting covered by his minute handwriting. When Tom mentioned Sieber, Joe got up from his chair and by a gesture of his hand indicated that the visit is over.

Both men got up and said good-bye to Horn while Rick assured him that he would come again tomorrow. They walked silently downstairs. In the sheriff's office Coble asked Snow if the Deputy U.S. Marshal LeFors was present. Snow nodded and pointed at a short guy sitting in the adjacent room, dressed all in black with a massive gold chain on his vest. When they stepped in, he got up, looked at them inquisitively for several seconds and then asked about the purpose of their visit.

Coble didn't waste any time and went straight to the point. "Could you explain to me how you can arrest a person without solid evidence, without witnesses, just like that? What do you have to support the charges? The stories of two men who having consumed a good amount of booze bragging about their exploits? The judge will laugh at you!"

LeFors was obviously entertained, smiled and calmly responded, "Well, that occurred to me, too, so I did get witnesses." Then he turned around, walked back to his desk, opened the drawer and pulled out a large red folder. He opened it and in front of agitated Coble placed two sheets of the typed text. When he saw the blank stare in Coble's face, he began with poorly hidden irony explaining, "You see this paper is the transcript of shorthand recording which was taken by a court official and Deputy Sheriff Snow. Here is every detail recorded of what I said and of what Tom Horn said. Both witnesses were hidden in the closet here under the steps where they could hear every word Horn and I uttered. In other words, Horn does not have a chance if he thinks he can deny everything. And the argument that he was drunk won't hold water because both witnesses can swear that he was quite sober."

Coble turned noticeably pale, opened his mouth and stuttered something in the sense that the lawyer would know how to handle this and a number of influential people would stand behind Horn. Then, followed by Rick, he quickly walked out of the sheriff's office.

Chatting with the Chief of Indian Scouts

Based on interviews with Tom Horn and prepared by F. Jackson.

My name is Tom Horn. I was born November 21, 1860 not far from Memphis in Scotland County in Missouri. It was a difficult time and anybody who was born in Missouri had to get into trouble sooner or later, as our neighbor old Bill Nye used to say. As a boy I had plenty of troubles. Most of them were connected to Sunday school and its location. It stood about a mile away from our farm and the road to it led along a creek and woods. Anybody who lived on a farm knows that once you leave the house you will run into tracks of all possible animals, particularly varmints which stalk at night the henhouse and the only thing they have on their mind is to kill a hen or a duck. Of course no farmer could afford to lose a good layer. When such a misfortune befell us, my mother was the first in the family who brought me a rifle and with words like, "Don't come home without the skin of that bloodthirsty beast," sent me on a hunting expedition. Out of eight children I was the only one who was entrusted with this noble task because mother knew that it wouldn't take long and the neigh-borhood would be short by one skunk, fox or lynx. Now it would be selfish of me if I did not admit that actually there were two of us who got this job, me and our dog Shedrick which we called Shed. Shed was a mutt but he could track like the best hunting dog. In the summer I had to neglect this passion because of the field work but as soon as the winter set in I tried to catch up.

My mother also saw to it that I was familiar with the Lord's scriptures and so every Sunday she sent me to school to listen to the sermon. But once I took several steps away from the house I glued my eyes to snow because in it I could read better than in the Bible. Here walked a marten, further up a skunk, and a little bit up the road a fox covered its tracks and a deer came to the creek to drink. Then near the woods a raccoon went for a stroll.

When I left the house in the morning I always had the good intention to make it all the way to school, but I just could not resist the temptation to look at least a little bit how far this or that animal went.

When my curiosity was finally satisfied, school usually started and there was the danger that the pastor would pull my ears for being late. So I figured if I should have trouble, let's at least make it worth it. Since I carried a rifle to school anyway, all I had to do was to get back closer to the house, whistle at the dog and the hunt was on. I returned home usually toward evening and the quarry indicated that instead of listening to the preacher I listened to the wind in the treetops and the sounds of the forest. The price I paid for such excursions was usually appropriate scolding or sometimes my ears got boxed, and if it happened too often then my mother borrowed my father's belt and I couldn't sit on my rear for several days. During such thrashings she had eyes full of tears but she swore that she would beat these Indian manners out of me for good. Of course I never saw a real Indian in my life, so I could only speculate what kind of manners she was talking about. Sometimes I complained about this treatment to my best buddy and partner in these away-from-school adventures, but he would look at me and I could see in his large brown eyes that he could not understand how anybody could prefer sitting in a school bench to a good hunt in the woods.

On many occasions I could establish the fact that Shed was extremely smart dog. Not far away from our farm lived the Griggs. Their oldest son, Sam, had a hunting dog and wherever he went he kept bragging that this dog was the best coon dog in the entire world (and since he never left home he probably meant the whole state of Missouri). Once I called his bluff and took him on a coon hunt. The dog really picked up the scent and rushed forward. After a while we heard him barking like crazy and when we caught up with him, there really was a raccoon sitting on a branch. Sam, who wanted to prove at any cost that his dog was a real hot shot, suggested that he would climb up the tree, reach the branch and shake the coon down. All I would have to do was just to watch the genius, how he expertly would bury its teeth into the coon and kill it. Sam then reached the branch but the coon backed away almost to its end. Sam followed him and shook the branch but because it was not too strong I suddenly heard mighty cracking and there crashing down went Sam and the coon. Now what do you think that dog of his did? As he was all excited instead of going after the coon he jumped on Sam and bit him on his ear. Well, such a stupidity Shed would never do.

Then the following year an event took place which changed my life. A short distance from our farm a wagon train of emigrants was passing by. The wagons headed west to the Oregon Trail. I stood at the road and watched one wagon after another and then, when the last one went by, two boys came by sitting on a grey mare. The older one held a shotgun and from his facial expression one could tell that he thought he owned the whole world. I could not help myself and made a remark that whoever goes to hunt with a shotgun won't be probably much of a hunter. The boys stopped, dismounted and the older one asked me if I knew what would happen to me because I had offended a "man". In spite of his age, he could have been about two years older, I just laughed and the fight was on. It didn't take long and the "man" was lying under me and I was giving him a good whipping. His younger brother saw that things were not going the way they had planned, put down the shotgun and joined the fight. Shed observed this scrapping from a distance and pretty soon he realized that this was not a fair game. He bared his teeth and went after the boy. The kid started to scream, more by fear than pain, so I let the older one go and with a victorious smile watched as both of them,

rather humbled, climbed on their horse. But their anger won over the common sense. The older boy, mad over the humiliation, raised the gun, aimed it and pulled the trigger. A shot thundered followed by a painful scream. The boys wasted no time, kicked the mare into canter and tried to catch up with the wagons while I was bending over a wounded Shed. Crying I carried him home and around midnight his soul departed for dog heaven.

That was the first time I encountered the human malice which cost my best friend his life. I got depressed and wanted to leave. Any time I passed the Shed's grave I got reminded of the whole incident and I ran away to the woods where I wanted to be alone, but there again I got reminded of all those joyful moments we spent together when hunting. On the other hand that wagon train made an indelible impression on me. Those people were leaving for far away where they wanted to start a new life and that was exactly what I wanted. To start a new life so I could forget Shed's death.

When I once mentioned it at supper, my father took off his belt and put it meaningfully on the table, saying, "Don't even think about it. Now, when the field work is about to start, I'll need every hand at home."

When I saw the belt, something snapped in me. No, no one will ever beat me again. At night I packed my things, put a half of loaf of bread and a big chunk of cheese into my hunting bag and slipped out of the house. I visited Shed's grave for the last time to tell him good-bye and then headed west.

I don't have to tell you that it was a long hike. Sometimes I stopped at a farm and when the farmer's wife was at home. I didn't have to worry that I would be hungry. One of them, I think her name was Mrs. Peters, she even washed my clothes so when I left their place I looked like leaving a church and not a person having covered on foot over hundred miles.

After about a week of walking I made it to Kansas City. You can imagine that excitement for a boy whose longest trip was to the county seat. But soon I had to worry about the basic stuff such as where to sleep and what to eat. I sold my rifle and started looking for a job. For a while I worked at the railroad near Newton and then, after about a month of killing work, a certain Mr. Blades asked me if I wanted to go with him to Santa Fe. He needed someone who would help him with his team of oxen. I didn't hesitate a minute and the next day we were on the way. We reached Santa Fe around Christmas 1874.

Well, then things were moving pretty quickly. In January, of the next year, Mr. Murray, the superintendent of the local postal service, hired me as a shotgun messenger for the stage coach. I had to sit on the box next to the driver holding my brand new shotgun but because I never had to use it, I believe it was rather for decoration or to impress the passengers. My route was from Santa Fe to Los Pinos and Bacon Springs and then all the way to Arizona to the Beaver Station at the Verde River. My monthly salary was fifty dollars and I was firmly convinced that my life dream had come true.

At that time I got an offer from a certain Mr. Hansen to take care of oxen which delivered lumber to the military garrison at Camp Verde. The monthly salary was seventy-five dollars plus food. Well, I took it but it was a boring job so I kept looking for something more interesting. Here I have to mention that at that time I was no longer that confused kid from Missouri. I was sixteen but I could make decent money, owned a horse, a new saddle, a rifle and among other things I spoke Mexican almost like a native.

Well, it didn't take long and an opportunity arose. Not far away there was Fort Whipple which also served as a distribution point for the

Fifth Cavalry horses. Once a year the wranglers drove in four hundred heads all the way from California and handed them over to the quartermaster. He then placed them into several large corrals and hired a couple of watchmen to make sure that the Indians wouldn't steal them. So overnight I became an employee of the U.S. Army. The trouble was that the individual troops gradually picked up the horses, and whatever was left of the herd the Army sold to the local farmers or ranchers so I was again without a job.

Then, as if by an act of Providence, I met Al Sieber.

Sieber introduced himself as the Chief of the Indian Scouts and asked me if I was interested in going with him south to San Carlos Indian Reservation to work there as an interpreter. I would have the same salary and all I would have to do was to accompany him during his travel in the reservations and interpret from Spanish to English and the other way around. He asked me if I also knew the Apache language. I said that I only knew a few words but he waved his hand saying quite confidently that I would learn it pretty quickly. So in July 1876, I entered an Indian reservation for the first time.

San Carlos Reservation was spread over a rectangle whose one side was about sixty miles and the other one hundred twenty miles long. In this area up to three thousand Apaches lived and they resided in several villages each belonging to a special Apache tribe or a band. In this reservation Al Sieber and a handful of Indian and white scouts were supposed to keep some semblance of order. I was all eager to start my interpreting work, but Al was only smiling. He would scratch his graying head and keep saying that there was no rush and that eventually it would come to it. My only task now was to shoot a deer once a while, watch his horse and in the evening to clean his rifle. Needless to say I didn't argue with him because this kind of life was quite agreeable to me. The only thing I couldn't get was why he needed an interpreter when he spoke not only fluent Spanish but the language of the local Indians as well.

Only about a month later I learned the real reason for my being here. Sometime in the beginning of October we visited an Indian camp at the confluence of the White and Black Rivers. We were welcomed by an older Indian and judging by his and Sieber's gestures they must have been old friends. They talked in Apache for a while and of course I couldn't catch any details but somehow I figured out that they talked about me.

When they finished, Al took me aside and simply said, "Tom, this is the real reason I brought you here to the reservation. The Army needs scouts who are fully familiar not only with the Apache language but also with their customs and way of life. Chief Pedro is my old friend and friend of the white people. He is willing to keep you here in his village as his adopted son. You will live, behave and think like an Apache and I'll come back for you in the spring. You will be paid on a monthly basis and you can either collect your salary or the quartermaster will keep it at Fort Apache and you can pick it up later. Think about it and let me know tomorrow after the sunrise."

As I knew Al Sieber, this was probably his longest speech he had ever held in his life. Needless to say, I hadn't even dreamed that somebody would make me such an offer. Due to the excitement I didn't sleep the whole night. Then in the morning when we were having breakfast, I told Sieber that I accepted.

The old scout grinned friendly, slapped me on the shoulder and then without saying a word went to Pedro's wigwam. There he discussed some details about my stay and when they parted, he called for his horse.

He mounted and then leaned toward me and speaking in English so that no Indian would understand him, he said, "Don't let these Indians fool you. They are on our side. The others are not that friendly. And one more thing, if you hear the name Geronimo, try to remember in what connection it was used." Then he paused for a second or two and added, "Geronimo, the chief of the Chiricahua Apaches." Then he straightened up and took off.

Of course at that time I had no idea who this Geronimo was so I only nodded, but over the years I had not only the opportunity to meet this chief in person but also to be a witness of his rise and inglorious end.

4

On a dirt road leading from the railroad station in Iron Mountain appeared a buggy. A spotted, spirited horse kept tossing his head and a young man looking like a lawyer or land speculator because of his derby hat and a black suit tried to reason with it.

"Just slow down. Take it easy. Save your strength. We've got another ten miles ahead of us. You will need it for the way back."

The brown and white Paint, however, did not share his opinion and judging by its prancing it was probably shut somewhere in a stall for days and now full of energy and on an open road it felt like racing with the wind. Finally after ten or fifteen minutes, it settled down to a sharp but even trot. The man in black whose appearance would fool many of his friends was Rick Jackson. Now he loosened up the reins and began to pay attention to the landscape he was passing through.

The road was winding between the vast pastures which in some places were interrupted by a wooded hill or a small valley with a creek. In spite of the fact that it was already May and the range was turning green in many a shaded ravine, he still could see the white strips of snow. There was no doubt that he was driving through the land belonging to a large cattle company because there was not a single fence in sight since he left the railroad. Watching the grazing herds of cattle, he had to think of Tom Horn. This was the land where he operated. Here he spent days or sometimes even weeks. He used to ride through the ravines which offered a perfect hideout for the rustlers or sat on the neighboring hills and surveyed the pastures with his binoculars to make sure that a group of strange riders does not try to drive away a cow or cows which did not belong to them.

It had been about a month since he had talked to Tom for the last time. After he had parted with John Coble, he met him several times and during these short visits in the jail he collected enough material that *The Denver Post* could inform its readers about his adventurous career regularly in its Sunday supplements. As to the questions about his recent past, Tom was evasive or just didn't answer them at all so Rick had to be satisfied with his narration about the fights with the Apaches. Then one day he received a letter from Cobble suggesting that he get in touch with Miss Kimmell who was at that time teaching at the country school near Iron Mountain.

Miss Kimmell was actually Tom's girlfriend and it was quite possible that she could provide additional information he could later make public. Rick promised that he would do just that but about a month passed with no word from her. Only a week before had she sent him a short letter signed "Glendolene Kimmell" in which she instructed him to come on Sunday by train to Iron Mountain, to borrow a buggy from the local blacksmith and to drive straight to school near Miller's ranch. She pleaded with him not to stop anywhere and not to talk to anybody along the way.

From the moment he stepped off the train everything went as planned. To find the smithy was only a matter of minutes because there was only one there and when he introduced himself to a guy in a long, leather apron, the black smith just waved his hand at his helper and he readily stuck a whip into Rick's hand and led him out to a buggy with a hitched horse. Rick would swear that they were expecting him. At the same time it crossed his mind that all of those days as a kid when he was helping around a livery stable were not wasted. Now the skillful handling of the horses he learned there will come in pretty handy.

After about a half hour drive he reached a fork in the road. Following the instructions mentioned in the letter, he turned to the left and entered a picturesque canyon confined from both sides by steep slopes covered by tall pines and aspens. Rick suddenly realized that while watching the distant hills from the train window he was mistaken when he believed that the big ranchers who grabbed the pastures in the flat lands were much better off than the poor settlers who had to do with the rocky plateaus in the mountains. Now, quite surprised, he stared at thick forests, rushing freshets, and herds of deer and elk. The plateaus offered a good pasture and the forest building material for houses and barns while the ranchers in the lowlands had to pay top price for each board and quite often fought over access to water.

The road began to rise. The Paint slowed down, its breathing became more rapid and visible whirls of steam rolled out of its nostrils. On the left they passed a lime kiln and shortly thereafter they stopped at a simple gate made out of barbed wire. Rick got out the buggy, opened it and led the horse through. They entered the land belonging to Miller's ranch. He shut the gate again and after another ten or fifteen minutes he spotted a small, one-story building constructed of peeled pine logs. He had reached the country school. It stood secluded and its location was chosen in such a way that most of the children from the neighboring ranches had to walk about the same distance from their homes.

Rick tied up the horse to a hitching post and walked up the wooden steps to the door. He saw a little school bell hanging on a cross beam and he was already stretching his hand to ring it, but then he suppressed the temptation, stepped to the door and knocked. For a while there was no response but then he heard tapping of heels and caught a glimpse of a female peeking out of the side window. In no time the key rattled in the lock and a young woman opened the door curiously looking at Rick.

At the moment when Rick was about to introduce himself, she asked, "You are Rick Jackson, right?" Rick nodded and the woman stretched her hand saying, "I am Glendoline Kimmell. Come in."

The small classroom reminded Rick of one-room school in Kansas he had attended until the age of twelve when his parents moved to Denver. There were simple benches in two rows, pictures of Washington and Lincoln on the front wall, and between them a blackboard of which the original black varnish had cracked and turned grey over time. There was a big-bellied Franklin stove in the corner and a pile of exercise books with homework on the table waiting to be corrected. However, instead of a strict male teacher with a switch he saw a young, good looking woman with slightly slanted eyes. Rick was itching to ask if one her ancestors had come from Asia, but it was Miss Kimmell who started asking questions.

"Did somebody from Miller's ranch see you? Who else knows that you are here? And how about Tom? When did you see him last time?" she rushed one question after another. Rick took off his hat, sat down on one of the benches and assured her that except of several cowboys near Iron Mountain he had not seen a living soul, and only Coble and Rick's boss Pete Swain knew about his trip. As for his last visit to the Cheyenne jail, it had taken place about a month ago.

The teacher visibly calmed down and apologized for her concerns. "You know, since Tom's arrest this place is teeming with newspaper hacks and scribblers of the worst kind. They all are trying to dig up some dirt and appropriately embellish it in the paper, and if Miller found out that we met, he would start immediately suspecting me of scheming or conniving behind his back."

"Miller? What does he have to do with Tom's arrest?" asked Rick quite surprised.

"You know, that's a long story." Miss Kimmell smoothed with her hand wrinkles on her skirt, sat down next to Rick and continued in a low voice.

"From the day when young Nickell was shot, the Millers were suspected of this awful deed. There were many reasons for it. The animosity between those two families goes back for several years. It all started when old Nickell bought a piece of land which included a road leading to Miller's pasture. The original owner assured Miller that he would have his right-of-way recorded for him at the land office, but Nickell didn't like it. In the end he agreed to it, but as time went on, the road became the true bone of contention. Nickell stretched a fence there and built a gate on the road. Miller was furious because any time he went by, he had to get of the box and open and close the gate. Then, just out of spite, he used to leave it open. It was only a matter of time until Nickell's cows got out and that meant trouble. Nickell used to watch out for Miller and when he saw him driving to the gate, he would stand there and wait to see whether Miller would shut it or not. This led to an argument and on one occasion Miller stabbed Nickell with a knife. The sheriff from Iron Mountain came. Miller was arrested, tried and eventually sentenced to several months in jail. Fortunately, it was superficial wound but from that time on Nickell never left the house without his Winchester."

Rick listened carefully, and then he pulled out his always-ready notebook and started to take notes.

"Then there was the incident with Willie, that is, with young Nickell. Just by accident when Miller was driving home, he ran into Willie. He immediately thought that Willie had been waiting there to report to his father if Miller had shut the gate or not. Miller got mad, called Willie a rotten bastard and, hoping he would chase him away, hit him with the whip but Willie stood his ground and didn't run. Miller then reached for his shotgun, aimed it at him and pulled the trigger. The gun did not fire, but was it because it was not loaded or because it misfired? Only Miller knows. Well, a year later it happened. They found Willie dead, lying in a pool of blood several feet away from the sheep corral.

"When the sheriff and coroner from Cheyenne came and asked whom he suspected, Nickell readily answered that he suspected Miller and his two sons, however, nobody could prove anything to them. Now, when they arrested Tom, old Miller was scared to death that Tom's lawyer would focus on him and that's why he forbid everybody who lives at his ranch to talk about those past incidents, particularly to strangers. As the school is on his property and I have to live in his house, this prohibition applies to me as well."

Miss Kimmell paused for a few seconds and then she added, "Rumor has it that Miller gave to the Deputy U.S. Marshal LeFors, who joined the investigation five hundred dollars this winter to look for the killer somewhere else and not in his family. So you can see one cannot be careful enough."

"No kidding?" Rick reacted quite surprised. "Five hundred dollars? That's a pretty big sum of money for a small rancher like Miller. LeFors took it?"

"That I don't know. I guess only the court can find out the truth. Right now it's just a gossip."

Rick wrote down a few more notes and then he asked, "Now, what happened to the sheep?"

The teacher frowned. "Well, to tell you the truth, Nickel should have thought it through. It was really irresponsible of him. My impression is that somebody in Cheyenne talked him into it and just convinced him that sheep were a gold mine. There is not so much work with it like with the cattle. They multiply like rabbits and he can get a pretty penny for wool. However here owning sheep is a kiss of death. There is an unwritten law among the local ranchers that sheep must not be allowed on pastures with cattle. I am sure you know what a herd of sheep can do to grass. In a couple of years even the best pasture turns into a desert. When Miller found out that right in his neighborhood there was herd of sheep, he was mad like a rabid dog. They say that Nickell started getting threatening letters, but he ignored them. Then, just to prove that nobody could break him, about a week after Willie got shot he hired a shepherd, an Italian, and sent him with a herd of sheep directly to Miller's pasture. Obviously, he could not come up with a bigger provocation. The next day somebody fired thirteen shots at him. It is a genuine miracle that Nickell actually survived it. To top it off, shortly after they took him to the hospital in Cheyenne, the same person or persons bludgeoned to death several dozen of his sheep. Again the sheriff came, questioned Miller, but he and his sons had alibi. Allegedly they were at home at the time of the crime."

The way Miss Kimmell uttered the last sentence made very clear impression that she had serious doubts about Miller's alibi and that she knew more that she was willing to tell. The room fell silent. The teacher stepped to the window and looked at the horse and the buggy. The Paint was obviously getting tired of waiting at the hitching post and impatiently pawed the ground. Rick in the meantime looked at the notes and summarized in his head all the information he had heard. Then he realized that while they had talked about the feud between those two families, Miss Kimmell didn't say a word about Tom. Since he spent lots of time in this area, he had to meet the Millers as well as the Nickells. Whom did he side with?

"How about Tom? What did he think about all that?" indirectly Rick asked.

"Well, Tom was a good judge of people. When he met Miller and Nickell he came quickly to the conclusion that the trouble was rooted in the fact that both men were at about the same level, material as well as spiritual. Moreover, Miller was a hardheaded weirdo and Nickell very short tempered. Tom believed that if one of them had been richer or more intelligent he would have ignored the other."

This answer, however, didn't satisfy Rick. "Did he come here often?"

"Yes, mainly because of the sheep. He wanted to make sure that it was not on the pastures of the big ranchers who hired him, but before that he came quite rarely. Neither Miller nor Nickell had the reputation of being rustlers so Tom didn't harbor any suspicion toward them."

Rick raised his head, looked at the teacher and then slowly, as if he knew that this question will not be received with great understanding, he asked, "Was Tom here at the time when young Nickell was killed?"

Her black slanted eyes flashed. She quickly turned away from the window and sharply said, "Yes, he was, but I hope you are not looking for any connection between his presence and that dastardly crime? Tom spent two nights at the Millers, from Monday to Tuesday and from Tuesday to Wednesday. Then in the morning he left. Based on the coroner's report Willie was not shot until Thursday morning."

"And what brought him to the Millers?"

"Somebody called the Double B Ranch to say that Nickell's sheep was on their land. Tom rode there and Tuesday morning inspected all their pastures, but there was not a single sheep there. When I think about it now, it looks to me as if someone purposefully lured him over here so that later on he could be blamed for this murder."

Miss Kimmell raised her voice, "Please understand that all small ranchers in this area hate Tom because on one hand he looks after the interests of the cattle companies and on the other hand because only a few newcomers have a clean conscience when it comes to cattle rustling."

Rick shrugged his shoulders. "I believe you but let's not forget Tom's reputation."

"Reputation?" Quite irritated she retorted, "I'll tell you something about his reputation. One half of it is slanders and gossips and the other half he made it up by himself. Ask somebody at the cattle association. Wherever Tom shows up, the rustling stops dead in its tracks. Why? Just because of this reputation. He couldn't come up with a better weapon. Don't tell me that you believe that he rides from ranch to ranch and shoots all the rustlers. If that were the case he would have cut down the Wyoming population of small ranchers in half by now.

"You should have heard him when he spent those two evenings at the Millers. Tom is a great narrator and once he gets going, his fantasy knows no limits. He was telling them how he had caught five outlaws who had robbed a train in Colorado. That happened years ago when he worked for the Pinkerton Agency. According to his version he tracked them down and after a dramatic gun fight he killed them all. Of course, it was not true. When he found and arrested them on the Colorado - Oklahoma border, there were only two of them and then he handed them unharmed over to the local sheriff. Old Miller and his sons, however, were listening with their jaws dropping and they were firmly convinced that there was no more dangerous gun slinger wide and far than Tom. I know he has many enemies in this area, but do you know who his greatest enemy is? His own mouth, particularly if he has some whisky under his belt and then he declares any violent incident for his own.

"Otherwise Tom Horn is a true gentlemen and a man of honor, the kind of which there are not too many around. Moreover, he is quite bright and well-read. He not only speaks fluent Spanish but also Apache. By the way, do you know that Tom was the only white man Geronimo trusted? When he was arrested after his last escape from the reservation, he insisted that only Tom would do the interpreting. Tom also showed me books he had carried in his saddle bag. He used to read them at the campfire when he was alone on the range. On several occasions he told me that if he had written down all the events he was involved in during his time in Arizona, that it would have been mighty interesting reading."

Miss Kimmell paced quite excitedly between the benches accompanying her words with lively gestures. Her black hair got loose, her black eyes flashed and her cheeks got a reddish hue. Then she stopped in front of Rick and with the tone in her voice which did not allow any compromise she resolutely declared, "I am convinced that Tom Horn never killed anybody intentionally, let alone a fourteen year old boy. Recently when he was in Cheyenne, he bought food for three ragamuffins and because they were barefoot he bought them shoes also. Just ask Coble about it. He was there with him. No Sir! A man like that does not shoot children!"

Rick made a quick note about Coble and the three ragamuffins at the railroad station, then turned the subject back to Willie and his father. "Do you think that the murderer really wanted to shoot young Nickell or that he mistook him for his father?"

The teacher stopped, ran her hand over her hair and in a little bit calmer voice answered, "The newspaper claims that it was a tragic error. When they found him, Willie had on his father's raincoat and hat. The fact that a week later the unknown person fired at Kels, that's old Nickell's first name," she quickly added, "would confirm this theory. However, according to the coroner's report Willie was hit by two shots and both were mortal. In the case of his father, thirteen shots were fired, only two hit him and the wounds they caused were not serious. As far as I am concerned, I believe that two different people were involved. Of course there are a slew of speculations and conjectures. I have my own opinion about it but it doesn't make much sense for me to make it public before the trial takes place."

Rick got up, stretched and because his journalistic instinct was telling him that he was not going to learn anything else, closed the notebook and put it in his pocket. At the same time he had this visceral feeling that teacher had not told him all she knew about this sad affair. On the other hand, he understood the urgency to be careful due to her mistrust of all reporters, including him. If she knew something that could help Tom, she would probably save it for the hearing. To divulge important information now would either warn the killer or killers, or enable the prosecution to prepare the counterarguments. LeFors and Stoll, the prosecutor, were convinced that Horn was guilty and would do their level best to prevent introduction of any information that would weaken their position.

Just out of politeness Rick asked a few questions which had nothing to do with the murder, like how big the class was, if she was the only teacher there, and then finally the question which was burning on the tip of his tongue. "Where are you actually from?"

"From Hawaii. Why?"

"No special reason." Rick hesitated and then a bit abashed added, "Because of your facial features."

Miss Kimmell laughed, "You mean because of my eyes? That's easy to explain. My father was a German, but my mother's mother was a Korean."

"I see," blurted Rick out and in order to cover up his embarrassment he pulled out his pocket watch, looked at the dial and just remarked that it was getting late and therefore it was time to hit the road.

The teacher first looked out of the door to make sure that no one would witness his departure, then held the horse and wished him good luck. Once the buggy disappeared from her sight, she returned to the classroom. For a while she walked around and tried to think about this visitor and all the information she gave him and when she convinced herself that none of it could hurt Tom, she sat down to the pile of exercise books and began to correct them.

Chatting with the Chief of Indian Scouts

Based on interviews with Tom Horn and prepared by F. Jackson.

Out of those ten years I spent in Arizona, the stay with the Chief Pedro was the best time of my life. All I did day after day was hunting, learning the language and getting acquainted with the Apache customs and traditions. From time to time I rode to Fort Apache to draw my salary, and then stopped at the Indian Agency at San Carlos which was the meeting place of many traders who brought any kind of goods including horses, saddles, bridles and colorful Mexican blankets. On such an occasion I bought some gifts for Pedro and my adopted brother Chi-Kis-In and his sister Sawn who took care of our household. By that time I knew all Apache tribes and at a distance I could reliably recognize Tonto, Chiricahua and Cibique warriors or Indians from San Carlos, White Mountain or Warm Springs. There were many ways to tell the difference - by the way they dressed, their skin tattoos and also their hair-dos. I also knew who Geronimo was and where he was hiding. Geronimo was a Chiricahua and that meant trouble.

Pedro kept me also apprised about character of individual tribes and their relations to the white people. The San Carlos Indians, to whom he also belonged, buried the war hatchet a long time ago and they did not harbor any hostility toward the whites. They regularly visited the Indian Agency, picked up their food rations or money and did not refuse to be counted. Very few left the reservation and many served under Al Sieber as scouts or policemen. However, as to the Cibique, Pedro believed that they were incorrigible devils and every decent Indian should avoid them. When the evening talks at the campfire turned toward Cibique, he usually said, "If it were up to me, I would take a hundred of my best warriors and fix them once for all. However, for some reason the people who are in charge of the reservation don't like this idea."

The worst ones, however, were the Chiricahua and the Warm Spring Indians. They sought refuge in Mexico, regularly raided the Arizona ranchers and then they returned with the loot back to Sonora or Chihuahua. There, on the other side of the Mexican border, they felt secure because they knew that the U.S. Cavalry was not allowed to cross the border and no officer was willing to take the blame for causing an international incident.

Another interesting thing to mention is the fact that in a specific tribe one could find "strangers" or namely warriors from different tribes. The main reason was usually a character of an individual Indian. For example, if there was a young man among the San Carlos Indians who did not like the peaceful way of life, he would join the Chiricahua or Cibique and the other way around. If a Chiricahua warrior got tired of raiding and risking an early departure to the eternal hunting grounds, he moved to San Carlos.

The blissful stay with Chief Pedro, however, ended in the spring of the next year. Sometime in April Al Sieber came to Pedro's camp, but unlike earlier when he just wanted to check on me and the progress I was making, this time he came to take me to the military headquarters in San Carlos. There a bad news was waiting for us. As of January 1st the army took over the administration of the reservation and the man in charge was Major Chaffee. The reason for replacing the civilian oversight with a military one was rather embarrassing. The former Indian agent was accused of corruption and fraud, particularly illegal sale of goods which was slated for the Indians. He used to sell them cheaply to the local traders and when charged, he defended himself by saying that there were fewer Indians than originally believed. Trouble was that the books didn't show any surplus. In another words, money made by these sales went to his pocket. The army then decided that until this mess was straightened up, payment of salaries for all civilians would be stopped. Since any civilian who was not employed by the agency was not allowed to stay at the reservation, it was announced to us that we should pack our things and clear out. When we asked the major for how long, he just shrugged his shoulders and remarked that probably for several months. This decision applied not only to me, but to Sieber and all white scouts and men who were in charge of draft and pack animals.

As you know, if the high brass makes a decision, there is no appeal. So we spent the rest of the day by weighing our options. Sieber frowned and cursed all thieves and embezzlers who put us in this unenviable situation. Toward the evening, however, he came up with a saving solution. Ed Schiefflin, his old buddy and a renowned prospector, wrote him a letter saying that he planned to look again at the deposits of silver east of Tucson he discovered some time ago. Then the Chiricahua drove him away, but since they are now in Mexico, it should be pretty safe to put together a group of prospectors and trappers and do some mining. If he wanted to try his luck, he would be welcome. They could all meet in Tucson in about two weeks.

After Sieber had read the letter aloud so we all could get the details, he then asked us who would like to join him. Only six of us were willing to take this chance. However, I insisted that before we depart, I would like to visit the old chief and say good-bye to all my Indian friends. Sieber didn't mind, so I filled my saddle bags with gifts and we set out to the confluence of the White and Black Rivers. Saying good-bye took two days. Chief Pedro arranged a major get-to-gather in my honor, the game was roasted on several spits and one dance followed the other. Then it was time to distribute the gifts. When I handed out all of mine, several squaws brought me a bridle braided from rawhide, a lariat and another bridle, this time braided from the black and white horse hair.

Apache squaws and even some warriors are quite skillful at this craft which requires years of experience and endless patience.

A week later we were on the way to Tucson and there we met Schiefflin and his partners. They came all the way from California and once they recovered from the trip, they were ready to pack the mules and move out. After three days of travel through the desert Schiefflin pointed to a small grassy hill. Somewhere over there was his mine. In the evening we reached the destination and camped at a deep shaft. Next day we divided the digging plots. Schiefflin just renewed his old claim and the rest of us could push a shaft or a tunnel where ever we wanted. First, I fell for this quite excitedly, but as days and weeks passed I realized that enthusiasm and hard work with a pick are not enough. One has to know something about rock formation, silver ore and all those tricks of successful prospectors. While the guys from California were quite satisfied with the results of their work we, the greenhorns from the reservation, didn't make enough to buy a pack of chewing tobacco.

Nevertheless, pretty soon the word got out that this area was really rich in silver ore and by the end of summer several hundred miners were opening new mines there. By the fall, the original camp became a town with brothels, hotels, saloons and even a stage coach station; and so the famous town of Tombstone came into existence. Of course so many people had to eat and because the supplies delivery didn't work too well. I saw an opportunity. I decided to throw away the pick, grab the rifle and start hunting and in this way provide additional food. Needless to say, it was a much easier way to make living. I used to ride to the nearby mountains and then return with two or three packhorses loaded with game. Quite often, thanks to my hunting skills, I made in a day or two more money than in a week of drudgery with pick and shovel.

One day, I believe it was the beginning of October, a cavalry unit appeared in Tombstone. Its commander was Lieutenant Schroeder and in his saddle bag, there was among other things, an order from the regional commander General Wilcox concerning Al Sieber and the former scouts. Our status was renewed so we should immediately report to Fort Whipple and consider ourselves again the civilian employees of the U.S. Army, specifically of the Sixth Cavalry. I don't have to tell you that he couldn't have brought a more welcome news than that one.

Frankly, not only me, but Sieber and all other formers scouts were getting damn tired of the life in Tombstone and we all longed for our old jobs. The next day we announced all over town that our diggings were for sale and the very same evening I got two thousand dollars for mine. Whether the chap who bought it had greater luck than I did, that I don't know, but according to my opinion it was not worth a dime.

On the way to Fort Whipple Lieutenant Schroeder informed us, privately, that all sorts of hell had broken lose in San Carlos. The Indians did whatever they wanted to, such as making *tis-win*, a kind of Indian whisky which was prohibited and they kept leaving the reservation to steal cattle belonging to the neighboring ranchers. It was simply a genuine anarchy. The Sixth Cavalry was at a loss as to what to do so it dawned on General Wilcox that the best solution probably would be to call back Al Sieber and his scouts to restore some semblance of order.

After our arrival to San Carlos we just waited for the next orders. The unit of the Indian scouts was restored with Sieber at its head and my salary was raised to one hundred dollars a month. Shortly thereafter I set out to Pedro's camp again. This time my task was to recruit a group of young men who could serve as scouts to expand the Sieber's unit and also to gather information about the Apaches in general. According to Pedro the situation was not good. Even though many young men wanted to sign up, he approved only the most reliable warriors. When parting, he remarked, "Apaches are about to dig up the war hatchet against the Pale Faces again. You will have a hard job to tackle. I am afraid that the desert sand will turn red by blood of many warriors before the peace will be restored."

5

In the morning on October 7th, 1902 the Cheyenne Courthouse looked more like a nest of angry bees than a building housing a peaceful public institution. The second floor where the district court was located was jammed by dozens of people, mainly reporters and invited witnesses, and through this noisy crowd a couple of messenger boys were trying to find their ways from one office to another. Then in the cacophony of voices coming from the courtroom one could hear creaking of tables and chairs being pushed which the bailiffs were bringing from the other rooms, trying to set them up into several rows to the right from the door.

Outside, the street in front of the courthouse was filled with cabs and private carriages bringing not only the members of the cattle association, but also big ranchers from the neighboring states. On this day after many delays and legal maneuvering, the trial of Tom Horn, the person accused of killing William Nickell, was about to start.

Horn's defense team - John W. Lacey and his assistant Timothy F. Burke - was already present. Both lawyers sat at a table, not far from the judge's bench, where from time to time they looked at a pile of papers and without saying a word observed the commotion in the courtroom. Lacey and Burke were considered among the best in southern Wyoming.

Lacey, a tall and well preserved fifty year old man with a protruding aquiline nose, was originally from Indiana and came to Wyoming when he was appointed the chairman of the Wyoming Supreme Court. His frowning face clearly indicated that something deeply bothered him. The street noise was getting inside through the open window and occasionally one could hear the yelling of the onlookers standing in front the building. Some of them voiced loudly their opinions and brazenly demanded the death penalty for the defendant.

Lacey got up, stepped to the window and remarked to his companion, "Look, there comes the jury. Instead of being fully isolated from the public as I demanded yesterday, the members of the jury have to walk through an excited mob which insists on capital punishment and threatens them if they decide differently. The panel which selected them publicly announced their names which is in clear violation of the law. As soon as *The Cheyenne Examiner* got hold of the list, they made it public so the whole of Wyoming now knows whose hands Horn's life is in. When I filed the protest and demanded selection of a new jury, the judge told me that it would be unnecessary waste of money." Lacey paused and then sarcastically added, "And this unbiased and uninfluenced jury is supposed to make a just decision."

The prosecutor, Walter Stoll, was restlessly pacing on the other side of the room, perhaps ten feet away from the jury box. He was about forty years old, a stocky guy and almost completely bald. In his right hand he held the opening statement and occasionally glanced at his assistant Clyde W. Watts. Stoll was born in New Jersey and after he graduated from the West Point Academy, he was stationed at Fort McKinney in Wyoming, not far from Buffalo. He had his practice in Cheyenne since 1882 and then, several years later, he was elected the county prosecutor. While Lacey and Burke were Republicans, Stoll and Watts were ardent Democrats.

Droning voices accompanied by the sound of chairs being pushed away suddenly increased. Everybody turned their heads toward the door where the bailiff was announcing the arrival of the jury. Lacey stepped away from the window and subjected them to a careful scrutiny. Most of them were small ranchers residing around Cheyenne. Two of them were cowboys from the Double B Ranch which was owned by Swan Cattle Company. During the selection process Lacey fought tooth and nail with Stoll, particularly when it was established that among the suggested names were ranchers accused of rustling. Now he had this unpleasant feeling that, except for the porter from Cheyenne railroad station and the blacksmith from Wheatfield, the rest had already made up their mind about Horn's guilt.

Lacey's contemplation was interrupted by the same bailiff announcing the arrival of the judge, the Honorable Richard H. Scott. The judge looked around the room, sat down at his bench and motioned everybody to be seated. Then he knocked the gavel on the desk and signaled the bailiff to bring the defendant.

Low murmur filled the room and again, as if somebody gave a command, several dozens of heads turned toward the door which a few seconds later opened and two armed deputies led in Tom Horn. All those present set their eyes on his over-six-feet-tall body which filled the door frame. Tom looked around the room as if he were looking for a vacant seat, but the bailiff quickly stepped up to him and pointed to an empty chair next to the table where his attorneys were sitting. The judge again knocked his gavel and as soon as the room calmed down, invited the prosecutor to deliver his statement.

Stoll spoke almost for half an hour. He spoke in ringing voice of an orator who is accustomed to speak in front of a large audience. He lively gestured with both his hands and paced from one end of the room where the jury box was located to the other end, to the table of the defense. He mentioned the arrogance of the big cattle companies and the unscrupulous ways they use to defend their interests. He emphasized that if they could not achieve their goals legally, they didn't shirk from hiring gun men and killers.

"One of them is sitting now in front of you." Then in conclusion he declared that the prosecution would introduce witnesses and present evidence, including Horn's own admission, which would prove the defendant's guilt beyond any reasonable doubt.

Now it was defense's turn. Lacey deplored the fact that the prosecution had tried to politicize the trial and reminded the jury that according to the American Constitution the defendant was innocent until proven guilty. He concluded with a statement saying that Tom Horn was charged of the aforementioned murder only on the basis of theoretical speculations and assumptions. His speech was a little bit shorter, delivered in a low voice and definitely lacked the fighting spirit when compared to Stoll's performance.

Rick Jackson was sitting in the first row taking notes and mentally was working on the cable which he planned to send during the lunch break to Denver. When the prosecution and defense finished their opening statements, Rick could not help the feeling that Stoll made more powerful impression on the jury and the rest of the audience than Lacey.

While Rick was writing down Lacey's last sentence, Stoll stood up, walked closer to the jury box and in a loud voice announced, "The prosecution calls the first witness, Mary Nickell."

The door opened and the bailiff brought in a tiny, old woman whose wrinkled face was marked not only by years of hard work but also immense suffering. Grey hair was showing from under her bonnet decorated with laces and her brown eyes looked scared at the unusual large number of people. Stoll stepped up to her and guided her to the Bible lying on the judge's bench. Mrs.

Nickell raised her right hand, the left one placed on the book, and repeated after the judge that she would tell only the truth and nothing else but the truth and concluded with the phrase, "So help me God."

Then she sat down on the witness chair and the prosecutor began the questioning, "Please state your name and place of residence."

"Mary Nickell, Cheyenne."

"Where did you live in July 1901?"

"At Nickell's ranch near Iron Mountain."

"Can you describe the events which took place on July 18 of that year to the jury?"

The woman slightly nodded her head and started to describe that tragic morning, "My husband was expecting a land surveyor and so Willie got the job to feed the sheep. It was raining so he wasn't too eager, but eventually he put on my husband's yellow rain slicker and hat and went to the corral."

"What time was it?"

"I don't remember exactly, but it was shortly after breakfast. We ate usually at six. So he left around six thirty or six forty-five."

Stoll nodded and Mrs. Nickell continued, "When about an hour later he wasn't back, my husband sent Freddie, that's our youngest," she quickly added, "to see what was holding him up. Freddie returned in about ten minutes crying that someone had shot Willie."

"Had you heard the shots?"

"Yes, but we didn't pay any heed to them. We reckoned that someone from the Millers went hunting.

"How many shots had you heard?"

"I heard two, but my husband believed there were three. Two following each other quick and then another one."

"Who went to the corral to pick up the body?"

"My husband and I."

The prosecutor stepped up closer to Mrs. Nickell and in a voice full of sympathy asked, "I know it will be hard for you, but could you describe the body of your deceased son? Where did it lie and what was its position?"

The woman in black deeply sighed and began to describe undoubtedly the most grievous moments of her life. "Willie was lying on his back about ten yards from the corral. His hands were next to his body but his shirt was open. It looked like somebody was checking where he had shot him."

"And how about the face? Was it covered with blood?"

"Yes, but …" Mrs. Nickell hesitated a moment.

"But what?"

"It was also covered with dust and little pebbles as if he had laid on his belly and someone turned him around."

The prosecutor continued his questioning. He asked if there were any weapons or spent cartridges lying around, how many people saw the dead body, and finally who informed the sheriff in Iron Mountain. Then he thanked her and looked at Lacey as if to ask if the defense had any questions. Lacey shook his head after which Stoll called the next witness, Kels Nickell.

Nickell basically repeated the testimony of his wife and just added that the soil next to the body was also soaked with blood. In this way he confirmed his wife's opinion that somebody had moved the body. When Stoll finished, Lacey got up, approached the witness and began asking questions. Unlike Stoll, he addressed a different subject.

"What was Willie's relation to the Millers, your neighbors?"

"What do you mean?"

"Well, was it friendly? Did he get along with Miller's sons? Were they all sort of buddies?"

"On the contrary."

"Could you be more specific? They were not just on talking terms, or did they even get into fights from time to time?"

Nickel looked at Lacey and slowly answered, "Well, I can't tell you exactly what happened because if there was some trouble, I wasn't there and I heard about it only from Willie, but as far as I can remember, they got into fights a couple of times."

"Did Willie mention an incident between him and Jim Miller, the father of both boys?"

"Yes, about a year before Willie got shot, Jim Miller hit him with a whip and threatened him with a shotgun."

Loud grumbling noise filled the room, but the judge readily restored the order with several strokes of his gavel.

"Do you know if the Miller boys carried any weapons?"

Nickell smiled as if surprised by Lacey's naiveté. "No rancher leaves the house without a weapon. He never knows what kind of varmint he can run into, including those two-legged ones."

"Do you remember what kind of rifle the Miller boys had?"

"Willie used to say that Victor had a Winchester 30/40."

Lacey paused several seconds and then unexpectedly asked, "And what was the relation between you and Jim Miller?"

At that very moment Stoll raised his hand and, without giving Nickell the opportunity to answer, emphatically said, "Objection! This question has nothing to do with the case. Jim Miller is not the defendant, Tom Horn is."

Lacey looked at the judge, but he nodded and curtly remarked, "Sustained."

The defense counselor didn't have a choice but respect the judge's decision and so he again changed the subject. "What did you do after you had brought the body home?"

"I returned back to the corral and looked for some footprints or simply something that …that was related to this crime."

"Did you find anything?"

"Unfortunately not. The terrain is very rocky. That's why I built the sheep corral there, but the Iron Mountain sheriff said that next to a big boulder he had found the imprint of a rifle stock. As if a Winchester was standing there leaning against the rock, or something like that. Yeah, and also an imprint of a small shoe."

"How far is that boulder from the corral?"

"About thirty-five or forty yards."

Lacey again made a brief pause, stepped closer to Nickell and said, "Now pay close attention to my questions. Do you know the defendant, Tom Horn?"

"Yes, he stopped at our place couple of times."

"Now as far as you can remember, has he ever threatened you or did you have a gut feeling he intended to hurt you?"

Nickell shook his head, "No. Nothing like that. He used to say that he couldn't care less who owned the sheep and who did not. The only thing he cared about was cattle rustling."

Lacey nodded his head, gestured that he had no more questions and resumed his place next to Burke.

Stoll got up, took Lacey's place in front of the jury box and called another witness Thomas C. Murray, the Denver coroner. Murray was a veteran of the Spanish-American War in Cuba and throughout of his carrier he has seen numerous wounds caused by rifles, hand guns and even Gatling machine guns.

After being sworn in, he opened his notebook and as a true professional began describing young Nickell's wounds. Both shots hit the boy from behind. One shattered his right shoulder blade and exited about two inches above the right nipple, while the other bullet broke the fourth rib, went through the heart and exited the ribcage two inches below the left nipple. Considering the trauma to the heart and lungs, both wounds were mortal. According to the size of the exit wounds one could judge that the murderer fired at a relatively short distance, not more than fifty yards. When asked what kind of caliber was involved, the coroner shrugged his shoulders. Since he had an opportunity to examine only the dead body, the size of the bullet is hard to determine. It could have been a Winchester 30/30 or 30/40. The problem is that the wound on a dead body is always a little bit bigger than on a live one.

Stoll then stepped up to his table and Watts handed him an open book, a manual for the military surgeons. The prosecutor then read a paragraph explaining that due to absence of the blood circulation the muscle tissue loosens up, so that originally a small wound could make the impression that it was caused by a larger caliber.

Then he shut the book and satisfied with the impression he made on the jury sat down at his table. Lacey then quickly asked, "Based on your expertise, is it unthinkable that the wounds were caused by a larger caliber than 30/30?"

The answer was unambiguous. "No."

Lacey thanked him, turned toward the judge and said, "The defense has no more questions."

The coroner barely left the room when Stoll stood again in front of the jury and in an eager voice announced, "The prosecution will now question Tom Horn."

Tom was startled. In his thoughts he was not in the courtroom, but at Coble's ranch during that week when somebody called the Double B Ranch that there was sheep on its pastures. He tried to remember all the details. It was Monday in the morning. He was standing at the ring and watched John Ryan working with a dark brown, broad-chested gelding which at the age of three stood already sixteen hands. It was in the spring and the sun has not bleached his summer coat yet, and so most of the cowboys would swear that he was solid black. The Brown had Coble's brand C.A.P. seared on its rump so everybody called it Cap. It had gone through basic schooling by now and all it needed was practical experience on the open range. Then Coble had showed up and said that he had a work for him, telling him that he should check out the pastures near Iron Mountain and in case he found sheep there, he was to tell the owner to get them out of there with appropriate warning that if it happened again, the sheriff would get involved. Tom had packed a piece of bacon and a half loaf of bread into the saddle bags, and just when he started looking for a horse he saw John leading Cap out of the ring. That three-year-old could use several days under saddle he figured and waved at John. He then held the horse while Tom snapped on the holster with his Winchester, mounted just wearing a shirt and a vest and jogged out of the ranch gate.

Only now, when he heard his name, Tom returned back to the present. He looked at Stoll, but at the same time the bailiff stepped up to him and led him to the Bible on the judge's bench to be sworn in. As soon as he sat down on the witness chair, Stoll began in strict official voice the questioning. "Please state your name and the place of residence."

"Tom Horn, as of this time the Cheyenne jail."

"Why are you jailed?"

"I am accused of killing William Nickell."

"What was your place of residence in July 1901?"

"Bosler, exactly John Coble's ranch."

"What is your profession?"

"I work for cattle companies as a stock detective."

"Detective?" Stoll's voice became markedly ironic. "Could you then describe your detective work for us?"

"Certainly. The ranchers who got troubles with rustling hire me to spend some time on their pastures and make sure that nobody drives away the unbranded calves. Sometimes I check the cattle at the slaughterhouses or at auctions to see if they have proper sale papers. Basically, I collect information about people suspected of stealing cattle."

"What do you do when you run into a rustler?"

"Either I detain him and turn him over to the sheriff or get hold of the stolen cattle and report his name to people who hired me."

Stoll shook his head, "And how long have you been carrying on this activity?"

"Eight years."

"Eight years, hem?" Stoll repeated, "But looking into the records of reported thefts for the past five years, there is only one case that you arrested the thief and handed him over to the sheriff. On the other hand, there are here four cases of people who were suspected of rustling and were found dead, shot from an ambush. Could you explain this discrepancy?" The last sentence carried not only iron logic, but also sharp sarcasm.

Tom was already opening his mouth to explain it, when Lacey readily raised his hand. "Objection! This question has nothing to do with the crime the defendant is accused of."

Judge nodded his head, sustained the objection and asked Stoll to rephrase the question. The procurator, knowing that he had made the desirable impression on the jury, just waved his hand and turned the questioning toward the places where Horn was present during the time of the murder.

"Where were you on July 18, 1901?"

"In the morning or in the afternoon?"

Light laughter filled the courtroom, followed by energetic knocking of the gavel.

Stoll caught by surprise blinked couple times and then quickly added, "The whole day of course."

"On the eastern pastures of the Double B Ranch."

"What brought you there?"

Tom leaned back in the chair, looked at twelve jurors who were waiting for his every word and began to describe systematically every step he had taken that day, from the moment he left Coble's ranch till Saturday morning when he came back. He mentioned the two evenings he had spent at the Millers, he described all places he had been riding through the pastures and making sure that there were no sheep there, including the spots where he camped Thursday and Friday nights.

When Stoll questioned whether somebody saw him, Tom answered with certain sarcasm that one precondition of a successful detective work was to be seen by as few people as possible. The prosecutor in the meantime studied the records which contained last year Horn's testimony obtained only several days after young Nickell was killed, and he had to admit that except for some minutia such as estimation of distances the current and the last year's statements were practically identical. Nevertheless, there was one issue. Stoll had a witness who was willing to testify under the oath that he had seen Tom on Thursday in the morning in Laramie. The only reason for Horn to show up in this town thirty miles distant from Nickell's ranch on the day of the murder was to have alibi.

Stoll for a while pretended that he did not object to the precise description of Horn's movements in the vicinity of Miller's and Nickell's ranches and then suddenly barked out, "And what did you do on Thursday the 18th in Laramie?"

Horn looked at the prosecutor and surprised asked, "On Thursday in Laramie?"

"Yes, on Thursday in Laramie," insisted Stoll.

"As I told you, on Thursday morning I was at the Mule Spring and in the evening I camped on Fitzmorris' pasture. I came to Laramie on Saturday afternoon, after I returned to Cobles' ranch."

Stoll sharply turned away from Horn and looking at the bailiff announced, "The prosecution calls Frank Irwin, a Laramie resident."

A short, stocky fellow whose round and clean shaven face made the impression that he was a lawyer or a doctor rather than a local rancher entered the courtroom. After he was sworn in, Stoll motioned Horn to return to the defense table and Irwin took the vacated chair.

Stoll thought for a couple of seconds about the best way to formulate the question and then asked, "Could you tell the jury what you did do in Laramie on Thursday the 18th of the last year?"

The witness cleared his throat and slowly answered, "The night from Wednesday to Thursday a couple of my cows got lost, so in the morning I set out to look for them. Returning along the road leading to Iron Mountain I ran into Horn."

"Which way did he go?"

"From Iron Mountain."

"Where was he going?"

"To Laramie."

"How did you know?"

"I followed him."

"What kind of horse did he have?"

"Dark brown, almost black gelding."

"Would you say that the horse was fresh?"

"Oh no, on the contrary. It was pretty played out."

"What do you mean?"

"It was all lathered and covered with dust. Walked slowly with its head down."

"What time was it?"

"I would say between eleven and twelve."

"Was the defendant armed?"

"Yep. He had a Winchester in the holster."

"On which side?"

"I think on the right."

While Stoll was spouting one question after another, Horn studied the witness's face. Then he leaned toward Lacey and whispered something to him. The lawyer nodded that he understood and as soon as Stoll finished, he asked the judge for a lunch recess. The judge looked at the prosecutor, but Stoll only shrugged his shoulders saying that he had no objections and actually it wouldn't hurt to eat something. The judge's gavel then announced that the trial was adjourned till two o'clock.

Immediately the noise of chairs being pushed around and shuffling feet accompanied by loud voices filled the courtroom. The ranchers and reporters formed little groups and slowly headed for the door. In the corridor one could hear voices criticizing or praising the prosecutor as well as the defense counselor and many of the men present continued the heated discussion all the way out on the sidewalk and then to the nearest saloon.

Rick made his way through the crowd of people standing in front of the courthouse and was about to run to the office of Western Union to send the cable when he caught glimpse of Coble. Right next to him stood Burke who was explaining something to him. Coble kept nodding his head, then grabbed Burke by his arm and led him to his carriage. Once they got in, Rick heard Coble telling the driver to drive to the Cheyenne Club.

Shortly before two o'clock the courtroom was again full of people. The dramatic course of the morning hearings and testimonies aroused enough interest among many Cheyenne citizens that now there was not a single vacant seat in the whole room. By the striking of two the judge reopened the trial, the bailiff called in the jury and Tom Horn took place next to Lacey and Burke. Both attorneys were leafing through a stack of papers and broad smiles on their faces indicated that they were quite happy about something.

Frank Irwin took again his seat on the witness chair and Lacey began the cross examination. He reminded him that he was still under oath and began to verify some of his earlier statements. He asked him several times if he was sure that it was really Thursday when he saw Horn on the road to Laramie and then suddenly asked an unexpected question.

"How did you get acquainted with the defendant?"

For a moment Irwin looked puzzled and then he slowly answered, "Well, I met him several times in the local saloons."

"How about some other occasions?"

Irwin's eyes wandered from Lacey to Stool and drops of sweat broke out on his forehead. Finally, he pulled himself together and in firm voice he answered, "I don't remember."

"You don't remember? Okay. Let me refresh your memory a little bit."

Lacey stretched out his hand and Burke handed him a several sheets of paper.

"How about May 20th, 1895?"

Irwin leaned his head slightly to the side, making an impression that he was thinking really hard. "No, unfortunately I have no recollection."

"On May 20th, 1895 Tom Horn paid you a visit at your ranch. What was the purpose of his visit?"

Irwin kept staring at the counselor but didn't say a word. Lacey straightened up and facing partly the jury and partly the witness announced in icy voice, "On that day Tom Horn removed from your place three heifers carrying the brand of the neighboring ranch and told you that if it should happen again, he would report it to the sheriff. After his return to Cheyenne he informed the cattle association about the whole incident. Now, are you sure you saw Tom Horn in Laramie on Thursday and not on Saturday?"

The audience roared. Even though the judge tried to restore order immediately, several ranchers managed to yell, "Try cattle rustlers and not Tom Horn!"

Once the courtroom calmed down, Lacey turned to the judge and without trying to hide his satisfaction stated, "The defense has no more questions."

Stoll watched the disastrous performance of his witness with perfect calm. He suspected right away that the request for the lunch recess was only a pretext, but that Irwin would get discredited in such a colossal way, never crossed his mind. Damned Irwin! He probably thought that Horn would not recognize him seven years later after that incident with the heifers. Now the big ranchers were rubbing their hands and gloating, "Didn't we tell you that every other of them is a thief?" Out of all those who were willing to testify against Horn, only a few could be sure that their police record was clean.

The prosecutor realized that to insist on the question when Irwin saw Horn was no longer important. On the other hand, the bad impression Irwin made had to be neutralized as soon as possible. In order to win this game, one has to put into the battle the big guns, in another words, to introduce the key witness. Stoll stepped up to the bench and in a ringing voice announced, "The prosecution calls the Deputy U.S. Marshal Joe LeFors."

LeFors sitting in the second row got up, stroked his thick mustache and stepped up to the Bible. He raised his right hand, rattled off the prescribed oath and sat down on the vacant chair. After the initial questions about his name, place of residence and profession, Stoll asked him to inform the jury about his activity from the day of the murder until the moment the defendant was arrested. LeFors looked around the room and began to describe individual events. He spoke matter-of-factly, focused, and one would even say that his speech reflected certain narrating skills. He mentioned his visit at Nickell's ranch when Kels Nickell was in the hospital and assured Mrs. Nickell that he would do everything in his power to catch the killer. During the preliminary investigation he came to a conclusion that the crime had been committed by a professional. No traces of evidence were found at the crime scene and both wounds were mortal indicating that the murderer was an excellent shot. Then he heard rumors that Tom Horn had bragged about this crime on several occasions, and that was the decisive factor.

By sheer coincidence he had received a letter from Montana sometime in December in which the local sheriff asked him for help to fight a band of rustlers. He needed someone reliable and experienced with this kind of job. LeFors thought immediately of Horn. It also occurred to him that it would be a great opportunity to chat with him about the events related to the death of young Nickell. He knew that Horn stayed in Bosler and so he sent him a telegram. Horn immediately responded and, because he was lately sort of jobless, he immediately expressed an interest to take this job.

He met Horn on January 12th in the morning at the Inter-Ocean Hotel. They drank up several shots of whisky and then around noon he asked Horn to wait for him there. He excused himself and under the pretext that he had to take care of some official business he went to the courthouse. There he asked for someone who is good at shorthand. The man recommended was Charles J. Ohnhaus. Shortly after lunch Ohnhaus and Deputy Sheriff Snow hid in his office in the closet under the steps and LeFors went back to pick up Horn.

Both men returned to his office and LeFors showed the letter from Montana to Horn remarking that it was a private matter and he should not mention it anywhere. Horn laughing answered that he could rely on him because he knew how to keep secrets. He, LeFors, could ask the local ranchers if he ever got anybody into trouble. They discussed some details related to this job and then LeFors turned to the subject of young Nickell. Gradually, based on Horn's comments, he came to a conclusion that Tom Horn was the real culprit. As soon as Horn left, Ohnhaus retyped the stenographic copy and about an hour later the judge issued a warrant.

Leslie Snow arrested Horn next day in the morning in the lobby of the Inter-Ocean Hotel. Horn paid his hotel bill and was about to leave for the railroad station to catch the train to Montana. He did not resist the arrest. He just did not believe that Snow was serious.

LeFors finished with a confident smile on his face. During his speech he played with the gold chain at his vest and Lacey who watched him very closely, noticed, that the marshal not even once looked in the direction where Horn was sitting.

Stoll then handed out each juror the retyped copy of Horn's testimony obtained in LeFors' office and distributed several copies also among the present reporters. In order to strengthen the effect of this document he also read it aloud with an appropriate emphasize on all incriminating passages. Rick, who didn't miss a word from the text, felt that something was not right. The testimony was full of cursing and vulgar expressions, but during all the time he spent with Tom listening to his stories from Arizona he didn't curse even once.

The prosecutor finished reading and grave like silence filled the courtroom. Horn's friend and enemies alike were so baffled by LeFors' testimony that they were utterly speechless. Lacey glanced at Tom, but his face did not betray in the least what was going through his mind. The silence disturbed only by buzzing of a fly at the window pane was finally broken by the judge's voice.

"Does the defense have any questions?"

Lacey nodded and with a paper full of notes stepped closer to LeFors. First, he asked about some details related to his initial steps he took during the investigation, and then he wanted to know whether Horn was under influence of alcohol when Ohnhaus was recording the conversation. LeFors readily obliged him by explaining that they drank a little bit more than usual when they met in the Inter-Ocean Hotel, but in the afternoon when they were in his office, Horn was absolutely sober which Ohnhaus as well as Snow could confirm.

Lacey realized that it is practically impossible to prove that Horn acted in the state of drunkenness and focused directly on the marshal. He asked a question which immediately got the attention of all present men.

"During the consultations I had with Tom Horn, the defendant informed me that shortly after William Nickell had been shot you offered Horn a possibility of working together. In the case you or he would succeed in capturing the killer, you would split the announced reward of one thousand dollars. Why did you make him such an offer?"

"Tom Horn, working as a detective for large cattle companies, had excellent knowledge of the local terrain and people. He used to see the settlers and ranchers in the vicinity of Iron Mountain almost on a daily basis so I could hardly find a more suitable partner," LeFors answered calmly.

"Did the defendant accept your offer?"

"No."

"Why not?"

"He kept saying that he had enough worries to keep after the rustlers."

"Did you make him this offer only once or several times?"

"Several times."

"And Horn always refused?"

"Yes."

"When did you give up on asking him?"

"At the time when I heard that he was bragging in the saloons that he had done it."

"When was that? Approximately."

"Toward the end of October."

"Wasn't that about the same time when James Miller gave you five hundred dollars to drop him from the list of the suspects?"

LeFors got red in face, jumped up and exclaimed, "That's not true! That's a God damned lie!" but his loud protest was drowned in the storm of excited voices accompanied by numerous strokes of the judge's gavel. Stoll ran out from behind his table and gesticulating with his both hands he objected to this question. His eyes were flashing and he insisted that the question be immediately deleted from the official record since the defense just referred only to unsubstantiated rumors circulating among the locals.

After a while when the courtroom finally became quiet, the judge ordered the recording clerk to delete the question. Lacey shrugged his shoulders, stepped up to his table and pulled out of a folder a small piece of paper which looked like a bank receipt. Then he turned toward the jury and holding it in his fingers quite undisturbed said, "The defense has no more questions but is asking the jury to consider the fact that James Miller withdrew five hundred dollars from the Iron Mountain Bank in the middle of October."

This time the audience limited its expression of surprise only to a few loud remarks and it became silent even before the gavel hit the desk. Stoll readily assured the jury that he would account for every dollar of the aforementioned amount and called the next witness. An older man in a black worn out suit walked in, took the oath and answered the questions about his name, place of residence and profession.

"Frank A. Mullock, businessman residing in Denver."

The first question sounded like a crack of a whip. "Do you know that man?"

Mullock looked in the direction Stool's hand was pointing.

"Yes."

"Where did you meet him for the first time?"

"In Denver, in the Scandinavian Saloon."

"When?"

"Last year, at the beginning of October."

"On what occasion?"

"We were sitting at the bar drinking whisky."

"What did you talk about?"

"Oh, all possible stuff, but mainly about killing young Nickell."

"How come?"

"Well, Horn," Mullock pointed at the defendant, "had a newspaper and kept showing me the reward for catching the murderer. He said that he was a detective and that he knew every rock in the area where the murder took place. When I asked him why he didn't try to find the killer and collect the reward he said that he couldn't do it. He is the best detective in Colorado and Wyoming but also the best shot west of the Mississippi, and that young Nickell was his best shot."

"Are you sure you are not confusing him with someone else?"

"No, I am pretty sure. I saw him in that saloon several times. Only at that time he didn't have the mustache."

Stoll spread his arms and turned toward the judge. "Prosecution has no more questions."

Judge looked at the defense counselor and asked if he wanted to cross examine the witness. Lacey nodded.

"Could you be more specific about the date of the conversation you had with the defendant?"

"Well, I don't remember the exact date, but it was Saturday or Sunday the week after the rodeo."

Lacey scribbled the information on a piece of paper and was about to sit down when he quickly asked, "Could you think of someone who would support your testimony?"

Mullock hesitated for a moment and then answered, "Certainly. The barkeeper was standing right there."

"What is his name?"

"George. George Roberts."

Lacey resumed his place at the table and the judge looking at his watch asked Stoll if he intended to call more witnesses. The prosecutor, being a veteran of many trials, knew that it would be too risky to strain the jurors' memory and attention. They had heard more than enough for one day. He shook his head and the judge knocked with his gavel, announcing that the trial was adjourned till nine o'clock next day.

The deputies stepped up to Horn, handcuffed him again and led him back to his cell. The courtroom was slowly emptying. The last to leave were Stoll and Watts. The prosecutor felt satisfied with today's work. The jurors listened eagerly to his every word and the defense could not present anything that would crack the iron logic of the charge. The only thing they could do was try to discredit the witnesses and that was always a sign of weakness. Lacey would have an opportunity to show how good he was tomorrow, but if he did not come up with something really big, the jurors will not wreck their heads about Horn's guilt for too long.

Chatting with the Chief of Indian Scouts

Based on interviews with Tom Horn and prepared by F. Jackson.

An old squaw carrying a message from the main Chiricahua Chief Nana came to the reservation in the spring of 1878. She arrived on a played out mule more dead than alive. She was hungry and barefoot. On the way here she ran into a dust storm and the mule got lost. When she finally found it, most of her food packs were gone. Nana and Geronimo were thinking about returning to San Carlos but before they would do so they wanted Al Sieber to meet them in Mexico in the Terras Mountains. Sieber was the only white man they trusted, and they were willing to talk over the conditions of their return with him. They didn't want to talk to the soldiers because most of the officers in San Carlos had come recently and the chiefs didn't know any of them.

Sieber scratched his head, then ordered me to give her some food and took off for Fort Whipple to see General Wilcox. The general didn't mull over it for too long and in the end decided to comply with their request. When Sieber returned to San Carlos, he picked me and another scout to accompany him and several days later we were on the way south. Near the border we reached a small river called San Bernardino which led us all the way to Mexico. At the place where it empties itself into the Bavispe River another messenger from Geronimo was waiting for us. He stood on a cliff and watched us crossing the river. Then he rode down to the bank and addressed Sieber while pointing his finger at me. Sieber explained to him that I was a new scout and he gave him my name. This warrior was the first hostile Indian I had met. At first glance he looked quite affable, smiled friendly and no one would have suspected him of any bad intentions. However, Sieber quickly dispelled this notion and informed me that Hal-zay, which was his name, had on his conscience lives of many American and Mexican ranchers.

His task was to wait for us and then deliver Geronimo's message that he would wait for us on the top of Terras Mountains at the place called Tu-Slaw. To my question if he was going to accompany us there, he shook his head, jumped on his horse and rode off. When I remarked that it wouldn't do him any harm to take us there, Sieber smiled and said, "Where do you think he went? Several miles back to make sure that there was no U.S. Cavalry troop behind us plotting a trap."

We reached Geronimo's camp before dark. It was spreading on top of a mountain plateau, and judging by the amount of campfires there must have been at least one thousand Apaches there. Along the trail a young boy, perhaps ten years old, was waiting for us and brought us to the spot where we could put up our tent. We barely unloaded our horses when several squaws came with food and shortly after them another boy brought the message that the talks would start tomorrow after sunrise. At dawn the same squaws came again with roasted meat and corn pancakes, so all we had to do was to make coffee and have a mighty big breakfast. After sunrise Sieber waved his hand to follow him. From his own experience he knew that the pow-wow would take place somewhere in the middle of the camp because that's where the big chiefs usually have their wigwams. Sure enough, after a short walk we came to an open area where about three hundred warriors were sitting on the ground and wait-ing. The squaws, children and dogs were gone and the loud ruckus of an Indian camp was replaced by silence and an atmosphere of respect.

When we came closer, the gathered warriors stopped talking; an older tall man rose to his feet, stepped up to Sieber and friendly shook his hand. This war chief whose real name was Goyahkla (The One Who Yawns) got the nickname Geronimo from the Mexican soldiers who were asking St. Geronimo for his protection when they had to fight this feared Apache. Geronimo set his piercing eyes on me and I had such an unpleasant feeling like he could see all the way into my soul. Of course I pretended that meeting this famous chief did not make any difference to me, but actually I was pretty shaky. He was looking at me for awhile and then he asked Sieber who would interpret his speech into English. Even though Sieber understood Apache quite well, he had a hard time following Geronimo because he spoke not only in a very flowery way but also very quickly. Sieber pointed at me and Geronimo asked me if I really thought that I would be able to translate everything he would say. I don't know what got into me, probably the typical puerile self-confidence, and I said yes because the great chief had only one mouth and one tongue. When I think about it now, it bordered on arrogance and disrespect, but amazingly Geronimo smiled and apparently he was mighty pleased with my answer. He motioned us with his hand to sit down and the great council began.

Well, to call it a great council was not actually the correct way to put it because only one party was speaking, and there could be no doubt that this chief knew how to speak. First he listed all the injustice he had suffered from the Indian agents, soldiers, White Mountain Indians and the Mexicans. Then he declared that he was willing to return to the reservation but under the following conditions: The government has to issue to him and his people new rifles and an unlimited amount of ammunition so they could keep hunting. For all his warriors he wanted a regular supply of horses, for the squaws mules and for all the children new shoes. For himself he wanted free movement away from the reservation, two Mexicans who would make him mescal, and so it went on and on. I was sure that if he had been familiar with the Sears catalogue, he would have wanted everything in it.

Sieber listened and not even by one word or gesture did he let any-

body know what he was thinking about it.

When Geronimo finished, the old chief of scouts got up, looked down into the valley as if he wanted to admire the beautiful scenery and told me, "Tom, tell Geronimo just what I am going to say, no more and no less." Then he stepped up to the chief and said, "You have asked for everything that I know anything about, except to have these mountains moved up into the American country for you to live in. I'll give you till sundown to talk to your people and see if you want these mountains moved up there or not. If you are entitled, by your former conduct, to what you have asked for, then you should have these mountains too." That was all. Sieber turned around, walked out of the council and the Indians reacted to his sarcasm by distinguished silence. Geronimo then announced that the council was postponed till the evening.

When I returned, I found Sieber lying on blankets next to the tent. He asked me to leave him alone because he had to think about what he was going to tell that old wolf later that night. He told me I should take the webs of fabric we had brought with us and give it to several squaws he knew from the reservation, and then come back around noon to make him coffee.

Toward evening we went back to the spot where the morning council had taken place. This time it was Sieber who held a long speech. If my memory serves me well, it sounded something like this:

"Geronimo, this morning you asked for many things and you knew I could not give you many of the things you asked for, and I do think that you asked for most of them because you love to talk and not because I could or would do as you asked me. Anything I do promise, you know full well, you will get because I never lied to you and I never promised anything I could not fulfill. I am not the fluent orator that you are, neither do I ask for or try to get that which I know I can never obtain. Now this I say to you: Go to the reservation and do as you will be advised to do by the government and you will get all that the government can give you. You know what the government can give you for you have lived there and have drawn your rations, as many Indians are doing now. A blanket will also be given for each of you and other things just as you have received before, but I can promise no more for it has been spoken by my government that you shall get no more.

"Geronimo, I have no idea if you will do as I say, for you do not love peace. You are a man of war and battle; else you would not be a war chief of the Chiricahua tribe. You could go to the reservation and stay maybe one season or maybe only one moon, but within this camp there may be some who do really want to settle down to a peaceful life. Any and all such I will take safely back, and most of your people know what they will get. Twice I have taken you there and twice you became uneasy and left. Never did a complaint come to my government that you were not fed. Never did you complain of not having enough clothing and blankets. However, if there would be a row between this tribe and some of the other tribes, or if someone would sell you a lot of whisky and you would all, or a great many of you get drunk, away you would go. Until now you have not complained of not getting what the government promised you.

"This cannot last. The white men are as the leaves upon the trees. There are hundreds and hundreds of white men to one Apache. It is true that many cannot protect themselves against such warriors as there are here, for it is my opinion that there are none better in the world. Still all the Chiricahua and Agua Caliente warriors who are within hearing my words cannot stay on the war path and not be eventually exterminated.

Slowly, of course, but one by one they will be captured or killed and how will you ever replace them? True, you can say that the Americans will not be allowed to come here into this Mexican country, armed and in force to fight you. Such have been the conditions so far, and I know you have no fear of the Mexican soldiers, and I have heard the Apache women say they would whip the whole Mexican army. But I say that within a short time, may be a year or two, a peace talk will be held between the Mexican and American governments and arrangements will be made to allow the American soldiers and scouts to enter these mountains in force and in pursuit of you and then you will be doomed, for as I said before, the American soldiers are without number. I have spoken words of advice to you in this council. I have never told you a lie and no warrior here will say that he thinks I talk two ways. Consider well what I have said to you. I'll leave in four days for San Carlos."

Sieber finished and motioned me to follow him back to our tent. Then at night we saw campfires burning way past the midnight. Geronimo held council with the other chiefs and the warriors consulted each other.

Shortly before the four day deadline expired, many squaws and old men who wanted to return to San Carlos began moving to our camp. I wasn't too eager to go back. Because of my knowledge of the Apache and the many gifts I brought with me, I became quite popular in the camp. I even managed to exchange two Mexican blankets for two pretty horses and two mules. The Indian I traded with and I were mighty satisfied. I paid for those blankets in Tucson only twelve dollars and the horses as well the mules were undoubtedly stolen from a Mexican rancher.

On the fourth day Geronimo came to say good-bye. He shook our hands and told us that he respected the wish of the others to return with us. Of course he didn't mind because leaving were only widows and old men who could no longer fight. When he shook my hand he just briefly remarked that I was still a young man and we would one day meet again, either at the battlefield or at the council fire. As long as I came on behalf of the government, I would be always welcome. I did not see Geronimo again until in 1883, but I'll talk about that next time.

6

Several sharp knocks of the gavel silenced the murmur in the courtroom and signaled that the second day of the trial State of Wyoming vs. Tom Horn could start. Now it was the defense's turn to present the witnesses who would testify in Horn's favor. Lacey as well Burke were fully aware of the fact that the smallest mess-up would break the thin thread on which Horn's life was hanging. Even though Stoll did not present any evidence which would prove Horn's guilt beyond any reasonable doubt, there could be no question that the transcript of Ohnhaus' shorthand recording made an indelible impression not only on the jury, but on the local population, too.

Lacey looked at the front page of *The Cheyenne Examiner* lying on the table next to Tom Horn. The splash headline was announcing that the murderer had confessed and consequently any effort to prove his innocence was a waste of time, and the legal maneuvering was not in the best interest of the public. Then he glanced at Horn and he got the impression that perhaps this man had no nerves. Such self-control was truly rare. Horn sat quietly on the chair, his hands folded and his face showing no sign of emotions or fear, as if he were just a spectator and not a human being whose life was at stake.

The judge gestured the defense attorney. Lacey got up, with the palm of his left hand straightened his hair and walked up to the jury box. Then he unfolded a sheet of paper with notes and began to summarize Mullock's testimony from the previous day. When he finished, he turned toward the bailiff and asked him to bring the first witness, William Davis, the Denver police physician. The eyes of the audience set on a tall grey-haired man wearing a police uniform. Davis stepped up to the Bible, swore that he would speak only the truth and nothing but the truth and sat down on the witness chair. Lacey quickly glanced at his notes and began the questioning.

"Could you describe the work of a police physician for the jury?"

"To offer first aid to the members of the police corps in case they get injured when on duty," briefly answered Davis.

"Only to policemen?"

"Also to the civilians if in the case of a police action they were injured or if police were called to an incident where a private person suffered an injury," sounded the answer as if quoted from the manual for the police doctors.

"Do you remember if you were on duty on October 1st last year?"

"Of course. On that day the annual Denver rodeo takes place, so several police physicians are always on duty."

"You were one them?"

"Yes."

"Did you have an opportunity to provide first aid to someone on that day?"

"Not during the day, but in the evening two patrolmen brought one chap with a broken jaw. According to their testimony a fist fight took place in the Pennington Saloon. The man with the broken jaw had bad luck because his opponent was a professional boxer. If I am not mistaken, he was even a Colorado champion."

"How would you describe his injury?"

"The jaw was broken on the right hand side..." Davis paused a second and then more to himself then for the jury remarked, "It must have been a left hook. His face was swollen and he could hardly talk. I bandaged his face and sent him to the hospital because in some cases with such a fracture, the bone has to be immobilized by plaster."

"Would you recognize him?"

"Sure. He sits over there, but at that time he did not have the mustache."

"Last question. Are you absolutely sure that was October 1st and not a week later?"

"Oh, yes. Just a moment, here. I have the extract from the book where we keep all injuries recorded."

The physician reached into the pocket of his jacket and pulled out a folded slip of paper. He ran his finger over several lines and then read, "Name: Tom Horn. Date: October 1st, 8 P.M. Injury: broken jaw. Treatment: starch bandage."

Lacey then walked to his table, opened the folder and reached for a letter signed by the hospital physician. The surgeon was describing in detail Horn's injury and toward the end stated that the patient could not speak for three weeks and communicated with the nurses and doctors only in writing. Then one copy of the letter was passed to the judge and the other one to the jury.

The judge looked at Stoll, but the prosecutor just waved his hand indicating he was not interested in the cross examination. Lacey could not believe his eyes. Why would he pass an opportunity to examine a testimony which practically nullified an important testimony of his witness? For a moment a burning question crossed his mind: *Which of the witnesses will he try to attack? Where does he sense a weak spot?* He quickly suppressed this unpleasant feeling and called several employees of the Inter-Ocean Hotel. One after other testified that they had seen Horn and LeFors drinking in the morning at the bar, and that by noon Horn was definitely drunk. He staggered, mumbled, and one of them confirmed that during the lunch time Horn was sleeping in an armchair near the restrooms.

Stoll sat at his table, squinted his eyes, and not even once tried to verify the information provided by Lacey's witnesses. He obviously did not want to waste time dealing with such a petty point of the defense that Horn had spoken in LeFors' office when drunk. It looked like he was saving his energy for something more serious.

Lacey called the next witness. A young dark-eyed fellow stepped out of the corridor, went through the swearing procedure and with a smile on his face awaited the questions.

"Please state your name, age, profession and place of residence."

"Otto Plaga, twenty-four years old. I live on a ranch not far from Iron Mountain. I work there as a cowboy," came the answer.

"How long have you been living in Wyoming?"

"Eighteen years."

"Do you know the defendant?"

"Yes, sir."

"For how long?"

"Since eighteen ninety-four."

"Do you know what kind of horse he rides?"

"Well, lately I have seen him riding a dark brown gelding."

"Does it have a special brand?"

"Yes, sir. Three letters: CAP."

Lacey paused for a moment and then continued.

"Do you remember where you were on July 18th of the last year, early in the morning?"

"At Mule Creek."

"What did you do there?"

"I did a little bit of prospecting."

"What do you mean by that?"

"Well, the old timers believe that way back one could find gold in them hills along the creek. So I went there with a pick to see if I could find any."

"How long did you stay there?"

"The whole morning."

Lacey now changed the subject.

"Do you know the location of Nickell's ranch?"

"Yes, sir."

"How far is it from the spot where you were looking for gold?"

"I'd say a good twenty miles."

"You said you had been there the whole morning. Did you see someone?"

"Yes, sir."

"Whom?"

"Tom Horn showed up there early in the morning. He was riding on the other side of the creek."

"In which direction?"

"Southwest."

"Would you say he was riding away from Nickell's ranch?"

"No, sir. Rather the other way around."

"What horse did he ride? That dark brown gelding with the CAP brand?"

"Yes, sir."

"Was he riding pretty fast?"

"No, sir, just jogging."

"In what shape was the horse? Was it all leathered? Did it look tired like after a long ride?"

"No, sir. It was dry."

"How far away were you from the rider?"

"About a hundred yards."

"Did he see you?"

"No, because he was riding along the creek and I was up on a hill."

"Do you remember what time it was?"

"Between eight and nine."

Even though Lacey made an impression that he was fully paying attention to Plaga's answers, he also kept an eye on Stoll. He soon noticed that after the second or third question Stoll concentrated on every word the young cowboy uttered and that he began taking notes. Lacey prayed that this good-hearted fellow would not make a mistake. He was the only witness who could save Horn's neck. It was close to twenty miles from Mule Creek to Nickell's ranch and if the murder took place between seven and eight in the morning it was absolutely unthinkable that about an hour later Horn was riding on a dry horse in the area where Plaga was hoping to find some gold.

As soon as Lacey announced that he had no more questions, Stoll swiftly ran out from behind his table and eagerly began the cross-examination. Already, the first question indicated that in this game he had no equal.

"Mr. Plaga, you own mining lots or mining rights along Mule Creek?"

The young cowboy quite surprised and wide-eyed answered, "No, sir."

"So you were actually prospecting on someone else's land, right?"

Plaga clearly embarrassed nodded his head, "That's true, but the land along the creek is open for anybody who wants to prospect there."

"But you have later applied for mining rights at the district court, right?" Stoll kept pressing.

"No, sir."

"So why did you prospect along Mule Creek if even a year later you didn't show any interest to seek the legal right to mine gold there? What actually did you do there? According to your previous testimony recorded last year, you claimed that you had been looking for lost calves in that area?"

"Well, that too, but when I came to the creek, I figured I'd look for the calves a bit later."

"According to your testimony you have known Tom Horn for six years. Am I right?"

"Yes, sir."

"Would you say that Tom was your good friend?"

"Certainly. We spent together many months in the saddle."

"A while ago you said that you had spotted Horn between eight and eight thirty in the morning on the other side of the creek. Did you talk to him or let him know that you were there?"

"No, sir."

"Could you then explain to the jury, why you did not call or wave at a man with whom, as you said, you had spent many months in the saddle?" Stoll raised his voice full of irony and sarcasm.

Plaga obviously didn't know what to say. First he looked at Lacey, then at Horn as if he were seeking help from them and finally, slightly embarrassed, blurted, "Well, I didn't want Tom to see me. I didn't want him to laugh at me because he didn't believe that there was any gold there."

Stoll doubtfully shrugged his shoulders and began to ask about Horn.

"How was he dressed?"

"He was wearing a yellow shirt, dark vest, and grey felt hat."

"Did he have a Winchester?"

"I don't think so."

The answer drew the prosecutor's attention.

"When Horn was riding along the creek, which side did you see?"

"The right hand side," Plaga responded without hesitation.

"Don't you guys carry the rifle on the right hand side of the saddle?"

"Not necessarily."

"One more question. Are you sure it was on July 18th? Couldn't it be a day earlier or later?"

"No, sir."

"Why not?"

"The mail was handed out the next day. You see, the mail is delivered to the ranch twice a week," readily explained Plaga. "Tuesday and Friday, and I was at Mule Creek the day before."

The procurator looked at the judge and threw up both his hands indicating that he had no more questions.

Lacey sighed with a relief. Stoll managed to raise some questions about the witness' testimony, particularly about his prospecting, but the issue of the date when he saw Horn, Plaga defended quite well. His statement about seeing Horn at Mule Creek matched the one he made last year. Lacey was now facing a dilemma. Should he call another witnesses to confirm that many things Horn mentioned during the conversation in LeFors' office were just fantasies, or should he grab the devil by the horns and let Horn himself explain them right now? He leaned to Burke and both lawyers whispered a few words. Then he straightened up and with a resolve announced, "The defense calls Tom Horn."

Horn sensed that the time when he would have to take the responsibility for his own words was coming. He was otherwise known for being quite a taciturn and reserved person, but right then it would have taken just a few more shots of whisky than usual and all caution and instinct of self-preservation gained and honed during the battles with the Apaches would have been gone. Only iron self-control prevented him from banging madly his head against the table at which he was sitting.

Horn got up, sat down on the chair Plaga had vacated a minute ago, and when Lacey reminded him that he was still under the oath, he almost imperceptibly nodded his head. Lacey opened the folder containing the retyped recording of Horn's and LeFors' conversation and then looked at an additional sheet full of notes. Yesterday evening he and Horn sat over this document almost till midnight. They went through it word by word looking for the smallest irregularity which could help prove Lacey's point that all those two men did was run their mouths. Even though Horn admitted that it was really a pretty close transcript, in several instances, however, he refused to confirm its correctness. Now it was up to him and Lacey to convince the jury that this evidence was false and therefore not legally valid.

The defense attorney took his place between Horn and the jury box, turned his back toward the bench and began asking questions.

"How would you describe the condition you were in when you were in LeFors' office? Would you say you were completely sober or you were still under the influence of alcohol?"

"Well, I was no longer drunk, but just a little tipsy. We consumed a good deal of whisky that morning."

"Were you aware of what you were saying?"

"Oh, yes."

"Could you then explain to the jury why you were saying such incriminating things?"

Horn scratched his head, looked at the jury, and then with obvious embarrassment answered, "LeFors, any time he could, made allusions that I was a paid gunman and I had a heap of human lives on my conscience. I noticed that he felt sort of important if he could brag in front of me how well he knew my past. So I didn't argue with him and, just to have fun, I also added something but in reality most of the stuff wasn't true. I was just joshing."

"Would you say the same if you knew that someelse was listening?"

"Of course I would. When one is joshing, it doesn't matter how many people are listening. The more the merrier," calmly Horn responded.

Lacey paused a few seconds and then inquired about some specific passages of that fateful conversation.

"The Deputy U.S. Marshal made the following statement, 'I don't know a man who could better cover his tracks than you. In the case of young Nickell, I didn't find anything worth a damn and at the same time, well, I don't want to brag but I am pretty good tracker.' You answered, 'I never leave tracks. To do such a job, the best way is to go barefoot.' LeFors had responded, 'But the ground is nothing but rocks and prickly pear. Your feet had to bleed pretty bad.' You answered, 'Well, that's true. For couple of days I could hardly walk, but that goes with the territory.' Did you mean that?"

"Of course not, but this kind of talk always made a hell of an impression on him."

On this occasion Lacey turned toward the jurors and asked them to remember this part of the testimony because he would come back to it later on. Then he quoted the next excerpt.

"To LeFors' question about where you had your horse, you responded, 'Far away.' What did you mean by that?"

Horn laughed, "Far away from the place of the murder because at that time I was sitting on it."

Several people joined Horn's laugher, but the gavel quickly restored the order.

Lacey waited until the courtroom was again absolutely still and then went on.

"LeFors then asked you if somebody used to bring you food and if you got hungry while out there. You answered, 'You better believe it. I got hungry, but no one brought me food. I can go without it for several days. The most important thing is to get the fellow I am after.' What were you trying to say?"

"If I suspect somebody is a rustler, I have to watch him sometimes three days or four days or the whole week. But if I run out of food, that doesn't mean that I drop everything and go home."

The attorney, satisfied with the answer, nodded his head and began to quote the most touchy part of the whole recording.

"LeFors had said, 'Tom, I never found out why Willie was shot. Was it because somebody had him on his list or was it a mistake?' You had said, 'Well, I think it was like this. Let's say that the shooter hid in the ravine near the sheep corral and Willie ran into him. So the man in question either shot him because he mistook him for his father or just because he was afraid that the boy would alarm the whole county.' Why did you say that?"

"Because LeFors wanted to hear my opinion. Of course it was just what occurred to me. After all, I repeated what was in the local paper."

"So you just speculated?"

"Exactly."

Lacey paused again and took a deep breath because now the worst was coming.

"When LeFors asked, 'At what distance was Willie shot?' you answered, 'About three hundred yards. It was my best shot, but also the dirtiest trick I ever made.' For God's sake, how could you have said something like this?"

Tom's restless eyes ran over the courtroom and then stopped at some point just above the jury box. Then he leaned back and stressing every word said, "This statement is not correctly recorded. I remember exactly that I said, 'That would have been my best shot but also the dirtiest trick I had ever made."

The courtroom exploded like a powder keg. The audience let go of their feelings. Frustration, anger and indignation accompanied by raised and wildly gesticulating hands filled the room. Some expressed their beliefs that this trial was nothing but an effort to frame Horn and was built on the basis of a doctored testimony to find him guilty. The others didn't hide their views that Horn was a monster, a scum who not only commited despicable crimes but, on top of it, he bragged about them. The judge kept pounding his desk with his gavel and only the threat he would have the room evacuated eventually calmed down the excited men.

Lacey and Horn stoically waited for this storm to blow over and once the room got quiet again, Lacey put the folder aside and asked an unexpected question.

"Have you ever been near the spot where young Nickell was shot?"

"Well, yes and no. Technically, no. I visited the Nickels several times, but I didn't care where they kept their sheep."

"Are you aware that there is no ravine there?"

"No."

"Do you know that Willie was shot at the distance of forty or fifty yards and not three hundred as you told LeFors?"

"I vaguely remember that the paper mentioned it, but I don't know exactly."

"In another words, what you told LeFors, you just made it all up?"

"Sure." Horn looked around and turned toward the jury. "I hardly knew the boy and with God as my witness, I had no reason to hurt him."

"What about his father, Kels Nickell?"

"The same thing. I never heard that Kels was suspected of rustling."

Lacey satisfied with Horn's answers turned toward Stoll and gestured him that the defendant was at his disposal.

The prosecutor was waiting for this moment from the very morning. Even though some defense witnesses could threaten his effort, the most important role in this trial Horn played himself. If he succeeded in convincing the jury that Horn was a dangerous individual who just lied and tried to worm his way out of this trouble, his work would be done. Lacey put all his eggs in one basket - that Horn was just joshing - but this kind of joshing kept repeating quite regularly and at many places. LeFors had signed an affidavit just the previous day saying that Horn admitted to killing Powell and Lewis in his presence and, on top of it, that he fired on Kels Nickell. An innocent and morally upright man would hardly make fun about such events and certainly not in several places. The jury must understand this simple logic.

Stoll walked around the table and like a hungry hawk attacking its prey came down on Horn.

"Your defense attorney mentioned yesterday that Deputy U.S. Marshal LeFors had offered you several times a possibility of collaboration. In all cases you have refused, haven't you?"

"Yes."

"Do you remember the conversation which took place here in Cheyenne in the Tivoli Saloon on August 14th last year?"

"I think I do, but I don't remember the exact date."

"On that occasion you refused saying that you were busy with the rustlers and didn't have time for this kind of work."

Horn nodded his head and then when admonished by Stoll to answer yes or no, said, "Yes."

"Do you remember what else you two had talked about?"

"Vaguely. He probably made allusions to my shooting skills and because he did it all the time, I did not pay any attention to it."

The prosecutor stretched out his hand and Watts put in it two sheets of paper with a typed text. Stoll waved them like a battle flag and turned toward the jurors.

"Here I have an affidavit signed by Deputy U.S. Marshal Joe LeFors stating that on August 14th, 1901 during his conversation with Tom Horn the following statements were made:

LeFors: I heard that you had shot Powell and Lewis by a six-shooter when they were standing next to a corral and that you had received for each of them six hundred dollars. Is it true?

Horn: Of course. I don't work for free.

So you didn't pay any attention to this, did you?" Stoll asked snappishly.

Horn was about to answer but Lacey immediately objected, "Horn is charged with the murder of William Nickell and any effort to introduce material irrelevant to the indictment is unlawful. Moreover it negatively influences the jury." Lacey looked asking at the judge but he rejected the objection.

At the same time Horn spoke, "Allow me to answer this. First, I would like to say that if LeFors had said I had shot them with the Gatling gun I would have gone along with it and if he had claimed that I had gotten ten thousand dollars or just one dollar and fifty cents, I would have agreed with him, too."

Light laughter was heard in the room but it stopped even before the judge had time to reach for the gavel.

"Second, in the case of Powell and Lewis, I was called to an inquest by the Natrona County Judge. The jury met several times, but in the end it ruled that during the time those two ranchers were shot I was not in the area. So who would resist a temptation to make fun of him?"

"Fun? You are saying fun, right?" Stoll reacted with higher volume of his voice. "And what about this?" The prosecutor looked at the papers he was holding in his hand and quoted,

"LeFors: How was it with Kels Nickell? You, such a great shot, fired a whole bunch of shots and he still survived it?

"Horn: Well, I was shooting against the sun, so I just saw his silhouette and on top of it the old Nickell was jumping left and right like a wounded Comanche, so I couldn't take a good aim."

"That's nonsense," Horn responded with incredible calm. "First, I don't remember I would have said anything like that, and second, at that time I was about eighty miles away from Nickell's ranch. I was at the Sellers. They were making hay so I was helping. All you have to do is go there and ask."

Stoll got red in face, threw the papers with LeFors' affidavit on the table and picked up another one. Then he stood in front of Horn and with eyes glistening excitedly announced, "The prosecution presents an affidavit signed by Robert Couseley of St. Louis, Missouri. During his business trip he stopped at the Scandinavian Saloon in Denver and there he overheard a man over six feet tall who was bragging that he had killed his first man when he was twenty-six and that shooting the troublesome ranchers was his business. He shot one boy by mistake, but he still has plenty of offers for this job, and as to the rustlers, he cleaned up the whole southern Wyoming. When Couseley later on saw the defendant's picture in the newspaper, he reliably recognized Tom Horn."

Stoll now decided that it was time for a psychological blow. He again raised his voice and with his forefinger in Horn's face he dramatically declared, "Mr. Horn, you are a common criminal, who offers his services to people who don't have stomach for this kind of dirty work. Moreover, then you hang around saloons where you brag about your murdering activity and when the law catches up with you and you should take the responsibility for your misdeeds, you cowardly lie and claim that it was all in fun."

A storm of loud voices broke out. From the row where Horn's supporters sat came exclamations like, "You should be ashamed!" "That's scandalous!" "What arrogance!" Immediately after that, many words were heard praising the prosecutor that finally someone said what everybody knew but was afraid to say aloud. Both Lacey and Burke jumped up and resolutely demanded deleting Stoll's verbal attack on Horn from the official record. The defense attorney became unusually aggressive, turned toward Stoll and threw in his face an ironic remark.

"Every law student knows that according to the American Constitution a defendant is considered innocent until found guilty!"

Stoll, his hands folded on his chest, however, observed the ruckus his statement had caused with obvious indifference. Even though from a legal point of view Lacey was right, the impression he had made on the jury was worth it. In spite of all that confusion, he noticed that several jurors nodded their heads in an apparent agreement.

The droning of voices and pushed around chairs interspersed with the hollow sound of the gavel pounding on the judge's desk lasted almost ten minutes. Even the threat of having the courtroom evacuated had to be repeated several times before the audience settled down. When order was finally restored, the judge asked the clerk to remove Stoll's statement and asked the jurors to ignore it. It was only the prosecutor's personal opinion and it should have no effect on their decision as to the guilt of the defendant. Everybody in the room, however, was aware of the fact that the uttered words cannot be taken back just like the damage they had caused could not be undone.

To the judge's question if he had any more questions, Stoll just shook his head and joined Watts at the table. Lacey glanced at Horn, who in the meantime had returned to his chair, but his face again resembled a sphinx rather than a human being. The attorney opened the folder with LeFors' testimony and read the passage where Horn said that he doesn't leave tracks because when he stalks a man, he walks barefoot. To LeFors' remark that his feet must bleed, Horn answered that it was true and that for several days he could not walk. Lacey closed the folder and asked the bailiff to bring Frank Stone, the former cowboy living in Laramie.

A minute later a middle-aged man with a handlebar mustache entered the courtroom. His hair was quite grey and he was limping. When he worked at Coble's ranch his horse stepped at full gallop into a gopher hole. It cost Frank an ugly fracture of his right ankle and even though Coble sent immediately for a doctor, the bones never healed the way they should have. The man looked around the room, stepped to the Bible and slowly and deliberately recited the prescribed formula. As soon as the final sentence "So help me God" came from under the mighty mustache, the bailiff motioned for him to sit down on the chair which only awhile ago had been occupied by Horn.

Lacey walked around the table, stopped several feet away from Stone and started with the obligatory question about the witness' name, profession and place of residence. Then more general questions followed.

"How long have you known Tom Horn?"

"Five years," without hesitation Stone answered.

"From where do you know him?"

"From Coble's ranch."

"When did you move to Laramie?"

"Three years ago when my horse fell."

"Have you maintained any contact with Tom after that or have you never seen him again since?"

"Oh, no," smiled Stone. "You don't know Tom. Any time he had some business in Laramie, he stopped by."

"How often? Once a week, once a month?"

"I would say once a month."

"Do you remember if you met him in July last year?"

"Yeah, I remember it quite well. I can't tell the exact date, but it was one Saturday toward the end of the month."

"Why does this visit stick in your mind?"

"Because we were at Jack's Saloon and Tom consumed a little more whisky than he could handle and I had to haul him to my house in a cart."

"Could you tell the jury what you did with him when you arrived at your home?"

"Well, what was I supposed to do? I couldn't leave an old buddy of mine outside. So I undressed him and put him in the bed."

"Did you take his shoes off?"

"Of course I did. You don't expect me to let him sleep in my own bed with shoes on, do you?"

"Did you also take his socks off?"

"Yeah, them too."

"When you were taking off his socks, had you noticed any bruises or scratches or any injury on his feet, especially on the soles?"

Stone looked quite surprised at Lacey and then readily with humor responded, "No, just needed them washed."

Lacey smiled and it was hard to tell whether he smiled because of the witty answer or he was pleased with the testimony. He then gestured to Stoll that the witness was at his disposal and sat down at the table. The prosecutor hesitated a while and it almost looked like he was going to skip further questioning when he suddenly grabbed the calendar standing on the table and began to leaf in it. Then he stepped up to the witness.

"Mr. Stone, you have electricity in your house?"

"No."

"So what do you use for the light in the evening?"

"Kerosene lamp."

"At what time did you return home with the defendant?"

"A bit after midnight."

"So the house was completely dark and the only source of light was the kerosene lamp?"

"That's correct."

Stoll nodded his head, then opened the calendar and matter-of-factly remarked, "The last July had four Saturdays. After the 18th when the murder took place, the next Saturday was on the 20th and the following, as you said by the end of the month, was on the 27th. In another words, nine days would have passed. Don't you think that if he had scratched his feet that by the time you were taking off his socks the soles could be healed enough that it would be almost impossible to see any scars or marks in the light of a kerosene lamp?"

The mustached fellow wrinkled his forehead, thought pretty hard for awhile and then slowly answered, "Wait, I don't remember the exact date, but one thing I remember quite well. Tom, among other things, complained that he had spent the whole day riding along the pastures near Iron Mountain 'cause somebody was supposed to turn lose the doggone sheep on the land belonging to Double B Ranch."

It hummed again in the front rows and Lacey's face was covered by a satisfied smile. If the jury does not get it that Stoll's arguments are based on speculations and unsubstantiated rubbish, then his further effort to prove Horn's innocence was in vain. The prosecutor gave the witness an incredulous look and was about to say something, but then just waved his hand, closed the calendar and returned to his seat next to Watts. The bailiff looked asking at the defense attorney, but when Lacey indicated that the questioning was over, he led Frank Stone out of the courtroom.

The bailiff returned and resumed his post next to the bench while the judge waited awhile and then asked both attorneys if they intended to call other witnesses. Stoll and Lacey requested a few minutes to consult each other after which the room became quiet again. The silence was interrupted only by four men whispering and the rustling of paper as they were going through the list of the other prospective witnesses. At the same time, they weighed the potential gains and risks which their testimonies could have.

After several minutes Lacey got up and in a firm voice said, "The defense will not call any more witnesses."

Stoll who was convinced that on the basis of LeFors' testimony the jury had already made up its mind, rose from behind the table and with a good measure of self-confidence and announced that the prosecution was ready to deliver closing arguments.

The judge nodded his head and declared the session adjourned until nine o'clock the next morning. A sharp knock with the gavel followed and the courtroom was again filled with the noise of shuffling feet and chairs being pushed around.

Chatting with the Chief of Indian Scouts

Based on interviews with Tom Horn and prepared by F. Jackson.

Several hundred Chiricahua returned to San Carlos between 1878 and 1879 but the situation in the reservation did not indicate that the government had a firm control over its administration. Major Chafee was transferred to Fort McDowell and his job was taken by a civilian, a certain Tiffany. Shortly thereafter, the garrison was pulled out of Fort Apache and the moment the Indians found out about it, the genuine mayhem started. The Chiricahua and Cibique started to leave the reservation and raided the American as well as the Mexican ranchers, stole their cows, horses and mules, and Tiffany, instead of trying to maintain some semblance of order, kept defrauding money and enriching himself on the account of rations slated for the Indians. When it got out and the whole affair ended at the Tucson Court, Tiffany's books showed a deficit of fifty-four thousand dollars and he couldn't account for a single cent.

The first major breakout from San Carlos took place in the spring of 1880. Considering the conditions in the reservation, it was only a matter of time and one could hardly blame its residents. About one thousand warriors, squaws and children and up to two thousand heads of cattle began marching south toward Mexico. In spite of the telegrams Sieber kept sending to the Bureau of Indian Affairs in Washington warning about the growing danger of a potential escape, nobody did anything to prevent it or even at least to be ready when it happened. Even the army didn't have enough horses to try to stop the fleeing Indians. The cavalry troops had to be satisfied with attacks on smaller raiding groups and reclaiming the stolen cattle and horses. The situation got better only in 1883. In that year the treaty between the USA and Mexico about mutual military operations on both sides of the border was finally signed. Now who do you think was the first to respond to this important event? Geronimo. He sent Peechee, one of his warriors, to San Carlos with the message that he had definitely decided to bury the war hatchet and return to the reservation with all his men. Among other things, he also insisted that General Crook who last year became the Department Commander come with a large military force to protect him and all Chiricahua on the way to the American territory against the Mexican army.

General Crook was an experienced soldier. Not only did he know the Indians, but he also believed that many of their complaints were quite justified. As soon as he found out that Geronimo was willing to negotiate, he sent for Sieber who was at that time at Fort Bowie and then they both met in San Carlos. The telegrams between Forts Whipple and Bowie and between San Carlos and Washington kept the wires hot for several weeks. In the end, General Crook had to go to Washington in person, but before he left he had sent Peechee back to Geronimo with a message saying that within two months he would respond to his proposal. When he returned, another messenger traveled to Geronimo's camp with a concrete offer, namely that General Crook would come to Sierra Madre to the Viejo River and there he would wait for a guide.

The preparations for this trip took about a week. Finally, about three cavalry troops were formed at Fort Bowie, plus about one hundred pack animals with food supplies not only for the soldiers but also for the Apaches and over fifty scouts headed by Sieber. The most interesting thing about this expedition was that nobody except for Sieber and several officers knew of its purpose. The local papers were falling over each other in speculations and when they found out that we carried food for two months, they were firmly convinced that the army planned a general attack on the Chiricahua hiding in Mexico.

Two weeks later we reached the Viejo River and who would you guess was waiting for us? Peechee whose name we changed to "Peaches". To make sure that the Apaches wouldn't think of any mischief, General Crook doubled the guards on both wings of the moving troops and the pack animals with the provisions were closely watched twenty-four hours a day.

We reached Geronimo's camp in five days. The countryside we were passing through was just gorgeous. Particularly we saw numerous peach trees whose branches were touching the ground under the weight of ripe fruits. "Peaches" readily informed us that these trees bear fruit twice a year. On the fifth day we saw abandoned wigwams and cold ashes of campfires. There was no doubt we were approaching a large Indian camp. Once we got really close, Geronimo himself at the head of small group of chiefs rode out to welcome us. After the exchange of pleasantries we were told that the big talk would start tomorrow and, symbolizing the renewed friendship, we could camp in a close proximity to their wigwams.

The next day the intricate diplomatic game was on. Both Al Sieber and General Crook knew that Geronimo liked to appear to the public as a great leader whose will was the law for all Chiricahua, but in reality, he needed a support of the majority of all male members of the tribe for any decision he made. In another words, Geronimo would agree to the departure to San Carlos only in the case that the majority of his warriors were willing to give up their raiding lifestyle and were about to accept the peaceful and not overly exciting life on the reservation. I was picked for the task to convince the present Apaches, mainly those who were not yet decided, to accept this idea. The potential trouble, of course, was Geronimo who personally was not too enthused about living in idleness. The old warrior would hardly come to terms with the kind of life whose greatest attraction or excitement was monthly distribution of rations.

When Geronimo asked who would interpret, General Crook waved his hand and one of the scouts, a certain Antonio Dias, stepped forward. Dias was a Mexican with some Apache blood in his pedigree. Geronimo looked at him, shook his head, and then resolutely said that Mexicans could not be trusted because according to his life experience they were all downright liars, and as they would be talking about rather serious matters, the interpreter had to be a person both sides could trust. To the question if he had someone in mind, Geronimo pointed at me. Then he added that the only white man who never lied to him was Sibi - that was his nickname for Sieber - and because he trained me, quite naturally I was the only one who had his trust.

Of course this maneuver would kill our plan, so General Crook tried his best to talk Geronimo out of it. He kept arguing that Dias was much more experienced than I, then that Sieber trained me as warrior and according to the traditions I could not interpret, but Geronimo kept shaking his head and so we had to give in. In this way I became the official interpreter and Dias assumed my role to influence the warriors in the camp.

The first person to speak was General Crook. His speech sounded about like this:

"Eleven years ago when I was the commander of this area, the Indians received the same rations as the white soldiers and nobody complained. At that time I would never believe that the Chiricahua would leave the reservation and go on a war path against the white men. Now many of them want to return which is a wise decision. Many Chiricahua warriors have also committed serious crimes against the civilian population, but if they return to the reservation, respect its rules and live in peace, they will not be prosecuted by the courts. They can settle in any open space free of the other bands so the conflict between them and the Chiricahua can be prevented. In order to maintain order in their villages the Chiricahua can even establish their own police.

"Recently I returned from Washington, which is the seat of my government, where I was also informed about the new treaty between the US and Mexico. According to this treaty Americans can pursue Indians all over the Mexican territory and the Mexicans can do the same in America. Those days when the Chiricahua could escape to safety of the Mexican mountains after a successful raid are irrevocably gone. The Chiricahua have to decide if there is peace or war between the white and red men. I am an old man and I don't like unnecessary bloodshed, but if the Chiricahua decide for war, I'll flood all the mountains along the Mexican border with soldiers in blue uniforms. My heart will be heavy, but I won't have another choice."

General Crook finished and returned to his camp. Sieber and I, we wanted to follow him, but Geronimo asked us to stay. Sieber sat down on a piece of skin and I remained standing as the Indian etiquette demanded it. Somebody once said that only an Indian can be by his silence quite eloquent. The only trouble was that this silent eloquence was getting on my nerves. How was I supposed to interpret this silence? Finally, Sieber asked Geronimo why he invited him to stay. Geronimo sighed and then just as any other human being without any formalities wanted to hear Sieber's advice. Not as a chief of the warring Apaches, but as an old friend. What does he think would be the best answer when he will face General Crook again tomorrow? Sieber nodded and asked when Geronimo wanted to hear his answer. The chief replied that he would send for him after sunset.

A man not familiar with the Indian customs would wonder why Sieber made so much fuss and didn't answer right away. Well, an instant answer would indicate a lack of respect to the other party, because the first party didn't bother to give a serious thought to the response. So the etiquette demanded that Sieber at least pretended that he would think about it and therefore needed a certain period of time. Geronimo sent a boy to take us to his wigwam around nine o'clock.

There is no need to tell you in detail what Sieber said to him. He basically confirmed the speech the general delivered in the morning and recommended Geronimo to return to San Carlos. Otherwise, the future of the Chiricahua people did not look good. It takes twenty years to raise a warrior while General Crook can put on the battle field hundreds of soldiers just within one day. Sooner or later these soldiers will penetrate the Sierra Madre Mountains and then the vultures will feed on the bodies of the Apache warriors. Sieber's advice definitely impressed Geronimo.

The chief sat at the fire and his stone-like face did not betray any emotion. He didn't say anything for quite a while and then he finally uttered just one sentence. "Even though your words filled my heart with sadness, I will consider them and tell the general my decision tomorrow."

The next day, shortly after sunrise, Geronimo came to our camp to respond to the general's proposal. He looked tired. Undoubtedly he spent most of the night in the council with his warriors and now he was ready to deliver a speech which would make proud even the most astute politician. It could be summed up like this: General Crook blamed the Chiricahua for many things yesterday, but he, Geronimo, was not upset because the white man sees the life in one way and an Apache in another way. The way of life of a white man is an early death for the red man. Geronimo admitted that many of his warriors took part in raids on the American settlers. That could not be denied because he and the "White-haired Old Man", Geronimo's another nickname for Sieber, met on the battle field many times. General Crook on the other hand must understand that Geronimo, even though he enjoyed respect and influence among his people, could not control every single warrior. There are many young men among the Chiricahua who prefer a heroic death in battle to the life in a reservation. Geronimo was an old man and was willing to abandon the warpath once for all. The soldiers in the blue uniforms and their scouts learned about the Indian way of life and the Indian customs and they also had an iron will to control their land. Geronimo wanted peace. He would go to the San Carlos reservation, but the general must give him time to send the messengers to the nearby mountains where the other warriors camp.

General Crook gladly agreed and ordered Lieutenant Gatewood of the Sixth Cavalry to hand out the rations brought for the Indians and count all present Chiricahua. After Geronimo's departure he then turned to Sieber and asked him what he thought about Geronimo's speech. Sieber, as it was his custom, scratched his head and answered that the speech was good, particularly the part about the peace, provided Geronimo means it, but as to those warriors camping in the nearby mountains, that was a dirty trick. Actually, all capable men will now try to steal as many horses and cattle from the Mexican ranchers as they can and under the protection of the American Cavalry they will march them to San Carlos.

General Crook got wide-eyed and readily asked how he could prevent it. Sieber shrugged his shoulders and not less readily answered that unfortunately he could not. The same day Lieutenant Gatewood reported that there were one hundred and ninety-three warriors in the camp. The following day their number shrank to ninety. When asked what happened to the others, Geronimo smiled and answered that some were carrying the message about the planned departure to the reservation and the others were looking for their horses stranded in the nearby canyons. The general having no practical way out of this predicament accepted this explanation and returned to the American territory.

Most of the Indians who joined the troops were old men, squaws and children. Only not far away from the border small groups of the Chiricahua warriors began catching up with us. They all drove a large amount of horses, so between twenty or thirty horses went to each man.

Once General Crook got the wind about it, he pounced upon Geronimo that these horses were stolen and they immediately had to be sent back. Geronimo again smiled and as cool as a cucumber explained to the general that if he tried to do that, all warriors would return to the mountains. So as always, the old fox Geronimo outsmarted General Crook just like all the other high brass before.

We barely had crossed the border when the rest of the warriors arrived. They drove with them close to one thousand horses; but this time, right behind them, there was a large group of Mexican ranchers hot under the collar. They were supported by the same size crowd of lawyers that followed. Needless to say, they all insisted on returning the stolen property, otherwise they would file a lawsuit against the American army which allegedly provided the cover for this roguery. Geronimo and all Chiricahua refused to participate in any negotiations and General Crook paced around the camp, mad as a gut-shot grizzly, hollering that at his age the last thing he needed was somebody making a horse thief out of him. In the end, in order to prevent bloodshed or a massive flight back to Mexico, the General offered to pay for the loot. The sum had to be pretty high and whether it was the Bureau of Indian Affairs or the War Department paying it, I never found out.

Geronimo and his people settled in the reservation near Turkey Creek, not far from Fort Apache and initially it seemed that some sort of peace was restored. Sieber now suffering of bouts with rheumatism decided to resign from his job as the Chief of Scouts. He settled in San Carlos and because there was not a better expert on the Indians far and wide, the government kept on paying him one hundred dollars a month for his advisory services. Thanks to his recommendation I inherited his job.

Shortly thereafter, a Mexican paper brought news that not all the Chiricahua had returned and that a small band kept terrorizing the local population. Whoever wrote that article was mighty well informed because he even mentioned the area where the band was operating. Pretty soon I was called to Captain Crawford. He shoved the paper with that article into my hand saying, "Take your men and make sure you find them. I want them here dead or alive."

So I just said, "Yes, sir," and several days later I was with my Indian scouts again on the way south.

7

The next day around nine o'clock in the morning, prosecutor Stoll passed his hand over the lapels of his jacket, swept away the tiny grains of ashes from the cigar he smoked a while ago in the corridor and looked around the packed courtroom. Then he turned toward the bench and by slightly nodding his head he let the judge know that he was ready. The gavel hit the oak desk several times, the murmuring of voices stopped and Stoll opened his folder full of notes. Numerous sheets of paper densely covered with his handwriting contained the draft of his final arguments constructed in such a logical way that the jury was bound to be convinced about Horn's guilt beyond any reasonable doubts. The prosecutor looked at the jurors and when he was sure that nothing distracted their attention, he began to speak:

"Your Honor, distinguished members of the jury, for two days you have been listening to the testimonies which should shed light on one of the typical crimes in this area, a premeditated murder whose victim was an innocent fourteen year old boy. The initiators of this deed did not have to bear the consequences, but the murderer whose hand extinguished the life of William Nickell, sits in front of you. It is now up to you to make sure that he receives the deserved punishment."

After this fiery opening, Stoll began to describe individual events and then analyzed the evidence and testimonies. He emphasized that the defendant had spent the night near Nickell's ranch and on the day of the murder he was seen about twenty miles away from the crime scene. After a careful study of the area it became obvious that using the shortcuts one could reduce this distance by half. If the murder was committed around seven o'clock in the morning and Tom Horn was near Mule Creek as Otto Plaga testified, a good rider, which Horn undoubtedly is, could reliable cover this distance within the mentioned time limit. Moreover he tried to create an alibi by riding the same afternoon to Laramie.

The most convincing evidence, however, are his own words. Affidavits of three independent witnesses mention an allusion to killing young Nickell.

Even though the defense claims that when the shorthand recording of Horn's testimony was obtained, the defendant was under influence of alcohol, Horn himself admits that he was fully aware what he was saying.

The coroner's testimony confirms that the weapon used during the murder was at least 30/30 caliber. The rifle which belongs to Horn and was confiscated on the day of his arrest is the Winchester of the same bore.

The silence in the courtroom was almost stifling. Stoll pulled out a handkerchief, wiped of his forehead and then pointing his index finger toward the table where Lacey and Horn were sitting and raising his voice declared, "The defendant admits that the murder of William Nickell was a mistake and that murderer intended to kill his father, Kels Nickell. Right after that he then claims that the big ranchers did not harbor any animosity toward Kels because he was not suspected of cattle rustling. Yes, the big ranchers did not harbor any animosity, even though they were not happy about his sheep being introduced to the cattle country, but how about Tom Horn himself?"

The prosecutor made a dramatic pause and looked into the faces of the spectators sitting in the front rows. Their eyes expressed maximum attention.

"According to the entry in the 1890 Cheyenne police records, Kels Nickell attacked Tom Horn's best friend John Coble during an argument about unbranded calves and stabbed him. Recovering from this serious injury, John Coble spent several weeks at the home of the Cheyenne surgeon Doctor Maynard."

For a moment Stoll enjoyed the impression the latest information made on the audience and then continued. "Yes, the defendant Tom Horn had a motive, namely to avenge Kels' rash attack on his best friend. Being influenced by James Miller, who undoubtedly complained bitterly about sheep being in his neighborhood, Horn arrived at a conclusion that Kels Nickell was a troublemaker and it was time to get rid of him. On July 18th, 1901, on that fateful morning Tom Horn was not riding by Mule Creek, but waited for his victim behind the boulders at Nickell's sheep corral."

The prosecutor quite excitedly gestured with both hands, dramatically raising and lowering his voice and with the help of his fantasy running wild began to reconstruct the crime in order to give his speech the appropriate finale.

"Horn knew either from the Millers or from his own observation that Kels fed the sheep every morning by himself. On that morning due to a tragic coincidence it was his older son, Willie, who went to the corral. As it was raining he wore his father's raincoat and hat. Horn spent the night in his hideout on the eastern side of the fence. He picked this position because he knew that he would have the rising sun in his back, therefore the sun rays would blind the man in the corral. However, the weather changed and the corral was covered with morning fog and drizzling rain was falling on the entire Iron Mountain area. The visibility was quite limited. Between seven thirty and seven forty-five Horn spotted a figure wearing the yellow slicker and a black hat.

"He wiped off the wet Winchester by his hand, flipped off the safety and waited. The moment Kels left the corral he would have him in his sights. Finally, the man in the slicker closed the gate and stepped out in the direction of the house. In that very moment Horn rose from his hideout like a rattler ready to strike, stepped closer and took aim while simultaneously he profanely cursed. Under the black hat he saw a boyish face and Willie Nickell's eyes widened by fear and looking directly at him. That was not in the plan. The boy quite horrified screamed and ran. What was going through Horn's mind is easy to imagine. What is for a professional killer more important? To spare the life of a fourteen year old boy or to protect his own identity? Judging by the distance the boy managed to run, he did not hesitate too long. Driven by the instinct of self-preservation he pressed his head to the cold wood of the rifle stock and aimed two shots at the back of Willie Nickell which were supposed to conceal his identity for good.

"What did Horn do after he committed this awful crime? If he listened to his conscience, he rushed to his horse standing nearby and fled. Or did he just blow the smoke out of rifle barrel, step up to the boy and turn him on his back to make sure that he was dead?"

Stoll made a pause. The audience sat in their seats mesmerized by his acting performance. Many a man who yesterday still was not so sure was now willing to go along with his arguments and believe that Horn was really guilty of this coldblooded murder. Rick Jackson sat in the first row and wrote down Stoll's every word. Then he curiously glanced at Horn. What was he thinking? Did he want to get up and scream that these are all fabrications, just goddamn lies, or did he somehow admire the eloquent prosecutor and how well he managed to reconstruct that July morning; but in his face not even a muscle moved.

Stoll stepped to the table and lifted the jacket Willie wore on the day of the murder. He put his fingers through the bullet holes, waived the jacket like a flag and then turned toward the jury box.

"Crimes like this are prevalent only because the perpetrators are rarely punished. The defense lawyers using technicalities and other legal tricks succeed in either freeing the accused murderers or convince the jury to recommend less strict sentences. Distinguished members of the jury, it is up to you whether such crimes will be stopped once for all or whether similar miscreants will continue their reprehensible activity. Remember last year's case when the jury found the indicted murder innocent after which he returned to the scene of the crime and killed off the whole family. Only you by passing a just verdict can make sure that the blood of your fellow citizens will never be spilled again."

Stoll finished his thundering oration, snapped the folder shut and walked to his table. Lacey, aware of the powerful impression the prosecutor made not only on the jury but practically on everybody, didn't waste any time. Before the Stoll's words struck roots in the juror's minds, he had to refresh any doubts they may have had about his arguments. The moment he caught the judge's asking look, he grabbed several sheets of paper with his notes and took his place in front of the jury box. Unlike the prosecutor, he didn't write the whole speech verbatim, but rather only the most important points.

The strategy of his defense was simple. First, none of the evidence presented by the state proved directly Horn's guilt, and second, the witness' character could hardly be considered irreproachable. Lacey turned his back toward the bench, waved his hand toward the prosecutor's table and emphatically declared, "Distinguished members of the jury, what you have just heard were only speculations, speculations and nothing else but speculations."

A light murmur agreeing with the defense attorney filled the courtroom and one could even hear some muted voices chiming in. Lacey didn't wait for the gavel to restore order and launched an attack on Stoll's first argument.

"The prosecution claims that Tom Horn had a motive, namely to avenge an attack on his best friend John Coble. However, Kels Nickell explicitly testified that Tom Horn had never threatened him and that he had never posed any danger to him or his family. He testified in this way not only shortly after the murder of his son, but also here, during the trial. On the contrary, Tom Horn when carrying out his duties visited the Nickells often and always behaved friendly. Therefore, it is quite speculative or even naive to believe that ten years after the mentioned incident the defendant suddenly felt a powerful urge for revenge. Not Tom Horn, but James Miller, according to last year's testimony of several witnesses, instructed his sons to shoot Kels Nickell should it come to any kind of confrontation."

The attorney made a short pause and looked at twelve men in the jury box to see if he gained their attention. Some of them quite surprisedly raised their heads and looked at him, but others didn't react at all. Lacey ran his hand through his hair and began systematically to analyze the depositions of the individual prosecution witnesses.

"The testimonies of Frank A. Mullock of Denver and Robert Causeley of St. Louis were effectively refuted. How could Horn brag in the Scandinavian Saloon that he had shot William Nickell if at the same time he was in a hospital with the broken jaw and communicated with the other people only by writing? Who is actually Frank A. Mullock?"

Lacey flipped one of the paper sheets and began to read to the surprised audience more than a dozen entries from the crime register.

"Mullock was charged and tried for numerous embezzlements, frauds and even for impersonating a Denver policeman and finally for an attempted murder. Now Horn is supposed to be found guilty on the basis of the testimony provided by such an individual? What kind of nonsense is the argument that Horn went to Laramie to have alibi? Why doesn't he resort to it? He's even got a witness." Lacey's voice turned quite ironic. "Frank Irwin is listed at the Cheyenne Association as a cattle rustler."

The attorney then stepped up to the table where Stoll and Watts were sitting, looked them in the eyes and hit the tabletop with his fist. "The show performed by your witnesses smacks not only of perjury but also of conspiracy!" Not waiting to see how the prosecutor and his aid would react, Lacey turned toward the jury and waved the folder containing Horn's conversation with LeFors.

"Here is the strongest argument of the prosecution, the so-called "Horn's confession". Confession? Confession is a statement which a remorseful person makes voluntarily and not a mish mash of utterances obtained under dubious circumstances. The reality itself confirms the doubtful value of this document. The visit of the crime scene has clearly proven that the distance, as well as the spot from which the murderer fired, do not correspond to what Horn said in LeFors' office. Even though the defendant admits that a number of statements were correct, the sentence, 'It was my best shot but also the dirtiest trick I ever made,' he emphatically denies. Confession? Rubbish spoken under the influence of alcohol. The one guy brags to impress and the other to lure out self-incriminating information. Only the facts count."

Lacey lowered his voice a bit and began to recapitulate the testimonies dealing with the distance and places of Horn's whereabouts. He emphasized that Plaga's and Horn's testimonies provided during the trial were practically identical with those obtained last year.

"This means that they both testified according to what actually happened and not according to some later on arranged scheme. Even if it were possible to cover the distance between Nickell's ranch and Mule Creek in a shorter period of time, Horn's horse would bear signs of a sharp and strenuous ride. It would be covered with dust and sweat. Plaga, however, claims that the horse was dry. What about the testimonies of the Cheyenne coroners Dr. Barber, Dr. Johnson and Dr. Conway obtained shortly after the murder? All three believe that the wounds were caused by a larger caliber than 30/30. Even the Denver coroner, Thomas C. Murray, concedes that possibility, and who living in the vicinity of Nickell's ranch owns a rifle 30/40? Miller's sons. Who left a foot imprint which could not be made by an adult, near the bolder where the alleged killer was hiding? Whoever it was, he did not appear at this trial."

Lacey looked at the jurors' unshaven faces. Twelve pairs of eyes kept staring at him and he had such an unpleasant feeling that their minds had wandered God knows where. They were either not listening to him or they were not able to understand the logic of his arguments. Therefore he decided to arouse their attention by appealing to their emotions and conscience in the closing part of his speech.

"If you find the defendant guilty, you won't condemn him to jail for several years, but you will send him to the gallows. Please understand that you will condemn another human being to death only on the basis of sheer speculations and conjecture. How will you then reconcile your conscience with the fact that, let's say a year later, it would be determined that Horn was not guilty? How are you going to undo this judicial murder?"

The attorney, leaning toward the sitting jurors, kept walking from one end of the jury box to another and with the raised voice he repeated several times this question. Some of them looked down. The others nervously fidgeted in their seats and obviously tried not to even consider this possibility.

Lacey stopped talking and slowly walked to the defense table. At the bottom of his heart he was convinced that he had done all he could for Horn.

Now his fate depended on those twelve men. It depended on how much they allowed themselves to be influenced by the local newspapers and how far the hatred toward the big ranchers suppressed their sense for justice and fair play.

The attorney sat down and pulled out his pocket watch. It was exactly eleven o'clock. He spoke for less than an hour. Stoll's speech was significantly longer.

The courtroom fell silent. The judge moved some papers on his desk and then ordered Horn to be taken back to his cell. The moment the deputies led him away, he began to instruct the jury. He went through all the points of the indictment and emphasized that they have to ignore all statements which were not directly relevant to it. Their task is to come to a conclusion whether the defendant is guilty or not. They will not be released of this duty before they decide one way or the other. If necessary, they will stay at the courthouse the whole night. Then he handed out a fascicle of typed documents containing all testimonies and asked the bailiff to take the jurors to the next room. Once the last juror walked through the door, two bailiffs took position in front of it so nobody could interfere with their deliberation.

The time was passing slowly. Some men remained sitting and quietly conversed, others left the courtroom and in small groups gathered either in the corridor or outside on the sidewalk to keep guessing about the verdict the jury would come up with. After a while, even Judge Scott got up from his seat and went to his office. Around noon, the door of the room where the jury was deliberating suddenly opened and in its frame stood the jury foreman. Those in the courtroom were convinced that the jury had reached the verdict, but it was a false alarm. The juror had only a couple of questions concerning the LeFors' testimony and wanted to see the judge. He also used this opportunity to ask the bailiff to bring all jurors something to eat. They still had to go through a pile of papers and that would take some time.

The hours dragged. The nearby tower clock struck one, two and then three in the afternoon. The elapsing time made the nervousness in the courtroom become palpable, particularly among those who were convinced that Horn was guilty. Stoll kept pacing restlessly between the windows and from time to time he wiped off his forehead. He was trying to figure out why it was taking so long for the jury to make the obvious decision. The logic of his arguments was iron clad. Lacey on the other hand was becoming more confident. Considering the fact that the jury didn't come back right away with the guilty verdict, his counter arguments must have created appropriate doubts in their minds. It was probably the statement about the judicial murder which had the right effect on them and now those twelve chaps are rethinking the whole case. Thank God they didn't fall for Stoll's sophistry and theatrics.

Rick was in the meantime going over the notes to be used for the special report for *The Denver Post*. He outlined the major points of both closing speeches and now a blank spot was just waiting to be filled in when the jury announced the verdict. Several times he also looked around to see if Coble was in the courtroom, but there was no sign of him. Rick suddenly realized that he had not seen him even in the morning, so it was quite probable that he didn't show up today at all. The only reason would be his nerves which could no longer take this stress.

Shortly after four o'clock, a dozen of people came from outside. After lunch they dropped in the nearby saloon to have a glass of beer and now they were bringing the news about the bets the Cheyenners were making. Some of them were allegedly more than one thousand dollars high. Strangely, most of those who made the wagers believed that the jury would find Horn not guilty.

Finally around four thirty, twelve men entered the courtroom and the foreman announced in a tired voice that the jurors had finished their deliberation. The courtroom became alive again. The bailiff ran for the judge and several men leaned out of the window and called out to people standing on the sidewalk that the verdict would be announced any minute. The noise of dozens of feet running upstairs filled the courthouse and in no time the courtroom was fully packed. The judge called for the defendant and once Horn took his seat, he then knocked with his gavel on the desktop and asked the jury if it had reached the verdict.

The foreman answered, "Yes, Your Honor," then got up, opened a sheet of paper and in the grave-like silence read only one sentence. "The jury finds the defendant Tom Horn guilty and in accordance to the Wyoming laws recommends death by hanging."

Rick quickly turned his head and glanced at Horn. He saw only a stone-like face which did not betray any sign of emotion. As to the self-control, Horn surpassed his teachers - the Apaches.

Chatting with the Chief of Indian Scouts

Based on interviews with Tom Horn and prepared by F. Jackson.

This trip to Mexico differed profoundly from the previous ones simply because I was in charge. In another words, I had to worry about where we were going and what we were going to do there while earlier it was all up to Al Sieber. Now I was responsible for its success and the one thing that worried me the most was that in case of failure or if I messed up, it would reflect badly on the old man because he recommended me for this job when the army was looking for a new Chief of the Indian Scouts.

Before we left, I had carried out an inspection of all men selected for this expedition. There were about forty of them and right away I detected trouble. Their rifles were not of the same make. So I talked to the garrison commander and they all got issued brand new Springfield rifles. The purpose for unifying their arms was simple. We didn't have to carry about ten different kinds of ammunition and in the case somebody ran out of it he could use the cartridges his live or dead buddy had.

My plan was not overly complicated. According to Geronimo about two dozen warriors decided to come to the reservation a little bit later. They assured him that once they found their horses, they would join him in San Carlos by the next full moon. Well, the next full moon was about a week away so we didn't have enough time to look for them in Mexico. All we could do was to jump them on the American side of the border as they were coming back. Since I knew the land between the border and San Carlos like the palm of my hand I placed the scouts in all the nearby canyons and arroyos along the route they used when returning from their raids on the Mexican ranchers. The scouts were not too far apart and I dare to say that a mouse wouldn't slip through. The guy I left in charge was a certain Micky Free who was kidnapped by the Indians as a young boy and who later joined the army as a scout. I myself then rushed to the Terras Mountains to the place mentioned in the newspaper article.

There I spent about three days. Being alone I could move quickly and undetected, unlike a whole company of the scouts, and it worked. On the third day toward evening I spotted a smoke signal on a mesa opposite of the place where I was camping. Shortly the answer came from another mountain wall not far away. One group of warriors signaled the other to wait with the return two more days. Needless to say, I was on my way back the same night and as I had to cover about seventy miles, I didn't spare the horse. The next day I stopped at Slaughter's ranch near the San Bernardino River, got a fresh horse and kept riding north to my men. I ran into one of them the same evening. At first he didn't recognize me because I was mounted on a different horse and had me in his sights for a while until I came closer.

As soon as we joined his group, I sent the messengers to the others to come to Tex Spring to conduct a war council. One man rode to Quadalupe Creek, the other to Skeleton Canyon and the third one to the southern edge of the Chiricahua Mountain. I, accompanied by another scout, rode to Tex Spring and once we got there I hit the blankets because I hadn't slept for more than twenty-four hours. Only after sunrise Micky woke me up saying that everybody was present. Then he asked me if they could make a fire to cook breakfast. Since the renegades were prob-ably still in Mexico, I told them to go ahead and then informed them what I saw in the Terras Mountains. After debating the next steps, we agreed that the best place to ambush them would be at the foot of the Chiric-ahua Mountain. By that time they would be all together and driving a large herd of stolen horses or cattle which would slow them down and limit their ability to maneuver.

In the afternoon one of the scouts brought the news that he had spotted a troop of soldiers coming from the north. I jumped on a horse and rode ahead to meet them to avoid a serious misunderstanding be-cause to mistake the Indian scouts for the renegades was quite easy. Then, rather surprised, I found out that General Crook had sent twenty sol-diers commanded by Lieutenant Wilder from the Third Cavalry to reinforce my unit. After we shook hands, Lieutenant Wilder handed me the orders signed by General Crook. Since it was a military opera-tion the lieutenant was supposed to take over the command, but when I told him that, he just laughed saying that I had much greater experience with the Indians and he would gladly follow my suggestions. So I made him familiar with our plan, namely to spend the night here at Tex Spring and then next day move to the Chiricahua Mountain. The lieutenant agreed and his soldiers set up a camp right next to ours.

The next day we moved out. After about an hour of riding, six cowboys from the San Simon Ranch joined us. They found out from my scouts that we were planning to ambush a band of Chiricahua who were terrorizing the ranches on both sides of the border, including the San Simon Ranch, and they obviously didn't want to miss an opportunity to settle some old scores with them. They were all armed to teeth and judging by the way they talked they couldn't wait for the moment when they would be able to pull the trigger of their Winchesters.

It became apparent that as long as somebody doesn't mess up, due to such a large force, the success of the operation was pretty much guaranteed. Toward the evening we camped at the foot of the Chiricahua Mountain and did the basic reconnaissance. Eventually we agreed that the most probable route the Chiricahua would pick would be Dry Creek Canyon. The canyon was relatively wide and several miles long so a large herd of horses or cattle could be comfortably driven through without being detected either by the military patrol or some local ranchers.

The night was peaceful. I expected the renegades at the dawn, but the sun cleared the mountain range and the canyon entrance still didn't show any signs of life. Only around ten o'clock, Micky Free who was patrolling on the western side of the canyon began to wave his hands like crazy to attract our attention. I ran across the canyon to find out what was going on and as soon as I came close to him, he just pointed his hand in the southern direction at a huge cloud of dust. The Indians decided to travel in the wide open space and ignored the mountain routes as if they suspected an ambush. Of course that changed our plans. Instead of surprising them from a much more advantageous position on the canyon walls, we had to fight them in the open terrain.

After a short consultation with Lieutenant Wilder we divided all our men into three groups. His unit would face the advancing Indians and my scouts, reinforced by the cowboys, would attack them from both sides. The Chiricahua were still about ten miles away so we had enough time to take positions and wait. The cloud of dust was slowly approaching and after a while we could recognize individual riders. The Indians felt incredibly safe. Some were laughing and the others even singing.

When they got really close and we were ready to open fire, the leading warrior apparently spotted one of the Wilder's troopers, raised his hand and yelled, "Un-Dah!" which meant the white man. There was no time to wait any more. I lifted my rifle, fired and the fight was on.

The Chiricahua, soldiers, cowboys and scouts, simply all men on the battlefield got mixed up and only thanks to the lieutenant's idea of having the scouts wear military jackets there were no casualties due to friendly fire. The deafening noise of rifle shots was permeated by wild neighing of horses and by high-pitch yelling of the warriors, but the Indian war hoops were getting weaker and weaker until they finally stopped. The fight lasted less than ten minutes and then it was over as suddenly as it started.

Once the dust settled and the horses calmed down, we began to count the dead bodies. We found ten warriors and two squaws. One squaw hid behind a rock when the first shot was fired and now scared to death she was waiting to see what would happen to her. I told the lieutenant to give her a slice of dried meat and handful of beans and when she realized that there was no imminent danger, she told me that there were fourteen people in the group - three squaws and eleven warriors. What happened to the eleventh one we never found out, but if he was wounded and tried to return back to the Mexican mountains, he probably died along the way. On our side there was only one dead cowboy and two wounded soldiers. Considering the amount of men involved in this fight we were extremely lucky. The Chiricahua were truly caught by surprise and they must have lost most of their warriors before they managed to return fire.

Then we rounded all the horses and tried to figure out what to do with them. The herd consisted of at least one hundred horses and because most of them were stolen, nobody wanted them. I didn't want them, Lieutenant Wilder didn't want them, so finally we convinced the cowboys to take them back to San Simon Ranch and announce in the paper that the original owners would be welcome to pick them up. Of course the chance that this news would reach the Mexican ranchers who probably owned most of them was not too great.

When we were about to bury the dead cowboy, one of his buddies told us that it had been his stupid idea to rope one of the Indians which brought him this misfortune. The loop actually caught the warrior, but when he fell from the horse, he managed to get on his knees and fire his gun. Whether this was a matter of a typical cowboy humor or whether this guy thought he would become a hero for the rest of his life, I don't know, but this rashness cost him his life.

So my first campaign against Chiricahua ended in this way. In the afternoon Lieutenant Wilder and I put together a report for Captain Crawford and having one female prisoner we headed back to Fort Bowie. The only thing I was wondering about was how Geronimo would react to the news that this band was now shorter ten warriors.

8

The front desk clerk at the Silver Horse Shoe Hotel politely bowed, put the money in the drawer saying, "Please, come again," and then handed Rick a receipt for twenty dollars. The reporter made sure that they charged him only for five days and it just occurred to him that four dollars a night was genuine highway robbery. A month ago they wanted only three and he would bet a bottle of the best whisky that now after the trial the price would go down again. Pete would fret that he should have stayed at a cheaper establishment and he wouldn't be happy that instead of sending him the results of the trial by telegram he used a phone, but the telegram office was beleaguered by the reporters not only from Wyoming, but also Montana and Colorado and if his report arrived after the deadline, he wouldn't like that either. What would he say if all Denver papers brought the news about the verdict except for *The Post*?

Rick stuck the receipt into his pocket and looked around the lobby. According to the clock on the opposite wall the train to Denver would not leave for another two hours. He could sit in the saloon where he met Coble in the winter and have a glass of beer or take a stroll through downtown and listen to the views of the local citizens about the outcome of the trial. In his mind he again saw the courtroom shortly after the jury foreman announced the guilty verdict. The prosecutor who was about to accept the fact that Horn would be set free, brightened up, rushed to the jury box and congratulated each juror to their decision. Lacey readily stepped up to the judge and told him his intention to appeal to the Wyoming Supreme Court. The audience realizing that there is no need to fear the judge's gavel any longer, dropped all restraint and exclamations expressing joy as well as condemnation were heard all over the room.

In all that confusion, he also saw Tom's motionless face. He wanted to step up to him and say a few consoling words that everything was not yet lost, that Lacey could insist on a trial in a different county because Cheyenne could not guarantee an unbiased jury, but the duty of a reporter led his steps to the nearest phone. Maybe before his departure he should pay him a visit, but he rejected this thought as well. Tom and Lacey are now probably busy planning the next steps and he would just waste their time.

Rick picked up his suitcase and was about to leave when he noticed two bellboys carrying bundles of fresh laundry. Nickell suddenly flashed across his mind. Sometime last year before the trial started he had opened a steam laundry here in Cheyenne. How about trying to make an interview with him? What was the story about the sheep and who he thinks fired at him? Miss Kimmel mentioned this incident but she didn't know any details, and during the trial the judge blocked any reference to the animosity between him and Miller.

Rick turned around and stepped to the front desk. To find out how to get to Nickell's laundry took less than a minute.

"It is the second street to the right of the railroad station. You cannot miss it. Plumes of hot steam keep coming out of a metal pipe and his chimney belches smoke like a locomotive smoke stack because old Nickell is penny-pinching and heats the boiler with lousy coal."

About twenty minutes later Rick stood in a dark street in front of a two-story brick house. From the darkness above the roof he heard the hissing sound of escaping steam and all around he could smell smoke and cheap soap. Peeking through the window he saw a half-naked man wearing a rubber apron and pulling washed laundry out of a large metal container. He then placed it on a long table next to a manual ringer. On the other side of the room an old woman in an open blouse sat on a small three legged stool and was sewing little strips of cloth with the names of customers on the individual pieces of laundry to be washed. Rick quickly glanced at the tangle of pipes which carried not only hot water but also steam to power the paddles in the wash machine, then grabbed the door knob and entered.

The man in the apron barely paid attention to the new customer, however, the woman who apparently took care of receiving the new laundry got up, threw a large scarf over her shoulders and asked Rick how she could help him.

"I am looking for Kels Nickell who owned the ranch near Iron Mountain," Rick matter-of-factly responded.

The half-naked man turned around and came closer. "That's me. What can I do for you?"

Rick thought about the best way how to make this guy talk all the way from the hotel. Reporters writing for the other newspapers and in quest of some sensation must have been all over him probably since the day he had moved to Cheyenne. Unquestionably, the new laundry owner could not stand any of them. Just to say, "Hello, I am a reporter and can you tell me something about Willie and the guy who shot you," wouldn't work for sure. No, when it came to old Nickell one must use a different tack. He was convinced that the Millers were behind all his misfortune and that had to be the starting point.

"You've got fixed up here pretty good," Rick began quite inconspicuously. "You see, this is the first time I've got a chance to see how such laundry works. And I bet you, this machine wasn't cheap, was it?" Nickell looked quite surprised at the stranger and at the same time tried to figure out what he wanted from him. He didn't carry any laundry, unless he came to pick up something he had brought last week. He looked again in his face and it occurred to him that he had seen him somewhere. Rick kept rattling something about the laundry business and how as the city grows, the number of customers will grow as well and then casually mentioned the trial.

"What do you think about today's verdict? I believe the real killer is running free and laughing his head off."

Nickell kept nodding his head and the moment Rick mentioned the trial, he remembered. He saw him in the courtroom. He sat in the front row and kept writing something down. He must be one of those damn paper scribblers.

Nickell frowned and bluntly asked, "What do you want from me?"

"I would like to ask you a few details about this case. You must have on your mind many things you didn't have an opportunity to say at the hearing. I am sure that the public would like to know."

"The public can kiss my ass," came the unfriendly response to Rick's suggestion. "And as to them newspaper hacks, I have had it up to here." Nickell gestured with his hand to his throat and then continued, "They all sniff around and if I tell them something they turn it upside down and write some crap which is not true. Anyway, don't you see I am busy? You are wasting my time."

Rick, however, was not yet ready to give up. "Well, if we do an interview, you won't get short." Saying that he saw immediately in his mind Pete's frowning face because one thing his boss hated were bribes, but when a person needs an extra motivation… Rick reached into his pocket and in his hand held a ten dollar banknote.

Nickell hesitated, then quite irritated grumbled, "You think I am for sale or what?"

Now it was time to pull out the last trump card. "Wait, it doesn't bother you that Miller and his boys got out of this trouble unscathed?"

This hit the raw nerve. Nickell got red in face and angrily shot out, "I don't want to even hear the name of that goddamn scoundrel!" Then he took two steps forward, pushed aside the apron and pointed toward his belly at a long scar. "Look here. That will remind me of that son-of-bitch for the rest of my life." Nickell's finger moved from his belly to the left forearm and then to the right arm pit. On the sweaty skin one could see clearly long scars surrounded by little red dots caused by numerous stitches.

"So you see, and when Lacey asked you about Miller, Stoll objected and the judge agreed. If you can think about something that could incriminate … I mean shift the suspicion toward Miller, let's have it. You don't believe that it was Horn who fired at you, do you?"

"Horn?" retorted Nickell and coarsely laughed. "If Horn was the shooter, I wouldn't own this laundry now." Then he suddenly reached for the banknote, put it in his pocket and saying, "Okay, let's go over here. Wife will watch the shop."

He led Rick into the next room. Nickell reached for the switch and the pale light illuminated shelves with neatly lined up packets of clean laundry waiting for their owners to be picked up and soap boxes stacked up on the floor. Nickell removed a bundle of dirty shirts from a chair, motioned Rick to sit down and he then seated himself on an empty soap box.

Rick pulled out his indispensable notebook, with a pocket knife sharpened a pencil and began asking questions. Nickell responded tersely, accompanying most of the answers with a steady stream of curses and he consistently referred to Miller as a son-of-bitch, scurvy scoundrel and a rotten bastard from hell. When he finished, another five pages of Rick's notebook were full. Nickell made a long pause now and Rick took this opportunity to recapitulate in his mind all events.

The attempt to assassinate Kels Nickell took place seventeen days after the murder of his older son Willie. Shortly after dawn, he went to the corral where he kept cows to check on a newly born calf. He walked around the pasture, found the calf which was doing fine and because he hadn't had breakfast yet, he turned around and walked back to the house. At that moment, a rifle shot cracked. He felt a sharp pain in his left side and then a hot stream of blood on his thigh. As there was no place to hide, he began to run toward his home.

Then several shots followed one after the other. As an old veteran of the Sioux wars he knew that he could not run straight but rather jackrabbit. The bullets were whistling by his head and even today it seemed to him incredible that he was hit only three times. In addition to his side he was hit also on the left arm and high on the right side of his chest. The doctors who worked on him in the Cheyenne hospital were just shaking their heads. They hadn't seen such luck yet. The only serious injury was on his arm. It looked like he wouldn't be able to use it. The other two shots didn't hit any vital organ and the bullets went straight through the skin without damaging any bones.

Once he made it home, the firing stopped. As soon as his wife managed to stop the bleeding, she sent their oldest daughter Julie to her brother Bill Mahoney who owned a ranch not too far away. Around noon he came with a wagon and they hauled Kels to the railroad station at Iron Mountain and then to the hospital. The children stayed at home behind the barricaded door and when they heard the wild bleating of sheep, they didn't dare to go out. Their mother returned the next day in the afternoon. The children were okay, but in the sheep corral all hell was loose. Over fifty sheep, including young lambs, lay dead with smashed heads. Miller and his sons were arrested the same day, but they had a firm alibi. On that day they were allegedly at home. When lying in the hospital, Kels came to the conclusion that Miller, possessed by devilish fanaticism, was willing to kill off all his family and that's why he decided not to take any unnecessary risk.

In mid-October they moved to Cheyenne, he got a job with the railroad and this year he bought the steam laundry, the cattle company Double B Ranch, then bought his Iron Mountain ranch.

Rick thought for awhile and then asked what happened to the shepherd who was supposed to take care of their sheep.

Nickell cut a scornful face, "You mean Jim White? His real name was Vingenjo Biango. He was an Italian, you know, but we just called him Jim White. He got scared to death. He fled and walked on foot all the way to Cheyenne. There he got on a train and never showed up here again."

The room fell silent. Rick wondered if he should ask Nickell why he had sent the sheep on Miller's pasture, but then he dropped that idea. There was no need to irritate him. On the other hand, he kept claiming that it was Miller who wanted to kill him. Was it just his imagination or did he have a concrete reason or evidence?

"And you are sure it was Miller who fired at you, right?" Rick continued asking.

"Of course. Who else?" The tone of his voice didn't allow any doubts.

"Can you prove it?"

"If the judge asked me, I would tell him."

"How about you tell me. I'll make it public and if it is something serious, Miller could get indicted." Rick correctly sensed that Nickell knew something and now he hesitated about whether he should share it with a reporter or not. The fact that the trial was over and he wouldn't have an opportunity to charge him of an attempt on his life publicly made him finally decide.

"Okay. So listen damn well. You are the first person I am gonna tell, and if the sheriff arrests that rotten bastard, I'll repeat it again under oath." Kels after this colorful opening made a short pause and then continued. "When I ran into the house, only my wife and Julie were at home. The other two small children, Freddie and Ida, were outside picking blueberries. When their mother milked the cow in the morning, she then added milk to them," Kels quickly explained. "When the firing stopped, they both ran home pretty frightened and when they calmed down, they told me they had seen two men riding away from the place where they heard the shots. They didn't see their faces, but they recognized the horses. The one was brown and the other grey, the same kind Miller has. And now comes the best part. Julie had hardly left when the other neighbor, Bill McDonald came saying that a while ago young Miller told him that someone had shot me. How could he know that? Nobody stopped at our place during the entire morning."

Nickell victoriously laughed and happily rubbed his hands. "All that's necessary now is to get that snake to the judge. This testimony would put a noose on his damn neck for sure."

Rick felt for a moment genuine satisfaction that those ten dollars were not wasted. It was million dollar information, but then a sober thought brought him back to reality. The trouble was that Horn was not charged with the attempt to assassinate old Nickel, but with his son's murder, and there was the rub.

"So you don't suspect Horn at all?" Rick was trying to be absolutely sure.

"No way! Horn never had anything against us." Kels waved his hand, got up from the box and walked to the door. Rick stuck the notebook into his pocket, put his hat on and followed him. When he was passing the washing machine, he glanced at the woman sitting on the three-legged stool. She didn't seem to register his presence. Stooped over a pile of dirty laundry she kept sewing little strips of cloth on bed sheets, towels and underwear of all kind. She made an impression that her thoughts were somewhere else, probably on the ranch in the mountains where she was listening to the wind in the pines and golden aspens and enjoying watching a cluster of playing children.

Arriving at the railroad station Rick bought a ticket for second class so he wouldn't have to listen to Pete's sermon about wasting money. The train from Casper pulled into the station shortly after eight o'clock and while the engineer was filling the boiler with water and the tender with coal, the passengers were slowly filling the vacant seats. Rick also noticed that many of them were present in the courtroom when the verdict was announced. When he got on the train, he found an empty seat right next to the window, so he leaned into a corner and began to think what would be the best way to use the information provided by Nickell in Horn's favor. The previous day Stoll introduced LeFors' affidavit in which Horn allegedly admitted shooting at Kels Nickell and he didn't manage to kill him because he was shooting against the sun. Even though this testimony was not directly connected to the murder of Willie Nickell, it could help charge LeFors of perjury. Horn denied saying anything like that and if LeFors lied in case of old Nickell, why could he not lie in case of Willie's murder?

His thoughts were then interrupted by the conductor calling "Aboard!" and the hissing sound of released steam and the puffing of the locomotive. The car jerked and the train was on its way. Rick watched sparks flying out of the chimney for a while and then the rhythmical pounding of the wheels and murmur of voices in the compartment rocked him to slumber. Half asleep he heard the names of stations - Fort Collins, Loveland and Longmont. When the train stopped in Boulder, the conversation in the car got louder, mainly because of a new passenger, an older man all dressed in black with a large silver buckle on his belt, undoubtedly an owner of some bigger ranch. He looked at the other travelers, then stepped up to a short fat guy wearing a Derby hat and shook his hand. From the conversation it became apparent that they had known each other for quite a while.

The man in black inquired about the purpose of his trip and his corpulent friend told him that he was coming from Cheyenne where he had spent three days at Horn's trial. The newly boarded passenger showed immediately an interest and because he wanted to hear more details, the guy in the Derby hat began gladly describing various testimonies and then, of course, the verdict. He also mentioned the LeFors' affidavit, which according to his opinion, helped convince the jury that Horn was guilty, particularly the part where Horn was bragging about this crime in the Scandinavian Saloon and how it must have made a powerful impression on the jurors.

Reference to the Scandinavian Saloon immediately attracted the attention of the man in black. He rubbed his forehead as if he were trying to remember something and then what he said immediately woke up Rick.

"You know, I have heard about this. Last year when there was rodeo in Cheyenne, several of my cowboys witnessed this conversation. But… and that's the most interesting thing… when Horn left, one of them asked the barkeep if this was that famous detective Tom Horn. And you know what he said? 'I don't know if this guy was a famous detective, but since I have known Horn for years, let me tell you, he just looked like him."

Rick stopped sleeping the moment the conversation focused on Horn. He had his eyes closed but listened to every word they said. Now he sat up turned to the stranger from Bolder and almost exclaimed: "What did you say?"

The man in black quite surprisedly looked at Rick and repeated: "Well, I said it quite clearly, didn't I? According to the barkeep who knew Horn for years, that guy just looked liked him. Maybe he was some sort of a double."

Rick suddenly saw the courtroom again and then Lacey leaning toward Stoll and pounding the desk with his fist. The attorney's words were now ringing in his ears. "The show performed by your witnesses smacks not only of perjury but also of conspiracy!"

Chatting with the Chief of Indian Scouts

Based on interviews with Tom Horn and prepared by F. Jackson.

Six months passed after the fight at the Chiricahua Mountain and it seemed that the conflict with the Apaches was permanently behind us. Unfortunately, it only seemed. Lieutenant Gatewood informed me on several occasions that the Chiricahua were involved in shady business with the white traders, mainly trading stolen horses and cattle for whisky, ammunition and new rifles. Moreover, they ignored the reservation rules; particularly, they refused to be counted on a regular basis and flooded the administration with dozens of trivial complaints.

When I asked Geronimo what was going on, I had to listen to a long tirade that most of the warriors were not happy with the life on the reservation and that they wanted to go back to Mexico. To my question if he realized what it would mean, he just shrugged his shoulders saying that the Chiricahua were willing to accept any fate except this kind of life which they viewed as a slow dying.

However, Sieber saw this issue in a more realistic way. Geronimo wanted to run an advantageous business. Being safe in the reservation he would send groups of warriors out to Mexico where they could steal horses and cattle, and then they would drive the loot back to the reservation where he could trade them for whatever he would like to. If he could not pull this off, he would leave the reservation. At the same time, of course, he would talk about the peace and injustice he had suffered.

First, I thought that Sieber was exaggerating, but sometime in the middle of November a command of the Indian scouts ran into a small group of the Chiricahua in Skeleton Canyon who were driving a herd of stolen cattle. The cows had the brand of the San Simon Ranch and, needless to say, they were driven toward the reservation. The scouts attacked and the thieves dispersed, but one squaw was not fast enough and was captured. She fought like hell and only when Micky Free threatened her with his gun, did she quit. About a week later when I was returning from the San Simon Ranch to Fort Bowie, I met a group of cowboys who were digging a well. From them I found that that there was a major breakout from the reservation and that all Chiricahua were on the way to Mexico. In another words, Al Sieber was right.

In the meantime, all hell was loose at Fort Bowie. The couriers were coming and leaving, Major Burke swore that this was the last time the Army would fall for Geronimo's peaceful intentions and a telegram was sent to Washington DC asking for General Crook's immediate return to Arizona. Within a few days we got the news that all Chiricahua crossed the Mexican border and now it was only necessary to find out where they planned to settle down. An answer to this question came from a least expected source.

One evening Micky Free came to see me. He looked quite serious and after a while he shared a secret with me. That squaw who put up such fight had one weakness, namely whisky. After the third or fourth shot she let her mouth run and among other things she blurted out that Geronimo planned to settle down in Sonora in the El Durasnillo Mountains. As I said, that was the information we were all waiting for. General Crook arrived in the spring of 1885 and in a couple weeks the preparations for the Mexico campaign were in full swing.

I was entrusted with a special task, namely to recruit about one hundred warriors to serve as scouts. The reason was obvious. Through all the Apache wars it became an unwritten law that only an Apache can find another Apache. Those warriors came mostly from the White Mountain bands. General Crook then ordered to build a dense network of heliograph stations and at Fort Bowie he opened a special school where the crews operating this latest means of communication were trained. The cavalry kept patrolling all sources of water in the desert and trains were bringing mules and draft animals all the way from Wyoming. At the beginning of June, individual troops accompanied by mules and wagons carrying provisions for a six-month campaign started moving to Mexico.

The headquarters were set up in the town of Nacori. It took a heliographic message about an hour to reach Fort Bowie. Additional stations were built on top of the hills, usually spaced about fifteen miles apart. Furthermore, the local population was urged to inform the crew of the nearest station in the case they spotted a band of Indians. In this way the Army could keep tabs on their every move. At the beginning of December when I was again at Fort Bowie, a message arrived that a band of Chiricahua had crossed the American border near a place called Agua Azul and was moving north. As the chief of the scouts I was supposed to find them. I placed my men in the Dragoon and Whetstone Mountains and waited for some reports, but that band disappeared into thin air. I was sure that sooner or later they would attack a ranch or a group of miners, but the heliograph was silent. Several days later we found out why.

This band didn't cross into the American territory to loot, but rather to avenge. They managed to slip into the reservation and murder the Nad-is-kis Apaches in the White Mountains. As all male members of this band were serving as scouts in Mexico, they killed their squaws and children - altogether twenty people. The neighboring Indians eventually killed one of the raiders and proudly marched with his head into Fort Apache. Well, you'd never guess whose head it was. The warrior who went to the eternal hunting grounds headless was Hal-zay, the same Apache who was waiting for us at the Bavispe River when Sieber and I visited Geronimo's camp for the first time.

The telegram sent from the reservation informed us that a troop of cavalry was on their heels and that it was up to me where we wanted to join them. I figured that they would not rush back because they might try to scare more families of those Apaches serving with the Army and if I picked up their tracks in Mexico, they could lead us to Geronimo's camp. I moved quickly to Nacori and there I waited for the next news. It turned out as I expected. The Chiricahua stayed ahead of the troop and maintained about a two-day start. They didn't draw unnecessary attention to themselves and raided the ranches only if they needed fresh horses.

Then finally the news came that the soldiers lost them when the band crossed the border near a place called Alamo Hueco. I contacted Captain Crawford and got the permission to take ten men and go after them. Near this place I picked up their trail and the hunt was on. I firmly believed that this band was heading toward the main Chiricahua body to brag about the results of their raid. We followed them for several days and then, judging by their zigzagging route, I realized that they could not find it and so we were "lost" with them. About a week later, however, they picked up the right direction and we followed them rather in a parallel fashion not to run into their rear guards. Once I was sure we were close to Geronimo's camp, I sent two men to Captain Crawford with a message that I was waiting for him and as soon as he caught up with me we could hit them.

Two days later both messengers came back saying that Captain Crawford was camping about an hour march from our camp. I immediately took off to see him because I wanted to make sure that Geronimo wouldn't get away, but above all because I hadn't had a decent meal for almost a week and I knew that his troop was accompanied by one of those wagons full of food supplies. After we enjoyed an unusually tasty dinner, we sat down to talk about the plan for the next day.

In the end we decided to divide all our men, that is the soldiers and the scouts, into four groups. I commanded the scouts and the troopers were under the command of Captain Crawford and Lieutenants Maus and Shipp. We moved to our positions the very night. I took the eastern side of Geronimo's camp, basically a rocky rise where I figured most of the Indians would look for refuge after the attack started. Lieutenant Shipp went to the western side between the camp and the Arras River. Lieutenant Mouse blocked the southern side and Captain Crawford was supposed to launch an attack from the North after sunrise. There was no need to hurry with the assault

on the Indian camp simply because we were going to shoot practically towards each other, and in a case like this you want to make sure that there was enough light on the battle field to avoid bullets flying into your own ranks.

The camp woke up at the dawn. The squaws began to make fires, children ran around and the warriors looked for their horses. Then just out of the blue two young warriors walked straight to the spot where I was hiding. I hoped they would stop and return because I was not supposed to start the fight, but they kept walking and when they were about ten yards away, five of my scouts raised their rifles and fired. Those two boys never smiled again. Needless to say, that those shots caused a havoc in the camp.

Geronimo ran out of his wigwam, jumped on a log and yelled, "Get the horses! Get the horses!"

Then he must have changed his mind and urged everybody to run to the river. Hundreds of people, men, women and children rushed toward the position where Lieutenant Shipp was waiting, but not a shot came from that direction. Something must have gone wrong and it looked like the Apaches would get away practically unscathed. In my mind I imagined Al Sieber being around and reacting to this situation with an expert stream of unique curses, but then suddenly one volley followed another. Shipp didn't fail.

As luck would have it, a small boy from the reservation who spoke a little bit of English heard Geronimo giving instructions to flee to the river, so he told Lieutenant Shipp and he just waited until this huge mass of people came close. Well, many warriors didn't make it to the river, but because the orders clearly prohibited killing women and children, and in this chaos warriors mingled with everybody else, most of the Chiricahua including Geronimo escaped after all.

My job was to keep control over the scouts, but it took a major effort since many of them lost their wives and children during the recent raid on the White Mountains Apaches. I cursed alternately in Apache and in English, threatened with the strictest punishment, and eventually managed to prevent the killing of non-combatants, but nevertheless many Chiricahua squaws and their kids did not escape their fury.

When the battle was practically over I saw an old Indian slowly running on the bottom of a ravine toward the river. The man was quite limping so it took me just a couple of seconds to catch up with him.

When I yelled to stop and surrender, he turned around saying, "Para sirvir usted (At your service)," and threw his rifle on the ground. To my major surprise, the old man was one of the main Chiricahua chiefs – Chief Nana. I picked up his rifle and told him to follow me to Captain Crawford who was now counting the prisoners. Nana was over ninety years old, but his ability to talk and talk equaled Geronimo's. Right away, he started complaining and his sharp sarcasm was aimed at his people.

"The best Chiricahua warriors today are those who are the fastest runners. Instead of fighting with their enemies they engage them in foot races. The Apaches used to fight the same way Sibi taught you to fight, but now they sit around the campfire, argue what to do and in the end they run. Geronimo had enough warriors to have a good fight with the Blue Coats and then in the evening to pull back into the mountains, but instead…" Nana quite disgustedly waved his hand and then continued, "You heard him. 'Run to the river, run to the river!' Why not 'Run the soldiers into the river'? Everybody on the reservation kept calling, 'To Mexico! To Mexico!' Didn't they know that for freedom one has to fight?"

I turned Nana over to Lieutenant Maus and when I was leaving I heard Nana saying that he was an old man, he was crippled and that he was not schooled in the new art of winning battles by engaging in foot races. The only thing he would like to do now was to go to San Carlos and die there. Somehow I felt sorry for the old chief that he had to see the inglorious end of his people, but on the other hand I was glad he survived the fight unharmed.

In the afternoon we began to liquidate the Apache camp. We tore down all the wigwams, collected horses running loose and collected all personal items the fleeing Chiricahua left behind such as leather bags, saddles, blankets and what have you. After some arguing about what to do with them, Captain Crawford ordered to pile them all up and burn them.

Around three o'clock the sky got overcast and then it began to rain. First we thought it was probably just a shower, but it was raining heavier and heavier and after a while we were walking in mud ankle deep. So we built simple shelters and the departure was postponed for tomorrow. Of course nobody knew that the main surprise was still ahead of us, but that is a story for next time.

9

The train from Cheyenne arrived to Denver quite late and Rick got to bed around midnight. It was the main reason why today he made it to his office sometime after nine. There was no reason to hurry. The news about the trial and the verdict was already printed and if the specific details or commentaries would appear tomorrow, it would not cause the end of the world. Rick passed the room with the familiar tapping of the telegraph and walked upstairs. He stopped in Jeff's office, asked about the latest events and then entered the office he shared with his boss. Pete was in an unusually good mood, undoubtedly because he was happy with today's issue. According to Jeff he stayed in the office until late in the evening and prepared the final version of Rick's report by himself. He didn't even complain that the raw information was dictated over the phone and not sent by telegraph as the unwritten policy called for.

As soon as Rick opened the door, Pete wiggled out from behind his desk and in spite of his corpulence he swiftly ran across the office floor to greet him. The rest of the morning they spent discussing various aspects of the trial and then how much space and time they should allocate for it in the newspaper. Rick suggested they continue to print the stories from the time Horn served in Arizona and also keep bringing news about the appeal to the Wyoming Supreme Court. On top of it he also obtained a large amount of information which was not published during the trial. Once he managed to fill some gaps and create a complete picture, he would write a commentary that would certainly stir up public opinion. Pete hearing the last sentence got a little bit restless and raised his eyebrows, but Rick immediately calmed him down saying that he still had to verify many details and separate speculations from the facts.

Then at noon he grabbed his hat, put two issues of *The Denver Post* in his pocket and headed out the door. When Pete asked if he should order lunch for him, Rick said that today he would eat out and ran out of the office. He thought for a while whether he should walk or not, but then he spotted a cab on the corner of Broadway and Colfax Avenue. He waved his hand, the cab-driver stopped, and Rick got in.

"Where to?"

"To the Scandinavian Saloon," and then he quickly added, "It's at Seventeenth and Blake."

The horse broke into a sharp trot and at the next intersection the cab turned onto Seventeenth Street. From there it was another fifteen blocks to the Scandinavian Saloon. Rick impassively watched the bustling life in the downtown and when he caught a glimpse of two brand new buildings which were much higher than the surrounding one- or two-story structures, he realized that the old, picturesque Denver of the end of the nineteenth century was slowly disappearing. The hotels with the Romanesque windows and saloons with false facades were retreating before cold modern high-rises which were to house offices of banks and mining companies. The colorful crowd of prospectors, cowboys and ranchers milling on the sidewalks was being replaced by office workers in dark suits and stiff white collars. The city quarters, which just several years ago were popular hot spots frequented by desperados of all sorts, soiled doves, and girls from the dance halls were now meeting places for prudish-looking matrons. And the saloon girls? They could be picked up any time by a policeman patrolling the streets. On Broadway where just several years ago Concord stage coaches pulled by teams of six horses rumbled in both directions, one could now hear the rattling of ugly looking tramways.

When they passed Arapaho Street, the exterior of the local buildings confirmed his gloomy thoughts. Those which were not completely abandoned made an impression that the owners were trying to get out of them a few more dollars, just before they boarded up the windows and left.

The cab pulled onto Nelson Street and stopped in front of the Scandinavian Saloon. Rick paid and got off. He looked around and was quite surprised. He had to admit that the saloon and the entire street were trying to resist the changes brought onto the rest of Denver. Most of the buildings were in good shape, the wooden windows were painted, and big as well as small establishments made an impression that they still enjoy relatively large clientele.

Rick opened the door and stepped in. Nothing had changed since he visited the place last time. The first room served as a bar and a gambling room while the adjacent space was reserved for dining. Rick passed a massive wooden bar and entered the dining area. There he sat down at a vacant table, ordered a hot roast beef sandwich and from time to time he peeked into the bar. Except for three cowboys playing the Faro and an older gentleman sitting in the corner reading newspaper, the room was empty.

Then he focused on the barkeep. He could be around forty. His slightly corpulent body was covered by a white apron reaching almost to his neck and above his jovial face shone pitch-black pomaded hair neatly divided in the middle. *So this is George Roberts.* Mullock testified that he had witnessed his conversation with Tom Horn when he bragged that killing young Nickell had been his best shot, but according to the Denver police physician Horn was at that time in the hospital with the broken jaw; and this very barkeep allegedly expressed doubts that it was the real Horn who in Mullock's presence boasted about his sharpshooting skills.

Rick finished his sandwich, put a quarter on the table and leisurely walked into the bar room. For a while he pretended that he was watching the Faro players and then took a seat at the bar and ordered a glass of beer. When the guy in the apron obliged him, Rick casually remarked, "No big crowd today, huh?"

"No, lunch time is sort of quiet, but in the evening it's pretty full. The roulette over there doesn't even have a chance to cool off," the barkeep explained friendly.

"I know when the word got out that Horn frequented this place, customers came just out of curiosity," Rick started to lead the conversation toward the desired topic.

"You're right. There is no question that the papers made us quite popular and it didn't cost the boss a dime."

"What do you think about the verdict? The jury found him guilty yesterday."

"Well, based on what I have read in the papers, it looked to me that they framed him pretty good. A guy like Horn is not so stupid to hang around the saloons and brag about something he hasn't done, particularly if that murder stirred up the whole area."

Rick's heart began to beat faster. This talkative chap could not only offer quite important information, but it also seemed that he didn't believe that Horn was the murderer. Now was the time to strike the iron while it was hot.

Rick looked around. The three cowboys were fully concentrated on their game and the man in the corner kept reading the paper and didn't seem to pay any attention to the guests. Rick lowered his voice. "What actually happened that evening when Horn bragged in front of Mullock that it was his best shot?"

The barkeep leaned toward Rick and almost whispered, "Mullock cannot be trusted. He is a crook and as such he has a reputation all over Denver. He'll do anything for money. If you pay him the right amount, he will be willing to swear anything."

"But in that case it could be proven that he committed perjury, right?"

"Yeah, it could be done, but you would need witnesses."

Rick was puzzled. Something was wrong here. He looked suspiciously at the barkeep and thought about that rancher from Boulder who said…

"But you had overheard that conversation, hadn't you?"

"Me? Oh, no. You have mistaken me for the guy who worked here before me."

Rick got wide-eyed and quite suddenly blurted, "So you are not George Roberts?"

"I am sorry to disappoint you, but he left a long time ago. Bob Wilson." The barkeep stretched his hand and Rick hesitantly shook it. At the same time, he kept calling himself a genuine idiot. He behaved like a beginner. Every reporter knows that before he starts an interview he must verify the identity of an interviewee.

Rick pushed his hat back and with certain embarrassment asked, "Do you know where I could find him?"

"I can't help you with that, but why don't you ask the boss over there." The barkeep turned around and pointed at the man reading the newspaper.

Rick paid for the beer and slowly slid from the barstool. He glanced at a color print of several naked beauties in a seducing position on a Turkish divan set in a large, gilded frame mounted on the opposite wall. Right under it sat the owner of the Scandinavian Saloon. Rick stepped closer and when he saw that the paper which kept the man oblivious to his surroundings was *The Denver Post*, he felt more confident.

"Sorry to bother you. I am looking for George Roberts. If I am not mistaken he worked for you as a barkeep."

The owner folded the paper and gestured Rick to sit down. Only now the reporter had a chance to get a better look at him. His wavy grey hair was combed back and from under his thick eyebrows a pair of brown eyes was curiously looking at him. His mustache was trimmed according to the latest fashion and long, slim fingers were playing with the gold watch chain on his vest. Rick also noticed a revolver grip inside his open jacket reflecting the bluish light of a gas lamp. He would bet his weekly salary that the grey-haired man was a former gun fighter or a sheriff who decided in his advanced age to make living in safer way.

"Police sent you?" the saloon owner responded.

"No, not at all. I am a reporter. I write for *The Denver Post*. Look here," Rick pulled out of his pocket two issues of *The Post*. "Writing about Tom Horn I mentioned your saloon, so you are now a sort of local attraction, but now I need your help."

The man rocked once or twice in his chair, stared at Rick for a while and then asked, "What do you want from him?"

"I would like to ask him about something in the connection with Horn's case. I need to verify something."

"You are out of luck. George is no longer in Denver."

"Really? And where is he?"

"In New Orleans."

Rick couldn't believe his own ears. He leaned back and stuttered out, "In New Orleans in Louisiana? How the hell did he get there?"

The saloon owner ran his hand over the folded newspaper and slowly, as if he were weighing every word, then answered, "Under pretty strange circumstances. Sometime in the spring. It was in the middle of April I believe. He didn't show up at work. I sent a messenger boy to his apartment and the boy came back saying that according to his landlady George had received an excellent job offer from a saloon owner in the French Quarter a day earlier - double the pay and a free train ticket. However, there was one condition. He had to go straight from his apartment to the railroad station. Since he was single, he just packed his personal possessions and the next day in the morning he was on the train heading east. The name of his landlady is Mary Swanson. She owns a house on Pennsylvania Street between Eleventh and Twelfth Avenues. She may tell you more."

Rick thanked him for the information, his head spinning as he walked out.

"Mary Swanson, Pennsylvania Street between Eleventh and Twelfth Avenues," he kept repeating to himself. Grasping this lead like a straw he tried to figure out what actually happened. If Roberts knew that the guy hanging around the Denver saloons bragging about killing young Nickell was actually Horn's double, then it was necessary to get rid of him. A murder would raise suspicion, but this way it looks perfectly normal. Roberts got an offer he could not refuse, so he took it. Who would suspect something nefarious; and above all they put him far away. Who would make an effort to go all the way to New Orleans to look for a former barkeep from Scandinavian Saloon in a city which is twice the size of Denver? The proverbial needle in a haystack would be a more realistic proposition than this.

Rick walked to Larimer Square and at Carrington Hotel stopped a cab to save time. Finally, luck was on his side. Mary Swanson was at home. She was an older lady, a widow of a cavalry major, supplementing her pension by renting three small rooms on the second floor of her house. She never had any problems keeping those rooms occupied. Just the fact that a few blocks away stood the opulent residence of Molly Brown, which even became temporarily the governor's mansion, attracted many customers. However, the information she could offer was truly insignificant. She basically repeated what he had learned in Scandinavian Saloon, and then she added that Roberts was an old bachelor from Texas who all the time complained about Colorado's winter, and when an opportunity arose to move south, he didn't hesitate a second. Forwarding address? No, he didn't leave any.

Back at his office Rick tried to do some work, but his thoughts were swirling around Roberts and Mullock. Is it possible Mullock was involved in this scheme? Probably not. Since he was a bribable type, who would want to involve him in such a delicate undertaking? For the right sum of money, he would blabber everything out. After all, it is quite possible that he just repeated what he had heard. With Robert's disappearance, the trail got cold. The only witness who could testify in Horn's favor and even uncover an attempt to commit a conspiracy has vanished.

Having picked several usable reports Rick pushed the today's telegrams aside. As he leaned back in his chair his eyes rested on a row of books on the shelf next to the door. The one book caught his attention. The golden letters on a red spine read *"The Newspaper Yearbook - 1902"*. Rick jumped up. That's it. *How come I didn't think about that. Looks like I am getting old*, he thought as he reached for the book. *All I have to do is place an ad in several New Orleans newspapers and there is good chance that Roberts will sooner or later notice it. If he got a job in a bigger joint, he must be surrounded by all kinds of papers. That's the only way to get hold of him and if Horn was born under a lucky star, Roberts will not only read the ad but also respond.*

Rick opened *The Yearbook*, leafed in it and ran his finger on a list of newspapers published in New Orleans. *The Yearbook* listed not only their names, but also addresses and a number of copies. He picked three dailies which ran about ten thousand copies - *The New Orleans Democrat*, *The Louisiana Observer* and *The Bayou Reporter*. Then he put together a short announcement and a messenger boy took it to the post office the same afternoon. Three brown envelopes addressed to the three biggest newspapers in New Orleans contained the following text:

George Roberts of Denver: Contact *The Denver Post* in connection with the Tom Horn affair. Mark your answer by the code words "The Double".

Denver Post   **August 8th, 1902**   **Sunday Supplement**

Chatting with the Chief of Indian Scouts

Based on interviews with Tom Horn and prepared by F. Jackson.

As I told you last time, we spent the night under canvas shelters, soaked and tired. I remember that I carried two ammunition belts, just like old Sieber taught me. He used to say the most important thing was to have enough ammo to last until dusk because then there was always a chance to disappear. Those two belts weighed eleven pounds, but toward the evening I felt like I was carrying a small size locomotive on my back.

The night was rather peaceful. The rain stopped and early in the morning a squaw showed up in our camp. Geronimo sent her. The Chiricahua were on the other side of the river and wanted to negotiate. Captain Crawford listened to her and then sent her back with the message that the command would leave around noon. If Geronimo wanted to talk, he could do it in the morning. Nana also let Geronimo know that he and all prisoners were returning back to San Carlos. In that respect, however, he was mistaken. He and the others were on the way to the prison at Fort Bowie. When he found out about it, he just remarked that he didn't care where he was going, he was willing to go even to end of the world, as long as he didn't have to take part in the foot races anymore.

The squaw disappeared on the other side of the river and we began to pack for the trip to Nacori when several shots cracked south of our camp. I ran up on the cliffs and could not believe my eyes. In the distance, I saw a company of Mexican soldiers getting ready for a frontal assault on our position. We all, including the prisoners, moved up the rocky hill and watched the Mexicans. Since none of our officers spoke Spanish, I waited until they got closer and then I began to yell at them that we were The Third Cavalry Command and in accordance to the treaty with Mexico we were allowed to pursue the hostile Chiricahua on Mexican territory and that was the reason why we were here. The Mexican officers, however, pretended that they didn't understand and their captain gave an order to attack. About one hundred and fifty soldiers broke into a trot and ran toward the hill we occupied.

Captain Crawford, trying to prevent the bloodshed, jumped on a rock and waved a white handkerchief. I told the scouts to shoot only if in imminent danger and again yelled at them that we were Americans and we had no unfriendly intentions.

Instead of a reasonable answer I heard an order to fire. I turned back and then caught a glimpse of Captain Crawford falling from the boulder he was standing on. At the same time I felt sharp pain in my left arm. I jumped behind the nearest rock and at the same time a volley out of about thirty Springfield rifles thundered right behind my back, and then another one. Within several seconds almost a half of the Mexican soldiers were lying on the ground. Later on I was told that thirty-six of them were killed instantly and thirteen were seriously wounded. Needless to say, this kind of answer cooled off their fighting spirit significantly. Then I ran to the spot where I saw Captain Crawford fall and tried to understand what the hell was going on.

The captain was unconscious and was bleeding from his head. Again several shots cracked and the bullets hit the rocks nearby. I dragged him to a safe spot with my good hand and then crawled among the boulders to Lieutenants Shipp and Maus. Both officers were so surprised by this attack that they believed Mexico had declared war on the USA. There was no other explanation. After a while, the firing stopped and one of the Mexican officers yelled at us.

"Who are you and what are you doing here?"

I was hopping mad. Didn't they hear me when I tried to communicate with them? I stuck my head out and yelled back at them that we were a bunch of toughs from el Norte and that we came down here to do some shooting. We really liked their attack and if his "valientes" tried again it would give us an extreme pleasure.

The Mexicans argued among each other for a while and then again wanted to know what we were doing here. So I repeated that we were pursuing the hostiles and that in accordance with the treaty signed by Mexico and the US we had the right to operate on Mexican territory.

For several seconds it was quiet, and then one of the officers replied that they had never heard about such a treaty. Now surprise was on our side. It was unthinkable that General Crook would have lied to us, so either nobody told these guys about the treaty or they knew about it but thought they could help themselves to the horses we took away from the Chiricahua, or even worse to our weapons. In the case of the horses, there was no problem because most of them were stolen in Mexico anyway but as to our weapons or ammunition, we wouldn't give them a single round. If they wanted to take it by force, they would be welcome. Not even a thousand soldiers could dislodge us from our position.

I was just about to say that I would go down to talk to them when a piercing Indian war hoop sounded from the left southern side of the hill and then I heard a familiar voice.

"Tom, give me the go ahead and none of those devils will leave this place alive. We'll kill them all and take their pinoles." Geronimo stood behind one of the boulders and was ready to fight the enemy he hated most. The idea of getting their hands on pinoles, which was dry meat seasoned in a special Mexican way and all Indians loved, only increased the Chiricahua's fighting spirit. This was something the Mexican valientes didn't count on. They again huddled and then the same officer announced that they were ready to talk.

The actual negotiations didn't last long. The Mexicans were aware that their situation was pretty hopeless and so they tried at least to save face. During the talks we found out that their Captain Corredor was killed and that it was the first time

they heard about the treaty. They believed that we were part of the military units which provided cover for the Apaches to return back to the US territory with the stolen cattle and horses and that was the main reason they attacked. Then they insisted that one of the officers go with them to Chihuahua and sign a report about this incident. Well, I have categorically refused, so the Mexicans eventually caved in but insisted on repossessing the horses. There was no argument there. We picked about forty horses for ourselves and when they began retreating, they drove with them up to three hundred heads.

They barely disappeared from sight when Geronimo accompanied by several warriors showed up. He behaved as if nothing happened and wanted to negotiate. In that respect I had to disappoint him. I told him I was grateful for his offer to help fight the Mexicans, but the only person who could negotiate with him was Captain Crawford who unfortunately was mortally wounded. However, if he wanted me to take a message for the high command at Fort Bowie, I would be happy to deliver it. Geronimo agreed and asked me to tell General Crook that he would like to meet him sometime in March. After that we parted.

Captain Crawford died in the evening and because we were running low on supplies, we pulled back to Nacori which we reached three days later. Once we arrived in town, the first thing we did was bury Captain Crawford with full military honors and then properly stored all extra ammunition. Having taken care of all that, we continued on to Fort Bowie to hand over the prisoners and report about the campaign directly to General Crook. He listened to us, that is, to me and Lieutenant Maus, with great interest. He particularly wanted to hear all the details about Captain Crawford's death and because Washington kept pressuring him to finally settle the Geronimo affair, he agreed to meet with him again. Maus and I got orders to go back to Mexico and wait till Geronimo got in touch with us.

This time we positioned ourselves about twelve miles south of the border near the San Bernardino River. We built a heliograph station to be able to communicate with Fort Bowie about the future date for the planned meeting and waited. You won't believe me but for six weeks we did nothing. We just kept staring at the surrounding hills and kept saying no to the generals' questions about whether Geronimo got in touch with us or not.

Finally one evening, there was a smoke signal on the top of the opposite mountain. I set out right away and there I met a messenger who wanted to know how long it would take the general to come for a meeting. I could tell him right away it would take four days.

We sent the message to Fort Bowie and four days later General Crook, accompanied by a dozen of officers, arrived at our camp. On the same day Geronimo came with twenty warriors and both parties met in De Los Embudos Canyon. Geronimo wanted to know when the big talk would start, so I took him to the general, but the big talk did not happen. The general was not in the mood to witness again Geronimo's rhetorical skills and when he started with his favorite tirade of complaints, he cut him off shortly. Geronimo and his warriors would either surrender and go with him to Fort Bowie where they would be held as prisoners until Washington decided what to do with them, or he could go back to the mountains. In that case, it would be only a matter of time until the remaining warriors would desert him and he would get caught either by the army or the Indian scouts. Nana informed him that there was a dissent in his ranks and most of his people finally understood that the old way of life was over and wanted to return to San Carlos. Finally, he told him if he wanted to talk to him again tonight or tomorrow morning he would be at the camp at the river. Without waiting for Geronimo's re-action, the general turned around and left.

Geronimo then began asking me how many soldiers were in the camp and why the general didn't want to talk to him. I explained to him that he was upset because the Chiricahua always promised some-thing but they never kept their word. Three years ago the general person-ally made a serious effort to solve the conflict between them and the American government in a non-vio-lent way, but now, when Geronimo chose the war path, the general looked like a fool.

Geronimo listened for a while and then he told me that he would think about it and let me know in the morning. However the next day when we woke up, Geronimo and his escort were gone. He probably sensed that if he attempted to see the general in the camp, he might walk into the trap and get arrested by the soldiers. So the general and I re-turned to Fort Bowie empty handed. Even though there were about two hundred Chiricahua in the fort's jail, the kernel of his warriors were still free which still meant a serious threat to the Mexican as well as American population living in the countryside. Of course the War Department was not too happy about this outcome and decided to entrust someone else with the job of subduing the hostiles. Shortly after his return from Mexico, General Crook was recalled and General Nelson Miles took his place, but we'll talk about that next time.

10

Lacey stood at the window and watched the afternoon traffic on the main street. Suddenly, his attention was attracted by a strangely shaped monstrosity on four wheels moving along Sixteenth Street from the Inter-Ocean Hotel toward the Tivoli Café. A pipe mounted under an open seat kept belching black smoke and an overwhelming noise which was a mix of puffing, hiccups and loud discharges echoing from the surrounding buildings was coming out from under a large bulge covered by red painted sheet metal. The owner of this modern transportation, whose parts shook as if having a seizure, kept rolling undisturbed toward the intersection of Sixteenth Street and Ferguson Avenue. Several people stopped on the corner, directly in front of Tivoli, either to have a closer look at this horseless carriage or they were just curious as to how much havoc this latest invention would cause among the nearby teams of horses. Lacey already had caught a glimpse of two horses rearing in front of a hardware store across the street, but then he heard knocking on the door and his secretary stepped into his office.

"There is a gentleman here who wants to see you. Here is his calling card." The secretary handed him a little white card with the black trim and waited to see how the boss would decide. Lacey looked at the card and grumbled just to himself, "Hmm. Rick Jackson, *The Denver Post*. Don't remember. Those guys in Colorado are not that bad, but here in Wyoming *The Cheyenne Tribune* and *The Buffalo Chronicle* would like to see Horn hang already today. One won't find a more bloodthirsty pack anywhere." His first reaction was to refuse to see him, but then he realized that it would not be smart to antagonize such an influential paper like *The Denver Post* because it could affect Horn's case or his own carrier. So he put the card in the drawer of his desk and without much enthusiasm told the secretary to let him in.

The secretary slipped out of the office and gestured the reporter to go ahead and step in. Mr. Lacey was ready to see him. Rick walked in, introduced himself and while looking around the room, the attorney was trying to remember where he had seen him. Oh yes, in the courtroom he had sat in the first row and he had seen him and Coble on several occasions talking together. What could be the purpose of his visit? It was rather unlikely that the Colorado readers were much interested in the fate of a cattle detective from a neighboring state.

Lacey asked the reporter to sit down on the chair at the window and he eased his over-six-foot body into a comfortable armchair next to his desk.

"What brings you to my office?"

Rick readily answered, "Two things. First, I would like to inform our readers about the next steps you plan to take in Tom Horn's case, and second, as a reciprocal service I can offer you some information which could strengthen your position."

Lacey had to smile. This was something unheard of. Usually these guys, if they know something, they open their mouth only when bribed or threatened by the law. How come this reporter was willing to volunteer some information just out of goodness of his heart? It was hard to believe. What are the next steps he plans to take? That's no secret. The public was informed about a week ago that he had appealed the verdict to the Wyoming Supreme Court, so he probably wants to know details about the specific arguments. I guess some of them I can tell him.

The attorney nodded his head and began to summarize the main points of the appeal. "Ad primum: Prosecutor Stoll seriously violated the standard procedures when he, in his closing argument, tried to psychologically pressure the jury by referring to a case when a man, three weeks after being set free, committed several murders in Montana. Ad secundum: The prosecution did not present any single direct evidence which would prove above all doubts that Tom Horn was guilty of the said crime. Ad tertiam: The main prosecution witness Joe LeFors presented a modified testimony which consisted of self-incriminating confession of the defendant who was under influence of alcohol. The defense with the help of the direct witnesses refuted all central points of this document. Ad quartiam: The defense obtained additional testimonies of reliable witnesses which would prove the defendant innocent. These will be introduced during the actual hearing at the Supreme Court."

Lacey paused for a second and then quickly added that the Supreme Court could not legally remove the actual charge against Tom Horn or nullify the verdict but could decide whether the trial had conformed to the constitutional requirements or not. In the case it had not, it could order a new trial somewhere else where an unbiased and above all uninfluenced jury could be assembled. According to his opinion they had a great chance that the Supreme Court would rule in their favor.

Lacey stopped talking, leaned back in his armchair and looked at Rick waiting for his reaction. The reporter made a few more notes in his indispensable notebook and then began broadly describing his visits to the Nickells and to the Scandinavian Saloon. Both men now changed their roles. Rick kept speaking and Lacey was taking notes. As soon as Rick finished, the attorney asked for clarification of some details, and above all he wanted to know if Nickell would be willing to testify again if the trial were renewed.

"You know, that barkeep from the Scandinavian Saloon, that's a long shot. It's true that his testimony would be relevant to the crime Horn is charged with, but the chance that we would ever see him is quite slim. On the other hand, if Nickell testified, he could pretty seriously shake up the LeFors' testimony and even convince the judge to throw the whole case out. When Stoll quoted his affidavit which contained the Horn's explanation that he didn't hit Nickell because he was shooting against the sun and Nickell kept jumping like a wounded Comanche, Horn categorically refused to admit that he had said anything like that because at the time of the shooting he was at Sellers' ranch. I talked to John Coble last week and he planned to go there. It's supposed to be somewhere on the Platte River not far from Laramie, but so far I have not heard from him."

Rick kept nodding his head and then assured the attorney that if Roberts responded to his ad, he would be the first to know about it. Lacey got up, shook Rick's hand and when the reporter was about to leave the office, he quickly asked, "I was wondering, why are you so interested in this case?"

Rick turned around and smiling replied, "Have you read those biographic stories I wrote for the Sunday edition?"

"Oh yes, but I was not familiar with the name. So it was you?"

"You've got it. And I would hate to see the last one having an unhappy ending."

From the lawyer's office Rick walked straight to the courthouse. The last time he talked to Tom was three weeks ago. He was sure that he would welcome the news that Nickell would be willing to testify and if Roberts got in touch with him and confirmed that the man in the Scandinavian Saloon was his double, the arguments of the prosecution won't be worth a pitcher of warm spit.

He signed in at the sheriff's office and when Snow had made sure that he didn't possess any weapons, one of his helpers took him upstairs. Rick found Horn quite busy. The prisoner was bent over large pieces of hide strewn on the chair and the table and with a razor blade attached to a wooden handle he kept slicing them into long strips about a quarter inch wide. Rick was just about to ask the guard what was going on when he caught a glimpse of a bridle and a pair of reins skillfully braided from two-colored leather strips. It occurred to him that he once saw a similar bridle in one of the Denver shops and it cost almost twenty dollars.

Horn raised his head and when he recognized Rick, finished the cut and laid the razor blade away. Then he pulled the chair close to the red line and sat down.

"I'll be damned," Rick stated jovially. "You got into the braiding business? Where did you learn it?"

Horn looked at the reporter and he could tell that Tom was not in the best mood today. "Oh, I learned it from the Apaches. The boredom was getting on my nerves so I asked Coble to bring me some hides and a couple of old razor blades and I got into braiding."

Rick wanted also to ask how long it would take to finish such a bridle, but then he figured that it would make more sense to spend time talking about more serious things and turned the conversation toward his visit at the Nickells and the Scandinavian Saloon. Basically, he repeated the same stuff he had told Lacey and now he expected that Tom would add some more details or at least he would feel pleased by this good news, but he only occasionally nodded his head. Rick had the impression that he wasn't even listening to him. However, when he mentioned Coble and his trip to Sellers' ranch, Horn began speaking. He spoke quietly and from time to time he looked into the corridor to make sure that nobody was listening.

"Look. Roberts, who could prove that it was not me who was bragging about killing young Nickell, disappeared. The other witness, who could testify that when somebody fired at old Nickell when I was miles away, disappeared too."

Rick moved closer to the bars and was already reaching for his notebook, but Horn stopped him. "The stuff I am going to tell you now must stay between you and me. I don't want to drag John into this filth. He did for me more than anybody else and if his name appeared in your paper, the local scribblers would blow it out of proportion."

Rick left the notebook in his pocket and Horn continued.

"John was here today in the morning. He told me that he had visited Sellers' ranch, but what do you think he found there? The place was deserted. John knew some people in the neighborhood so he asked around and he found out amazing stuff. Sometime this spring Sellers was getting threatening letters. Something about the day of the reckoning which was near and that for the crime he had committed, he and his whole family would pay. Sellers was not the type to be easily scared, but when one evening somebody shot through the window while the family was eating dinner and the following day another letter came mentioning the fate of young Nickell, he decided it was time to quit. He did so mainly because he had two young boys and obviously didn't feel like pushing his luck. He talked to his neighbors and told them that his place was for sale. He told them he had worked his tail off there long enough and all he needed was to worry not only how many calves would not make it through the winter, but also if somebody would kill him from an ambush. He also said that crude was discovered in the north and there were plenty of job opportunities there. First, he moved to Wheatland and when he managed to sell the ranch, he disappeared to no one knows where, just like Roberts. About Roberts, we at least know that he is in New Orleans, but as to Sellers, nothing."

Horn paused and Rick asked about the sentence which he didn't understand. "Sellers was getting threatening letters mentioning a crime? What crime?"

Horn nodded his head. "Yeah, that's the worst about the whole affair. Whoever wrote them letters, he was damn well informed. One cannot tell that he has committed a crime, but it is true that about seven or eight years ago he snuffed the life out of a cheating gambler. On one occasion he told me what had happened. At that time he worked in Montana not far from Helena as a cowboy. One day they drove a herd of cattle to town, handed it over to an agent and then they dropped by a saloon near the railroad station to wash down all the dust. It was toward evening when the foreman paid everybody off so in no time the boys were cutting loose. Seller didn't drink much, but he had one weak spot - he liked poker. At one table there were three men already playing, so they could use a fourth one. Two of them were also cowboys, but the third one, a short, rusty-haired fella made the impression that his hands never worked a rope. Well, not to make the story too long, after a while there was a pile of money in front of the red-haired guy and Sellers had only a couple of quarters left in his pocket. So they agreed to play one more game and then quit. It looked like Sellers was getting lucky that time. I don't remember what he had, royal flush or a full house, but he felt pretty confident and put on the table the rest of his money and even borrowed some from his buddies. There was almost one hundred dollars in the pot and so someone was to call. The other two guys folded earlier, so it was between Sellers and Rusty. That's what he used to call him. Well, when they put the cards on the table, Sellers' hand was not high enough.

"Needless to say, he cursed his luck including the moment he decided to play. Rusty cut a face, reached out for the money and then it happened. Sellers noticed a red edge of an extra card sticking out of Rusty's left cuff. He grabbed him by his hand, but then he was staring into the barrel of a gun. Sellers let him go, but at the same he feverishly started thinking about how to save his money. As he was leaning back in his chair, he kicked the table up and reached for his six-shooter, but Rusty was faster, jumped aside and pulled the trigger. Under normal circumstances the whole incident would end up by Sellers' buddies collecting some money for his funeral and returning to the ranch without him. But the gun misfired. It was simply bad luck which happens once in a lifetime. This time it was Sellers who pulled the trigger. When the sheriff came, Rusty was unconscious and by midnight his gambling soul was already in that big saloon in the sky. Sellers spent the night in jail and because those two other cowboys testified that it was a matter of self-defense, the next day Sellers was free. He saved his share, but as far as I remember, he never played cards again. For some time his conscience bothered him, but years later he let it go."

"And what was the real name of the red-haired guy" Rick asked.

"Frank Scott."

"Were those letters signed?"

"No, but they referred to the death of a brother, in other words the brother of the person who sent those letters."

"Well, I think I can take care of it. You said it happened about eight years ago near Helena, right? You see, I know some people in the newspaper business over there. I'll send them a telegram and they'll check it out." Rick thought for a second and then added, "John did a good job, that's for sure."

"John is the only friend who hasn't left me yet. The others melted away like snow in the afternoon sun."

"How about Miss Kimmell? She stands by you," Rick objected.

"Well, it may come as a shock to you, but she is gone too." Horn saw Rick's uncomprehending look so he explained, "She was transferred all the way to Missouri, to Kansas City."

"How come? Just like that?"

"Not just like that. Here, she wrote me... hold on, I'll read it to you." Horn reached into his shirt pocket and pulled out two sheets of paper covered densely by tiny female handwriting. His eyes ran over the letter and somewhere in the middle of the first page he began to read. When he finished, Rick could not believe what he had heard. Miller's wife and their small children moved to Cheyenne and old Miller and his two older sons vanished God knows where. In another words she lost a place to stay and at the same time the last handful of pupils. The nearest opening for a teacher was in Kansas City, so she moved there." Horn carefully folded the letter and put it back in his pocket.

"Does Lacey know about it?"

"You bet."

Rick pulled out his pocket watch and looked at the dial. The allocated thirty minutes for the visit were practically over. The Denver train was to leave in about an hour and if he wanted to send a telegram to Helena, he'd better rush. Listening to Horn's narration about the Apache wars definitely had to wait until the next time.

"Don't lose your faith. Everything will turn out alright, you will see. Lacey is convinced that the Supreme Court will order a new trial and in the meantime much new information will surface. Just the fact that the Millers high-tailed out of the area is a very important piece of information."

Rick got up from the bench, said good-bye and headed for the staircase. Horn's eyes followed him until the reporter disappeared in the dark corridor, then he returned to the table, took the razor blade and began to slice another piece of hide.

About two weeks later, in the middle of November, when Rick entered his office in the morning, he found a fresh issue of *The Cheyenne Tribune* on his desk. Right next to it laid a telegram. He hesitated a moment on what to reach for first, but then he looked at the front page and uttered an unusually profane curse. Pete, sitting on the other side of the office, quite surprised raised his head, but before he managed to say anything Rick was standing next to his desk pointing his finger at a large headline which read: "**Supreme Court Confirms Verdict. Date of Execution December 15th.**"

For a moment the room was gravely silent. Only after a while Rick remembered the telegram. Without saying a word he walked to his table and mechanically opened the envelope. On the form with the Western Telegram head he read one sentence: **"Frank Scott had no relatives."**

Denver Post   September 5th, 1902   Sunday Supplement

Chatting with the Chief of Indian Scouts

Based on interviews with Tom Horn and prepared by F. Jackson.

General Miles became the Department Commander in the spring of 1886 and once he found his footing, he started to reorganize. His administrative changes affected me as well. By the beginning of the summer the independent unit of the Indian Scouts was abolished and consequently also my rank as Chief of Scouts. I became only an interpreter and shortly thereafter I was sent to Fort Apache. The rest of the scouts were divided into smaller groups and attached to individual cavalry troops and their commanders.

I knew right away that this system would not work. Five scouts who were part of a military unit didn't have a chance against freely operating Chiricahua and that became quite obvious during the summer. Two troops of the Third Cavalry commanded by Captain Leebo stepped into a trap and after a short fight had to retreat with great losses. The Indians were so well hidden that the soldiers actually never saw them. Two days later the same happened to one troop of the Fourth Cavalry. Toward the end of July another Chiricahua band reached Fort Bowie killing two men and one boy and on the border it attacked four Mexicans who were making mescal and killed them all.

About the same time I chanced upon two newspapers. One was from Tucson and the other from San Francisco. Both publications tried to outdo each other in praising General Miles saying that finally the right man was put in charge of the Apache problem. Geronimo is practically finished and this guy Tom Horn is too. Well, the moment I saw my name there, I began to read the whole article more carefully and in doing so I found out that it was actually my fault that Geronimo was still loose. The author claimed that it was hard to tell whether I was an Apache or a Mexican, that I had full support of all Indians and I could freely move among them. On top of it all, officers were at my mercy because they didn't speak the Apache language. Then came the best part - thanks to my friendly attitude toward the Indians the entire conflict was dragging on and the number of the whites killed by the Apaches just kept growing.

Well, that definitely exhausted my patience. I went to the quartermaster, put the paper on his desk and briefly informed him that I wanted the rest of my pay which he owed me and that as of today I quit the Army. The quartermaster stared at me quite surprised, but when I showed him those two articles, he just nodded his head and produced the balance of my salary.

The same day I was on the way to a ranch in Aravaipa Canyon which lately had become my second home. I helped the owner work the cattle and in my free time I did quite successfully prospecting for silver, so I didn't have to worry about my livelihood. About a week later when reading again Tucson paper I learned that now since that "traitor" Horn was gone, it would be only a matter of time until they brought a shackled Geronimo to Fort Bowie

Weeks kept passing and one day, instead of a shackled Geronimo, several soldiers sent by the quartermaster from Fort Huachuca appeared at the ranch carrying a letter requesting that I report to duty. I wrote him back that it must have been a mistake because I no longer worked for the U.S. government, that I worked in a silver mine and, therefore, the Army

must find someone else. A week later another courier showed up, this time with a message directly from General Miles. He said that the General apologized for the rash decision to degrade me from the Chief of Scouts to an interpreter and that he would like to talk to me at Fort Huachuca, where his headquarters were now located, in the matter of the Chiricahua Apaches.

I thought long and hard about it. In the end it occurred to me that sooner or later Geronimo would fall into the hands of the Army and in that case it made sense that someone who was really fluent in the language should be present to avoid misunderstanding or unnecessary bloodshed. I arranged with my partners to put aside my share of silver, saddled up a horse and headed to Fort Huachuca. There I met with the general who backtracked some of his decisions. I got my rank back and soon was on the way to Mexico where I was supposed to contact Captain Lawton and with a group of his scouts to try to locate Geronimo.

I found the captain in Sonora at a place called Sierra Gordo. He had under his command two cavalry troops and twenty-five Indian and five white scouts. I organized the scouts into one unit, gave them assignments and several days later we were on Geronimo's trail. As Captain Lawton agreed to leave both troops in Sonora and move out only with the scouts, the distance between us and Geronimo started to get shorter. The fact that the Mexican soldiers patrolled the local ranches and prevented the Chiricahua from getting fresh horses and that the heliograph stations provided regular reports about their movements led to the reduction of their original head start of four days to just ten or twelve hours. Geronimo began to slow down. From time to time we saw dead horses or abandoned squaws with children who could not keep up with this murderous pace.

Then not far from Fronteras we received a heliograph message to stop further efforts to catch up with the Chiricahua and return to Fort Huachuca. It didn't make much sense, particularly now when Geronimo was within reach, but an order is an order and so we turned back. The next day another message told us to go to Fronteras and wait there for Lieutenant Gatewood who, accompanied by two Chiricahua warriors from San Carlos, was on his way to Mexico. General Miles allegedly got a missive that Geronimo wanted to quit and Lieutenant Gatewood was supposed to negotiate the conditions of surrender.

Well, several days later Lieutenant Gatewood and two Chiricahua really showed up. They rested a bit and then they followed Geronimo's trail. I estimated that within a day or two they should be in his camp, but on the fourth day Gatewood was back empty handed. The explanation was that his San Carlos Apaches got cold feet, they feared that as they entered Geronimo's camp, the other Chiricahua might kill them as traitors and so they refused to go on. Needless to say, we held a war council at which I suggested that I go there myself and see what I could come up with to solve this problem. Captain Lawton liked the idea, but Lieutenant Gatewood did not seem to be comfortable with my proposal. When we pressed him what was wrong with it, he, pretty embarrassed, admitted that according to General Miles' orders, I was not allowed to conduct any negotiations because it was strictly a military affair. So that was the general's game. I was good to find Geronimo but not good enough to deal with him. In this matter he just didn't trust me. Then it occurred to me that I could play this game, too. I suggested to Captain Lawton to send a message to Fort Huachuca, informing the general what happened and that I was proposing the following: I would contact Geronimo, but only myself because I could not guarantee safety either to Lieutenant Gatewood or to his companions.

The message was barely sent when a squaw dispatched by Geronimo entered our camp. Geronimo was willing to talk but only if the scouts left him alone and I would be present. I was about to translate everything to Captain Lawton, but then I figured it would be more effective if he heard it from someone else's mouth. I called one of the Chiricahua who came with Lieutenant Gatewood and asked him to translate the message for Captain Lawton. The Captain listened to him and then another message went to Miles' headquarters.

The answer came the following day. The general agreed that I should go to Geronimo's camp, find out under what conditions he was willing to surrender, and if he wanted to meet the general in person, I had the authority to negotiate the time and place of the meeting.

On the day of the departure when I was saddling up my horse, Lieutenant Gatewood stepped up to me and asked if he could join me. Since it was up to me to say yes or no and not the general, I assured him that it would be my pleasure to have his company and

if he stuck to me, no one would harm him.

The next day in the evening we camped at the foot of the Terras Mountain on the Bavispe River. The squaw who guided us told us to stay there because Geronimo would contact us by himself. Apparently, the instinct of self-preservation honed to an extreme by constant fleeing prevented him to disclose the place where the remnants of Chiricahua were hiding.

Geronimo and four warriors came shortly after sunrise and we spent practically the whole day talking about the best way to set up the meeting with General Miles. At this time I had no doubts that Geronimo was serious about quitting the war path. I could tell by his terse answers that they suffered a shortage of food and ammunition and the approaching winter could result in death of a sizable amount of his people. There was one thing, however, he was quite adamant about. He insisted that American soldiers should be near the meeting place because he was deeply worried about the Mexicans. He feared that they may take advantage of his presence, ambush him in a suitable place and so exact a bloody revenge for the past crimes Chiricahua committed among the Mexican ranchers. When I told him that there were cavalry troops in Fronteras so his safety would be taken care of, he noticeably calmed down. Lieutenant Gatewood then took off to deliver a message to Captain Lawton to be forwarded to General Miles, saying that the meeting would take place in Skeleton Canyon twelve days later. In this way both the general and Geronimo had enough time to reach the agreed upon destination.

Believing that everything was moving along just fine, I returned to Fronteras where Captain Lawton showed me the copy of the heliographic message sent to General Miles. An answer addressed to Captain Lawton arrived the next day. The general agreed with the date as well as with the place of the meeting, so I put his response in the saddle bag and headed back to Geronimo's camp. However, the moment Geronimo found out that there was no mentioning of my name in the missive, he became again highly suspicious and because he never met Captain Lawton, he refused to deal with General Miles through another intermediary unknown to him. So back to Fronteras I went. This time I personally sent another message to the general in which I asked him to send the agreement with the upcoming negotiations directly to me. General Miles responded immediately

informing me that according to the army regulations an official dispatch can be sent only from one officer to another, and since the highest officer in Fronteras was Captain Lawton the dispatch can be addressed only to him.

I have known for quite a while that as to regulations General Miles was a genuine stickler, but I also thought that considering the current circumstances he had learned a lesson. Well, it turned out exactly as I suspected. Geronimo listened to my desperate effort to explain to him the intricacies of the military bureaucracy for a while, but then he ordered to raise the camp and before he left, he had asked me to tell General Miles that he was willing to do the business only through one man and that man was Tom Horn. Once he agreed to that, he should let him know. The Chiricahua, altogether 136 people, disappeared in the southerly direction and I returned to Fronteras. There I reported to Captain Lawton what had happened and to Geronimo's words I added mine saying that I was going home and when the general gets over his bureaucratic hang-ups, I'd be happy to help him.

I rode the whole night and in the morning I arrived at Slaughter's ranch on the other side of the border.

I turned the horse in the corral, wolfed down something like a breakfast and went to bed. Around noon the neighing of horses and knocking on the door woke me up. It was a military patrol. The commanding officer pulled out of his saddle bag an envelope with the dispatch from General Miles, the same one he had sent several days ago to Captain Lawton, but this time it was addressed to me. As of this time I had full authority to negotiate all preparations with regard to the meeting in the Skeleton Canyon.

You can imagine what I thought about it. Last night I rode about forty miles and Geronimo covered about the same distance. He was going south and I was going north, so there were about seventy miles between us. Well, to make the story short, I caught up with him within a week, convinced him to come with me to Fronteras and then sent a message to General Miles, that the meeting was still on as originally agreed.

In the morning of September 4th, I brought Geronimo and several sub-chiefs to General Miles' camp. The general was ready to welcome us, but again it was not meant to go smoothly. He was accompanied by three military interpreters and that caused immediately a trouble. One of them, a young warrior from the Tonto tribe began to speak, but Geronimo didn't listen to him and just made a declining gesture and asked why I was not interpreting. The general remained calm and answered that I was not sworn in and therefore cannot interpret. Geronimo frowned and then sarcastically remarked that he always dealt with trustworthy people and never asked them whether they were sworn in or not. The most important thing was that they didn't lie to him, and the only white people who never lied to him were old Al Sieber and Tom Horn. Geronimo, the war chief of the Chiricahua, would negotiate only through the people he could trust and as far as he knew, General Miles had no reasons to doubt Horn's truthfulness.

The general wriggled and his vanity was obviously hurt. The old Indian came to surrender and now he had the nerve to lay down conditions. In the end he gave in, I took the oath and the big talk started. However, the general felt offended and so he just brusquely announced that there was nothing to talk about and if Geronimo was serious about surrendering, all he had to do was to follow him to Fort Bowie and there lay down the weapons. Then he uttered a sentence which had the most decisive effect on Geronimo's decision, namely that all his relatives were already in Florida and if he wanted to ever see them, it would be in his best interest to turn himself in. I didn't know anything about it because I hadn't been at Fort Bowie for more than two months, so I considered it factual information.

Geronimo asked for two days to cover the distance from Fronteras to Fort Bowie; General Miles agreed and that was the end of the meeting. Two days later about one hundred warriors and some squaws and children, the last remnants of Chiricahua, rode into the fort. General Miles ordered a whole troop of cavalry to line up in two rows at the gate which reminded me of a last honor to the defeated enemy. Geronimo symbolically handed over his rifle to the general and then dismounted. The other warriors followed him and when everybody was disarmed the guards led them to a big building erected for this special occasion.

As Geronimo entered, it would be hard to describe his surprise. There in the temporary prison he met all his relatives, sons, daughters and grandchildren who were captured during the previous months.

Several days later a special train pulled up in the station not far from the fort and about three hundred fifty Chiricahua guarded by the soldiers were transported east to one of the Florida Keys where they were held as prisoners of war. Chiricahua, the scourge of the American and Mexican settlers left Arizona never to come back. Later on, I read in the paper that they were resettled to Oklahoma, to Fort Sill and I believe they are there even today.

Geronimo never forgave General Miles for lying to him about his relatives. Many years later they both met in Oklahoma and the eighty year old chief reminded the general about this incident by saying that if he had known that they were still in Arizona, he would have never surrendered. Well, that was Geronimo. He liked big statements and he couldn't miss this opportunity to make one.

11

Horn finished his meal, put the plate with the spoon on a little stool next to the door and returned to the table at the window. For a while he sorted the freshly cut leather strips, then he picked out couple of them and began to braid. He promised John that he would make him in addition to the bridle a lariat and even though he would probably never use it, he could show it off in town or among his friends at the ranch because very few people could say that they possessed a leather rope.

The thoughts about Coble's ranch in Bosler made him stop working. His hands sank to his lap and Horn began to reminisce about the busy life among the cowboys in the neighboring county. He saw himself camping on the range where he spent long evenings alone, killing time by observing the stars or reading books in the light of the campfire. He thought of the dramatic moments when he followed the tracks left by a small group of riders driving a bunch of cows away from the pasture and trying to hide it in some deep hollow. Firing several shots from his Winchester usually got the attention of the thieves and once they found out who was on their heels, they abandoned the cows and tried to disappear behind the next hill.

Horn thought about the blissful moments in Coble's bathtub which he could use after a week spent riding the range, then about the smell of coffee and fried bacon. He also thought about the pleasant feeling of a fresh, clean shirt and the flannel pants he would put on before the trip to town and then about the rough fun in the saloons which sometimes ended in a fistfight. He thought about the pleasant aroma of the young teacher's hair and her naked body, about the time he spent with her on the top of Iron Mountain in the shade of tall pines where only the rustling of the wind in the treetops disturbed the ever present stillness.

All his life he had been incredibly lucky. Even though many times his life had been hanging on a thread, the tide had always changed and he had always gotten away from the stickiest situations unharmed - that was until now. Was it possible that fate wanted to finally collect the toll for all those favors it lavished on him earlier? He did not believe in God, but if He existed, He knew that he had nothing to do with the murder of that boy. True, many people died by his hand, particularly when he served as a scout in Arizona, but those he killed in an open fight. It's true, he shot Rush and Dart in Colorado from an ambush, but those were varmints in human shape who were not any different than the renegade Indians leaving the reservation raiding the local ranches and stealing cattle. They understood only the tough law of the West, the law of the gun, just like any other outlaw did. He, Tom Horn, always stood on the side of justice and never stooped to any dirt.

How many times had he stared death in the eyes? It had always backed off as if intimidated by his courage. Now it was stalking him cowardly from behind, disguised, wearing frocks of corrupted sheriffs, prosecutors and judges. All these so-called lawmen should appreciate what he did for enforcing the law. Now, when he was forty-two years old, he was supposed to become a victim of the new age - an age of weaklings, imposters and perjurers, people like LeFors or Ohnhaus who had no idea what honor or justice actually were.

Horn got up and began restlessly pacing in his cell. A week after the Supreme Court had rejected Lacey's appeal, he wrote Ohnhaus a letter begging him to tell the truth about the short-hand recording. Why were some passages missing? For example, the one when LeFors was bragging how many people he had shot. Why did he change that fateful sentence "It would have been my best shot"? Of course, he never wrote back. Who would voluntarily admit falsifying an important legal document anyway?

Horn stopped at the bed and put a blanket over his shoulders. November was pretty cold and the stove in the middle of the corridor didn't give much heat. On top of it the keeping fire in the stove was not on the priority list of the sheriff's helpers. The onset of the winter caused the old injury he suffered in Mexico in 1886 to begin to bother him. In that year during a campaign against the Chiricahua, Captain Corredor had gotten between the American command consisting of the Indian scouts and cavalry troopers on one side and Geronimo's warriors on the other with a company of Mexican foot soldiers. Believing he could help himself to their horses and food supplies, he had ordered an attack on the position of the Americans. The Mexicans had attacked in open terrain while his scouts had hidden behind the rocks on a hill. This suicidal idea had cost Corredor his life and had cost Horn a shot through his left arm.

Fortunately, that Denver fellow stopped by once a while. Otherwise the loneliness would have driven him crazy. From time to time, he got a letter or John paid him a visit but when that young reporter showed up, he brightened up for him the whole day. During those visits he returned back at least for half an hour to his youth and into a completely different world. Horn suddenly saw in his mind the American flag flying on a pole at Fort Bowie, the officers in blue uniforms with golden epaulettes and rows of cavalrymen accompanied by blaring sounds of the trumpet passing through the fort gate. He could see Al Sieber, the Chief of Scouts explaining to their commander where he spotted a group of Chiricahua who escaped from the reservation and suggesting a course of action. He vividly saw the Apaches who faithfully served under him during the entire war and he would never forget the pain in their eyes when they found out that Geronimo's warriors had murdered their wives and children just to take revenge on them for serving with the white soldiers. Then, of course, came the most memorable day of his life; the most feared Apache chief Geronimo had asked him to be his interpreter and advisor. He clearly recollected the moments at the campfire when the other minor chiefs with stone-like faces accepted Geronimo's decision to surrender, to become prisoners of war practically for the rest of their lives. At that time, he never knew what not only the next day but the next hour would bring. Now here, like a wild beast locked in a cage, he struggled with boredom and numbing monotony.

A key rattled in the door lock. Horn turned around and then following the prison rules stood next to the table while Joe was collecting the breakfast dishes. *Even this guy knows nothing else but his routine*, Horn thought. *He opens the door by his right hand, enters the cell, steps up to the stool and by his left hand collects the pots while by his right hand he holds the door. Then he slowly backs out, shuts the door and turns the key in the lock - the same moves day after day from the moment of the arrest.*

Horn stepped to the window and his eyes ran over the roofs of buildings blocking his view of the surrounding area. Some of them were already covered by light snow dust. Damn. He would give anything for an opportunity to leave this place at least for a while, be back at the range, sit in a saddle and feel rhythmical pounding of the hooves. The grey cell bars, however, reminded him of the futility of these thoughts and so he sat down on the chair and resumed braiding the lariat. It should be at least twenty-five feet long and that would take at least another week. If John took good care of it and regularly soaked it with grease, it would last a lifetime.

Shortly before noon he heard steps on the staircase. He was the only prisoner on this floor and since it was too early for the lunch, it had to be a visit. Horn put the thongs aside, walked to the door and stared into the dark end of the corridor. Soon he spotted the large frame of the deputy sheriff Snow and a short guy walking right next to him. When they both came closer, he noticed that the stranger's hands were handcuffed.

"Brought you a neighbor," Snow boomed with pretended geniality, then he opened the adjacent cell, pushed the new "guest" in and ordered him to put his hands close to the door. Then with a key ready in his hand, he skillfully unlocked the handcuffs, slipped them out through the bars and whistling a popular tune he returned to his office.

The new prisoner stepped to the bars and without hesitation addressed Horn. "You are Tom Horn, right? I am Hubert Herr, but you can call me Bert." Herr put his right hand through the bars to shake with Horn, but he ignored it, sat down on his bed and attentively studied Herr's face. He tried hard to remember if he had seen or met him before but he could not place him. The new neighbor could have been about forty years old with a receding hairline and blue eyes which gave his visage an image of honesty. The fact that Horn acted rather reserved didn't seem to bother him. He began to inquire about the food they served there in the prison, whether it was palatable and how often they got it.

Then the braided bridle caught his attention and he kept asking about it. When, finally his curiosity was satisfied and he stopped talking, Horn asked him why he was there and for how long.

"Bad luck. Just wanted to pinch a saddle. When I was putting it on my horse, its owner showed up, raised hell as if I killed someone and the judge gave me two weeks," Herr readily explained.

Horn just nodded his head and didn't say anything, but it crossed his mind that one would hardly find greater irony. In addition to all the disgrace that had happened to him, his neighbor was a common thief. Herr then made a few appreciative remarks about the cells saying that one could not break out of here even with the help of dynamite sticks and when he was about to compare this prison with the jail in Deadwood, Joe appeared in the corridor bringing lunch.

Herr, following Joe's order, stepped up to the window and Horn mechanically observed the food delivering routine. After lunch he went back to braiding. He made sure that the selected thongs were evenly wide and then he began to braid them around a hemp rope about one quarter inch thick. He tightened the leather strips as much as he could, and the new ones he placed one inch back under the old ones to prevent the ends from getting loose. So after about a day's work stooped over a pile of sliced hide, he added three feet to the new lariat. Herr watched him quietly and because after a while he got bored, he lay down on his bed and slept through the rest of the afternoon.

At seven in the evening the food serving ritual was repeated. Joe brought each prisoner a plate full of beans seasoned by a pepper sauce and a cup of black coffee. Half an hour later he came back, picked up the dishes and then he showed up once more around nine o'clock. He wished both prisoners good night and turned off the light. Horn barely buried himself in the blankets when he heard Herr whispering.

"Are you asleep?"

"No."

"So come over. I have to tell you something."

Horn first ignored his request, but when Herr insisted that it was extremely important, he finally kicked off the blankets and approached the bars.

"So what is it?"

"You know that story about the saddle? That was just a feint. Actually Coble sent me here with a message."

"What feint?" asked Horn. "The story about the saddle was phony?"

"No, I just feigned the theft. It had to look credible if I wanted to get arrested. Coble went to Omaha for couple of weeks so he won't be here and nobody will suspect that he had organized the whole thing."

"For God's sake, what thing?"

"Listen very carefully." Herr pressed his face against the bars and whispering he began to describe the real reason why he was in the Cheyenne prison. When he finished, Horn was speechless. He sat down on the chair and tried to make sense out of what he had just heard.

Because the Supreme Court approved the verdict of the Cheyenne court and set the execution day for December 15th, Coble decided not to rely on humanitarian feelings of the Wyoming Governor Chatterton, but to take an action. The only reliable way to save Horn's life was to help him escape. Even Providence seemed to support this effort.

President Roosevelt would be passing through Cheyenne on December 10th. The attention of the police, sheriff and his deputies would be focused on the railroad station where the president would give a short speech and a thank-you for the enthusiastic welcome in which, with the greatest probability, most of the local population would take part. Only old Joe would be watching the prisoners. If Horn succeeded in overpowering him and slipped unnoticed out of the jail, an unbranded horse with warm clothing, pistol and money would be standing at a hitching post on the second street in the direction of the Capitol. In the saddlebag there would be an itinerary from Cheyenne all the way to the Mexican border listing also places where reliable people would wait for him with fresh horses. The only thing he had to do was let Herr know whether he was going along with this plan or not.

The day before the escape there would be a large snow ball placed in front of the church - the one he could see from the window - as a sign that everything was ready.

Horn got up and walked back to the bars where Herr was waiting for his response. "There is something wrong with this plan. Why did John change his mind? He always begged me not to try to break out and suddenly he is planning an escape? How about if Chatterton is inclined to sign the clemency and then he finds out that I am on the run? That will just prove that I am guilty."

"I wouldn't count on it, and I'll tell you why. Chatterton will run for re-election next year, and the way the local papers influence the voters he is not going to risk losing it only because he changed the death penalty to life behind the bars on some guy whose name is Tom Horn."

"So why not wait to see how he decides?"

"Because there won't be another chance like this – a half empty town and Coble far away, free of any suspicion."

The logic of Herr's argument was iron clad. Horn felt cold rising from his bare feet and suddenly shivered.

"Okay, I'll think about it."

Horn turned around and slipped into his bed trying to get warm. He fell asleep only after midnight. Toward the morning, he had a strange dream. He actually managed to break out of the prison, the streets were really empty, only from a distance he heard the voice of somebody giving a political speech. First, he thought it was the president, but then he recognized the governor. Chatterton spoke about some awful crime saying that the person who had done it was undoubtedly guilty. Then the crowd kept calling, "Guilty! Guilty! Guilty!" He turned around and ran into the side street where a horse was supposed to wait for him. The roar of voices was getting closer and closer. Finally, he saw a silhouette of a horse. He ran to it and tried to untie it, but as the noise was getting louder the horse began to rear, striking with his front hooves and then he tore loose and ran away. He tried to catch it, but his feet became heavy as if made out of lead. He wanted to call the horse to come back but not a word came out of his mouth. Then the empty street got filled with people. He began to recognize familiar faces - LeFors, Stoll, Judge Scott and witnesses from the trial Nickell, Miller and now even the teacher Miss Kimmell from Iron Mountain and they all shook their fists and yelled, "Guilty! Guilty! Guilty!"

Horn woke up covered with sweat. Sun was rising and only Herr's snoring disturbed the quiet of the cell.

Shortly after breakfast, Lacey stopped by. He brought good news. Governor Chatterton was willing to consider the request for the pardon and listen to arguments of both parties - prosecution and defense. The hearing was set for December 15th and consequently the execution date was moved to January 9th.

12

The pealing of the church bell made its way into the cell through the window covered with bars. Horn got up, stepped up to the window and looked out at the other side of the street. The church janitor was just opening the large oak door and then gestured a crowd of church goers to step in. People muffled up in shawls carefully walked over the iced up steps and practically nobody paid attention to a large snowball lying next to the steps since yesterday. It was probably the neighborhood children who wanted to make a snowman, rolled up the ball and then something made them change their mind. They then left the snowball on the sidewalk and went to play somewhere else.

According to the tower clock it was ten in the morning. Horn sat down at the table, took two rectangular pieces of leather and bound them together through little holes along the edges by a thin thong while placing an old belt buckle between them. When he finished he carved with the razor blade strange patterns on its surface. After a while his fingers produced a nice leather covered belt buckle richly decorated with Indian motives. He was looking at it for a while and then mumbled something and put it in his pocket. Looking out of the window at the snow covered roofs it occurred to him that he could not have picked a worse time for his escape.

Herr left the jail about a week ago carrying the message that he was going along with the plan proposed by Coble. He couldn't make up his mind for many days. Just the fact that he did not participate in the preparation of this scheme made him nervous. Moreover those who had doubts about his guilt would doubt no longer. For the last two days he was going through all the details over and over and instinctively tried to foresee everything that could go wrong and if it did then what to do. How about if someone would be downstairs in the office? What if someone recognized him as he was leaving the building? How about if the president did not arrive at the expected time, or the horse was not at the right spot?

Horn walked to the table, took the lariat in his hand and ran his palm over its surface. He felt the tight rings of the drying rawhide. He shook it out and then coiled it up several times. It was not as flexible as it should be, but a little bit of oil would take care of it. He swung the lariat over his head and his thoughts carried him to Arizona, to Phoenix where in 1888 he took part in the rodeo.

Five men had made it into the finals - he, Charlie Meadows, Bill McCann, George Iago and Ramon Barca. The last event was calf roping. Bill was the first to ride into the arena. When he threw up his hands signaling that all four of the calf's feet were tied up, the time indicated by the clock on the grandstand was fifty-two and half seconds. Next was Charlie. He managed to do it in a mere fifty seconds. Everybody was convinced that he would take home first prize. Then it was his turn. The calf ran out of the shoot and he was right behind it. He swung the rope, the loop hissed through the air and landed in front of the calf's feet. A fraction of a second later he jerked the rope and the calf was lying in the dust of the arena with both front legs tied together. He slipped from the horse and pulled the rope attached to the saddle horn. Months of training now paid off. The horse took two steps forward, the rope got loose and to tie up the hind legs was a matter of seconds. He threw up his hands and looked at the clock. The clock hand stopped at forty-nine seconds. That he managed to tie up both front legs at the same time saved a whole second. The judge stepped up to him, nodded his head and the bleachers almost fell down by the roar of the spectators. Neither George, nor Ramon managed to finish below fifty seconds. That evening he paid for the whole saloon.

Horn sat down at the table and spent the rest of the morning by writing a letter to Lacey. First, he thanked him for everything he had done for him and then on two additional pages he explained the reasons which forced him to take these desperate steps. When he was writing the last sentence, the key rattled in the lock and Joe bringing lunch entered the cell. Horn put the pencil aside and watched Joe's every move. He counted the seconds from the moment when he placed the plate full of rice and cup of coffee on the stool next to the door to the moment when he stepped out and shut the door. Twelve seconds.

Locking the door Joe smiled and jokingly said, "Everybody is already at the railroad station. So it's up to me and you to watch this noble place. Imagine the commotion we would cause if both of us showed up there too."

Horn smiled, nodded his head and then asked about the weather outside.

"Not too bad. It has warmed up a little," came the answer.

As soon as Joe disappeared in the darkness of the corridor, Horn carried the lunch to the table and began to eat with relish. Realizing that this may be his last warm meal for a quite a while, he enjoyed every bite. When he finished the meal, he quickly drank up the coffee and put the plate and the coffee cup on the stool next to the door. Then he reached into his pocket and placed the leather buckle he made in the morning next to the dishes. For a while he kept looking at the stool, then he took a few steps back, looked at the stool again and moved it about a foot further from the door. After this minor arrangement he sat down on the bed and waited. Suddenly he heard the shrill sound of the locomotive whistle indicating that the president's train was pulling into the station. Several locomotives responded in the same way and then again the grave-like silence filled the cell. Minutes were slowly passing. Finally, the sound of the shuffling steps in the staircase. Joe was coming back to pick up the dishes. Horn suddenly felt a strange calm. All the nervousness was gone. Now he was again Tom Horn, chief of the Indian scouts who could lead his people into enemy territory and safely return back; a fighter who even in the most critical situations didn't lose his cool. Horn got up and when Joe inserted the key in the lock, he stood next to the table. He quickly glanced at the tower clock; it was one thirty.

Joe opened the door and with his left hand reached for the dishes.

"Joe, how do like that belt buckle? Would you like to keep it as a memento?"

Joe looked first at Horn, then his right hand let the door go and he took another step forward. The curiosity obviously won over the regulations and he leaned down over the stool to have a better look. At that moment the rope noose flashed through the cell and like a snake encircled both jailer's arms. Joe quickly turned around and was about to yell what kind of a stupid joke this was when the lariat jerked him to the middle of the cell. He tried to reach for his gun, but Horn's left arm clinched his neck, so when he tried to call for help, only a rattling sound came out of his mouth. Then he felt that Horn pulled his gun out of the holster and buried it in his ribs. Joe realized that he didn't have a chance against a much stronger Horn and stopped resisting.

The squeeze around the neck weakened and a quiet voice uncompromisingly ordered, "Sit down here on the bed and don't move!"

Joe obeyed and the moment he sat down on the bedside board Horn spun the rest of the rope around his body and his legs and secured it with a strap he cut for this purpose. Then he untied Joe's bandana, wrapped it around his mouth so he could not call for help and slipped out of the cell. He locked the door, and when he was putting the key in his pocket, it occurred to him that if he didn't run into anybody in the office, he would hang the key on the wall and so postpone the discovery of his escape.

Horn ran past the empty cells and stopped at the staircase. He listened for several seconds, but the staircase was quiet and neither a voice nor a sound was coming from the sheriff's office. He glanced at the gun. It was a Colt Peacemaker .45 with a short barrel. *Not too accurate weapon*, he thought. It was just good to shoot someone in the belly. He flipped the cylinder open, made sure that all the chambers were loaded and ran downstairs. He stopped at the door, pressed his ear against the panel and then jerked the door wide open and with his finger on the trigger walked inside. The room was empty and the door leading to LeFors' office was closed. In the dead silence of the office he heard only the ticking of the wall clock and rapid beating of his own heart.

Horn quickly stepped up to a cabinet where he suspected other weapons and ammunition would be stored, but a heavy latch and padlock reliably guarded its contents. For a second he thought he might try to pry it open, but he quickly rejected this idea. Carrying a rifle in the street would just draw an undesirable attention. Then he walked to the desk, opened the drawer, but there was no money in there, only some official papers and today's issue of *The Cheyenne Tribune*. Horn reached into his pocket, took out the key and hung it on a nail on the wall. Looking out of the window he didn't see a living soul. The street was deserted. He hid the gun under his sweater, opened the door and stepped out into the street flooded with the afternoon sunlight. A pleasant feeling filled his soul, good fortune, true, sometimes fickle, had not abandoned him after all.

With delight he breathed in the fresh air, gave the surrounding buildings one more look and brusquely walked toward Tenth Street. When he was passing the corner of Eleventh, he had an impression that the curtain in the window of the opposite building suddenly moved. He began to run. Then he sharply turned into Tenth Street, but then he literally froze. His eyes kept jumping from one hitching post to another, but at neither one stood a horse as promised. Maybe someone made a mistake. Clutching to this idea like to a blade of straw, he desperately ran to Ninth, but again he saw an empty street. There were plenty of hitching posts there, but nowhere a saddled up horse. He stopped, pressed himself into a recess of one door and feverishly thought what to do next. Something went wrong. Could it be that Herr didn't deliver his message? But that's not possible. There was the snowball at the church. How about if someone stole the horse? If true, fate could not have pulled off a more ironical joke.

Horn peeked out of his hideaway and at the end of the street and he saw a group of men hurrying toward the railroad station. He forced himself to start thinking rationally. To keep running from street to street and looking for a horse would be waste of time, but on the other hand he had zero chance reaching Mexico without one. Suddenly a sentence he once read in a book about an English king flashed through his mind: "Kingdom for a horse." Now he would give ten years of his life for a good and saddled up mount. Then he thought of those men on the way to the railroad station. They undoubtedly rode in from some small town or a ranch. Where did they leave their horses?

Horn returned to Fergusson Avenue and ran to Eighth Street. There he turned to the left and stopped in front of a livery stable. On the way he met several pedestrians, but they didn't pay him any attention. It seemed almost incredible, but there was not a living soul near the stable. He walked slowly around the large red painted building, passed a pile of fresh manure and opened the back door. It led into a long corridor with stalls on both sides. A quick look convinced him that it was safe to enter. Feeling on his face the damp warmth mixed with the familiar aroma of horse sweat and hay he shut carefully the door.

He looked again around to make sure that he was alone, but except for the sound of horses munching hay and occasional snorting, nothing indicated that someone could be in the building. Obviously all employees went to the railroad station and the horses were on their own. He took a few steps and in the second stall on the right he spotted a broad-chested bay. Now was the time to act. He took down the bridle hanging on a hook, opened the stall and stepped up to the horse. The bay backed a few steps and neighed, but when he felt the reins on his neck, it stopped and took the bit without any fuss. Apparently it was already getting tired of standing the whole morning in the stall. Horn led the horse out to the middle of the corridor and reached for a blanket. At the same time he couldn't help himself not to think about the facial expression of the owner who was probably one of those spectators welcoming the president when he returned.

At the moment when he grabbed the nearest saddle to throw it on the horse's back, he heard the front door hinges creak. Horn froze. The door opened and a young boy, perhaps fourteen or fifteen years old, stepped in and when he spotted a stranger trying to saddle up a horse, yelled at him: "Hey, you. That's not your horse!"

Horn dropped the saddle, sharply spun around holding the gun in his right hand. He leapt to the boy and aimed at his forehead. The youngster, wide-eyed and scared to death, stuttered, "You are Tom Horn. The killer of young Nickell."

Horn cocked the gun and calmly ordered, "Saddle up that horse and make it quick or you'll meet the same fate!"

The boy placed the saddle on the horse and with shaking hands buckled up the cinch. Horn put the gun in his left hand and with the right one he tightened up the cinch strap while thinking at the same time what to do with the boy. He knew that as soon as he left the stable, he would alarm the whole neighborhood, and there was no time to tie him up. Then his eyes stopped at the door leading to the feed room. He motioned the boy to get in and once he made sure that there was no way to escape from there, he barred the door and led the horse to the main gate. The bay was stepping high, but the saw dust silenced its every step.

Once I am in the saddle, I've made it, thought Horn. *Before everybody comes back from the railroad station and finds out that it is Joe who is in the cell, I'll be miles away.* He stopped at the gate, looked through a crack between the boards, but at the same moment he angrily kicked the gate and profanely cursed. There were deputies standing there and aiming their Winchesters at the gate. Then he heard Snow's voice.

"Tom, walk out with your hands up and without a weapon. If you have hurt that boy, not even the president will save you from the noose!"

Horn let the horse go and ran to the back door. Passing a window he caught a glimpse of more men holding the rifles. The stable was encircled and to try to shoot his way out with six bullets in the revolver would be a sheer suicide. Damn. How could they find out so quickly that he had gotten away from the cell and that he was here in the stable? How could they so quickly bring so many deputies? Now the boy will complain that he threatened him with a gun and Lacey will look like a fool when asking the governor to pardon him.

Having all these gloomy thoughts Horn walked slowly to the main gate. He put the gun on the ground, opened the gate a crack and exclaimed, "Don't shoot! I am coming out. The gun is inside."

Then he pushed the door open and with his hands raised he walked out. He took a few more steps and blinded by the sunlight he stopped and waited. Snow stepped up to him and with the stock of his rifle knocked him down on his knees. Then he twisted his arms behind his back and handcuffed him. By that time the street was full of people returning from the railroad station. They curiously surrounded the stable and waited to see what would happen next. Snow exchanged a few words with the nearest deputies and then asked the crowd to disperse. People moved but maintained a sort of a wall around the lawmen as if making sure that this dangerous criminal would not try to escape again. Then this mass of people, with Horn in the middle, set out on the way back to the prison.

It was five minutes to two on the tower clock. Horn's freedom didn't last even half an hour.

At the same time when the door out of the steel bars snapped behind him, Hubert Herr was getting off the train in Salt Lake City. There were five hundred dollars in his pocket which he received from the editor in chief of *The Cheyenne Tribune* for helping organize this fraudulent escape. About an hour later a typesetter of the same newspaper began to prepare a two page report including all details about Horn's prison break for tomorrow's issue.

13

The tension spreading throughout Cheyenne after the New Year was almost palpable. There was hardly a saloon or a restaurant in town where wild debates were not raging about the question of whether the governor would pardon Tom Horn or not. Moreover, the wagers, one way or the other, reached hundreds of dollars. Practically everybody knew that between December 15th and Christmas Lacey and Stoll visited the State Capitol almost every day to present to the governor one affidavit after another either in favor of the prosecution or the defense. Then on Christmas Eve Chatterton decided to close the whole case and during the last session with Lacey he asked for a one week recess so he could go over all the presented material including the trial recording. The week passed and people looked eagerly in the local papers for the date when he would finally announce his decision. The tension peaked January 4th when *The Cheyenne Tribune* brought a short statement that his Excellency would make an official pronouncement in the matter of Tom Horn the following day at three in the afternoon.

Small groups of people began to stream toward the Capitol shortly after two o'clock. The reporters and both lawyers - Lacey and Stoll with their assistants - were permitted to enter the circular hall of the building while the local onlookers were directed to the area in front of the main entrance. People trampled in the fresh fallen snow and if excited debates didn't keep them warm, then they took a swig of whisky from small flasks strategically placed in their coat pockets. Among the crowd one would find Kels Nickell, Frank Stone of Laramie, several local ranchers and even Otto Plaga had come all the way from Iron Mountain. Coble, however, was not present. Lately his gall bladder was acting up and so he rather stayed at home. Finally, at three o'clock, Chatterton's secretary appeared at the steps leading to the second floor and asked the defense and prosecution lawyers to follow him to the governor's office.

As both lawyers entered a tastefully furnished room, they were welcomed by the Wyoming chief executive, a man in his forties. A thick mane of brown hair was complemented by a long beard which didn't match his fine, almost feminine facial features too well. The bags under his eyes and pale skin indicated that he spent many nights studying this case and his brown eyes clearly reflected a desire for a good, long sleep. The governor stepped up to his desk and pulled out a thick fascicle containing numerous pages covered by his handwriting. He looked at all four men to make sure that they were ready to listen to his speech and then he began to read in a monotonous voice.

Listening carefully to his every word Lacey and Stoll were taking notes and paying extra attention to the legal jargon as they were trying to catch any hint or indication whose side he may favor. Chatterton summarized first the court proceedings emphasizing that he didn't find anything that would question the legality of the verdict and then he opined with regret that he had to agree with the decision of the Supreme Court. Pursuant the current laws and regulations the judge Scott acted correctly when he allowed retaining Horn's confession as a valid testimony which the jury had to consider. Even though the testimony of the other witnesses concerning Horn's statements in the Scandinavian Saloon may have been falsified, the testimony obtained in LeFors' office, however, was sufficient to determine Horn's guilt. Trying to establish the truth, he even looked at the shorthand recording written by Ohnhaus. In spite of Horn's claim that even this document was falsified, the original does not show any signs of additional changes or corrections. In another words while reviewing the whole case he did not find anything that would warrant a new trial.

Chatterton made a brief pause and then methodically analyzed the affidavits Lacey and Stoll brought to his office in the course of the last week. The way he talked about them, particularly his view that a statement of one party nullified or refuted the position of the other, Lacey found disturbing. Considering the fact that the trial was not to be renewed, the submitted affidavits represented the last chance to clarify the questionable features of the legal proceeding against Horn and prove that the verdict was not just. If the governor had taken them lightly...

Chatterton stopped talking and put the papers on the desk. Then he took a deep breath and in a tired voice said, "After long and difficult considerations I have arrived at the conclusion that it would not be in the interest of the law as well as the justice to pardon the defendant."

A grave-like silence fell upon the room. Lacey's eyes moved away from the governor and stopped at a bronze statue of a cowboy riding a bronco. The setting sun gave it a golden glow and Lacey felt for a moment almost mesmerized. The horse was bucking and with its head down and by a wild leap forward it was trying to lose this unusual weight. Its mane was flying, its muscles straining, but the rider sat firmly in the saddle. In his left hand he held the reins and in the right one a short whip.

Suddenly it occurred to him that he, too, was trying to free himself of an unpleasant burden, and that the whole year he had fought with forces which he legally could not defeat. He had no doubts about Horn's innocence. He had traveled to Iron Mountain and talked to several ranchers and most of them agreed that Horn had nothing to do with the murder. Then the ubiquitous reporter from Denver confirmed his view that they were dealing with a clear case of conspiracy, but any time it looked that he would have all the necessary evidence in his hand, the key witness had disappeared.

The feeling of a lost case is not a pleasant one. To hell with the money Coble paid him. The most frustrating was the fact that an innocent man believed in his prowess as a lawyer and then, after a year of nagging uncertainty, he failed him. Now he has to drain the cup of bitterness. The worst task was still ahead of him. From the Capitol his steps would take him to the prison where he would have to tell Horn that all his hopes were dashed away.

Lacey turned his eyes away from the sun reflecting statue, looked at Chatterton and in slow, hoarse voice as if he was weighing every word remarked, "Your Excellency, you are sending to the scaffolding a man who is not the murderer of William Nickell. I hope you will be able to live with it."

The governor turned pale and tried with several empty phrases to justify his decision, but Lacey was no longer listening. He just glanced at Stoll and his assistant Watts. Watt's indifferent face didn't betray any emotions, but Stoll's lips slightly curled in a victorious smile.

All four men politely bowed and without saying a word left the office. As they were approaching the marble staircase, the noise of many voices was getting louder. Once they appeared on the steps, the voices fell silent and several dozen faces turned upward, staring at four men who were bringing the news eagerly expected since the morning. Lacey looked at Stoll if he wanted to make the official announcement, but the prosecutor shook his head and by a hand gesture indicated that he would leave this honor to him.

Lacey took a few steps down the staircase, then he stopped and in low voice uttered a sentence which within several hours was carried by newspapers throughout whole of Wyoming: "His Excellency rejected the plea for mercy." Then he walked down to the lobby, made his way through the crowd of the excited reporters and left the building. Stoll, Watts and Burke remained and surrounded by men with their notebooks bravely faced the flood of questions.

One fellow, however, quickly parted with his colleagues and ran after Lacey.

"Wait! I'll go with you. Where are you heading now?"

The lawyer stopped and turned around. The guy all wrapped in a buffalo coat and with a warm cap pressed all the way to his ears was Rick Jackson.

"Now I'll go to the prison. If you want to, you can go with me, but they won't let you go upstairs to see Tom. You know, because of that breakout."

Rick nodded and silently followed Lacey. There were many questions racing in his head, but he didn't dare to bother him now. There could be no doubt that the lawyer was too preoccupied with thoughts of how to break this Job news to Horn.

The visit to the jail turned out exactly as Lacey predicted. Snow allowed only him to go upstairs and Rick had to sit in the sheriff's office and wait. Being a reporter and consequently motivated by a natural curiosity Rick asked Snow a few questions about the execution. Whose responsibility is it? What is the name of the executioner and who will be present? The deputy sheriff who was generally not a talkative person considered it a great honor to answer questions like that and above all he had an opportunity to show off his familiarity with the procedure. He readily emphasized that he was the man in charge and that the construction of the scaffolding would start immediately tomorrow. The man responsible for the actual gallows was a certain James Julian, a well-known Cheyenne architect. Rick, quite surprised, looked at Snow and asked why it took an architect to build a gallows. It could not be such a science to erect a pole with a crossbeam and tie a rope with a noose to it.

Snow laughed contemptuously at the reporter's ignorance and then he began explaining, "Ha, that's not just a common gibbet. In this case the condemned fellow will hang himself."

Seeing Rick's incredulous expression in his face, Snow went into the details which could be summarized about this way. The convict would step on a special trapdoor and the noose would be placed on his neck. At the moment when he would put his weight on both wings of the door, a string would pull a plug out of a large bucket full of water which was to be placed under the floor. The bucket would rest on one end of a long board and on the other end a special weight, lighter than the bucket, would be attached. Once all the water was gone, the weight would press the board down and with the help of another rope and a pulley it would knock down the wooden post from keeping the trapdoor closed.

"Simple, eh? And nobody gets bothered by his conscience that he helped his fellow man to the other world," Snow proudly concluded his lecture.

"And who will assist in this tragic event?"

"Me, Joe and Dick Proctor from the Court. Oh, yeah, I almost forgot, two doctors who will issue the death certificate."

"And the public?"

"The public will be shut out behind a high fence. People won't see anything; they can only speculate what will be going on. Horn, of course, can invite to this cheerful party anybody he wants to."

"And how about, if…" Rick hesitated. He just could not use the word *party* like Snow did. "How about if more of his friends would show up than you would feel comfortable seeing?"

Snow cut a face and quite confidently pointed with his thumb behind his back, "Do you see that?"

Rick's eyes obediently travelled in the direction of Snow's thumb, but except for a shapeless object covered by a tarp he did not see anything. Snow stepped up closer and jerked the tarp off. The astonished reporter was staring at a freshly oiled Gatling machine gun.

"Look here!" Snow opened a wooden ammunition box, pulled one shell and shoved it under Rick's nose. "The bullets have steel jackets and can penetrate a brick wall. This toy can fire two hundred and fifty shots a minute. The night before the execution we'll place it on the courthouse balcony and the crew that handles it will cover the whole area around the scaffolding. So Horn's cronies are welcome to try something."

Snow wanted also to mention the exact amount of the National Guard which would patrol in downtown, but then the door opened and Lacey walked in.

Rick quickly stepped up to him and whispering asked, "How did he take it?"

Lacey, a little bit pale, overcame his emotions and firmly answered, "Bravely, damn bravely. He just nodded his head and, as if he wanted to console me, said, 'Don't worry about it. You know, I was condemned even before this rotten trial started. But I still thank you for everything you did for me.'"

The lawyer made a pause and then added, "I know, you want to ask me about many things. Why don't you go with me to my office? There we can talk without being disturbed."

When they arrived at his office on Sixteenth Street, it was already dark. The secretary was about to leave, but when she saw her boss, she handed over to him several telephone messages and put on his desk two filled-out forms dealing with the sale of some local property. Lacey, as a matter of fact, was also making extra money by notarizing the deed extracts from the land register. He thanked her, wished her a good night and as the tapping of her heels faded away, he stepped up to a small walnut cabinet and took out two glasses and a bottle of whisky. He filled both glasses to the rim. One he handed to the reporter and the other one he poured down. Then he filled it up again, asked Rick to take a seat on the chair and he himself dropped his body into a comfortable armchair next to his desk.

For a while he kept staring at the opposite wall and then he turned to his companion and with poorly hidden gloom said, "Rick, I can call you Rick, right? I am afraid that the last story you will write about Tom will not have a happy ending, but God is my witness that I did my best." Lacey took a sip and began to summarize all the last steps he had taken to save Horn's life.

"You see, when the Supreme Court rejected my request for a new trial, because Stoll committed numerous procedural violations, I decided to change the strategy. I decided to present the whole case as a conspiracy orchestrated by LeFors and Miller. Even though Nickell repeated in the governor's office the same things he had told you, I still needed concrete proof or a main witness. For example, the barkeep from the Scandinavian Saloon would be a pot of gold, but he disappeared without a trace. Then, as if guided by Providence, a guy looked me up – a certain Jack Martin from Laramie. This fellow swore that LeFors bragged in his presence about getting five hundred dollars from Miller to drop him from the list of the suspects and that the reward for catching the killer was one thousand dollars. Among other things LeFors also said that framing Horn would be easy because anytime somebody gets shot near Cheyenne or Laramie, Horn wherever he can, declares it as his own doing. So I decided to build on his testimony. If you remember I presented a copy of a bank slip issued by the Iron Mountain Bank during the trial. Miller at that time really withdrew five hundred dollars.

'Then I wrote Miss Kimmell asking her if she could somehow support my line of thinking and she by return responded that whenever I would need it, she would send me an affidavit which would put an end to doubts about Horn's innocence once for all. Then the good fortune turned its back on me. Stoll managed to present receipts indicating how Miller spent those five hundred dollars - a new saddle, harness, seeds - simply accounting for every dollar. So I asked Martin to repeat in the governor's office what he told me, namely that LeFors focused on Horn not because of a substantiated suspicion but because of his reputation.

"When, however, the governor began asking about details and expressed doubts about some of his claims, Martin got upset and began talking rubbish. First, he insisted that there could not be any doubt about his veracity and reliability because he was employed as a guard in the Laramie jail. Then he began to claim that he was a prophet and that the end of the world was near. Stoll visited Chatterton the next day and brought an affidavit signed by several Laramie residents saying that Martin was a crackpot and as a liar he had no equal.

"So I tried to salvage whatever I could. I got in touch with the Laramie sheriff and he wrote an affidavit confirming Martin's testimony emphasizing that Martin was a person that could be fully trusted. For a while it seemed that Chatterton started to hesitate, that considering all those testimonies he didn't want to have the death of an innocent man on his conscience. At the same time I sent another letter to Miss Kimmell in Kansas City describing the current situation and asked her to send any information that would help. Unfortunately, I have not received anything from her so far. She either moved again and didn't leave the forwarding address or she believes that it is a lost case and decided not to get involved."

At that moment Ricked raised his eyes from the notebook and doubtfully shook his head. "I talked to Miss Kimmell last spring at Miller's ranch. I have not seen her since, but she made an impression on me as a very energetic woman, particularly when Tom was involved. One could suspect her of anything but not of giving up so easy."

Lacey shrugged his shoulders and continued, "Then we had that unfortunate attempt to escape. *The Cheyenne Tribune* got a hold, quite mysteriously, of information which was supposed to convince the public that if there was a conspiracy then it was among the big ranchers and not among the lawmen.

When I talked to Tom trying to find out what made him do such a foolish thing, it became suddenly quite clear to me. It was quite a transparent attempt to discredit him, and he, while under the influence of the Supreme Court decision, fell for it as the last chance on how to save his neck."

"You know, it would be great to find out if that fellow Herr knew that it was all sham or if he truly believed that he had delivered a message that could help Horn," Rick remarked.

"Well, I guess we will never find out. Herr disappeared without trace either being afraid that someone could permanently silence him as an undesirable witness who could betray the whole plot, or he was a first class scoundrel who stooped to this farce for money and now he is somewhere safely ensconced. At any rate when I talked to Coble about it, he swore on his mother's grave that he had nothing to do with it. On the contrary, he always tried to talk Tom out of any such idea. The old man always believed that justice would prevail in the end. I am afraid that Horn's death will be a blow to him."

Lacey paused, then took a sip of whisky and asked Rick, "What do you think made Chatterton reject the plea for mercy?" Rick just looked askingly at the lawyer. "It was the rumor *The Cheyenne Tribune* published two days ago that in case Horn's sentence would be changed to life in prison, then during his move to the Rawlins penitentiary a gang of his armed friends would set him free."

Rick, surprised, raised his eyebrows. "You are right. Now it all makes sense. First, a set up attempt to break out of Cheyenne prison to make an impression that many influential people are willing to free him at any cost and then, if it didn't work out, try again at a better opportunity."

"Exactly. You may not believe me, but I implored Chatterton several times to change the death sentence to life because sooner or later the real murderer would be found and as far as I remember this argument made a strong impression on him. Then it took just one false report in the paper and the governor backed down."

Lacey got up, walked up and down his office and then stopped in front of Rick. He ran his hand through his hair and then in a shaking voice said, "You may think that if a better lawyer handled this case, Horn would have been out of prison a long time ago, but that's not true and I'll tell you why right now. However, don't publish that, at least leave my name out of it because many people would respond to it by a lawsuit."

Rick nodded his head that he understood his concern and put the notebook aside.

"First, too many people have an eminent interest to see Horn hanging. Just think about it. Let's start with LeFors. A reward of one thousand dollars means pretty good money for a deputy U.S. marshal and perhaps a chance to be promoted to the rank of a chief of police. Then Miller. He and his sons will be permanently free of the suspicion that they have committed this crime. Ohnhaus. Now he will be able to sleep without fear that sooner or later he will be tried for falsifying an official document. Only God knows what LeFors promised him if he wrote the "confession" in the way that it would stick. Then the local small ranchers who have been rustling. They will have a warm feeling of revenge. Moreover, their nemesis, Tom Horn, will be gone forever. And how about his Excellency the governor? I have heard him many times condemning the executions in Denver and the neighboring states. Either because of religious or other reasons he always opposed the death penalty. Now, because of a miserable election, he decided to sacrifice a human life. If that is not hypocrisy than I don't know what hypocrisy is."

Lacey, quite excited, was now pacing and gesticulating. "It is all the dirty politics. You are certainly aware that crude oil was discovered here in Wyoming somewhere near Casper and Gillette. Now the local entrepreneurs need the eastern money boys to invest here. However, who will rush to a territory where the anarchy rules and law is enforced by individuals and not authorities? I would bet my annual income that some of these speculators reminded the governor of this fact. Do you remember Isaac Parker, the Oklahoma judge? The Easterners had a nickname for him, the Hanging Judge. The false moralists, corrupted politicians, and, please don't get offended, but also many people owning big newspapers in the East forgot that only thanks to his uncompromising attitude toward crime he managed to make out of Oklahoma a territory where at night people don't have to keep a rifle or a gun next to their beds. He was constantly attacked in the newspapers. They portrayed him as a bloodthirsty maniac and in the end he was recalled. The reason? Too many executions. Of course none of them could care less about how many innocent people were killed by the thugs he had sent to the gallows. And now just imagine that among these people who generally abhor violence, the news spreads that here in Wyoming there is a guy who dispenses justice from the barrel of his Winchester."

Lacey obviously exhausted by his speech slipped back into his armchair, dropped his head and more to himself than for Rick said, "Even the best lawyer wouldn't get him out of this. Horn was right when he said that he was condemned even before this trial. You see, Horn forgot that the world around him had profoundly changed and in this new world there was no place for people like him."

14

Horn rolled once or twice from side to side, then finally rested on his back and opened his eyes. He looked at the door of his cell and joyfully realized that he did not sleep through sunrise. Since that fateful day when Lacey brought the news that he had only four days to live, he always woke up early in the morning not to miss it. To watch the rising sun was his last pleasure he had in this world. It reminded him of the mornings on the range when the sun rays turned the drops of dew on the grass blades into tiny glittering diamonds, when the neighing of his horse bid him good morning and the gentle breeze carried the smell of bacon fried at the nearest campfire.

Finally the upper bars of his cell reflected the sunlight which meant that the sun was rising above the horizon. Horn kicked off the blanket, got quickly dressed and stepped up to the window. The sun made its way slowly through a strip of clouds, while from time to time illuminating the entire landscape and then eventually rose over the distant hills. Horn enjoyed the view of the snow covered roofs which now dazzled with a gold-like hue and then looked toward the railroad station. He could hear the rumbling of the cars moving from one rail track to another, the sharp sound of the steam whistles and the puffing of the locomotives accompanied by columns of black smoke. His eyes then slid to the right and stopped at a small wooden scaffolding. It was here where today he was to be…

He just smiled scornfully. Three days ago, early in the morning, he was awakened by hammer blows and the screeching sound of saws cutting lumber. He wanted to look out to see what was going on, but the window was covered. When Joe brought the breakfast, he asked him about it. Joe for a second hesitated and then told him that Deputy Sheriff Snow suddenly had become compassionate and ordered the window to be covered, so that Horn would not see the construction of the scaffolding for the execution. Horn then asked Joe to give Snow the message that he had seen death in many shapes and forms and that because of one gallows he did not intend to be deprived of the opportunity to observe the sunny mornings. Shortly before lunch the gunny sack which covered the window was removed so he could now watch both - the sunrise as well as the work on the scaffolding.

Horn's eyes returned back to the top beam dusted with snow. Pretty soon they would attach to it a noose which he had made by himself. They could not deny him this honor. When Dick Proctor brought him yesterday a hemp rope about three quarters of an inch thick, he tied at its end a noose with thirteen rings. At least he could be sure that all those bureaucrats and paper pushers who passed themselves as lawmen would not ruin the last day of his life by messing up the execution.

The silence of the cell block was interrupted by shuffling steps. Horn turned away from the window and saw Joe carrying a large tray with breakfast. Unlike the other days when he was served only corn mash, this time he saw several strips of bacon, fried eggs and potatoes and next to the slice of freshly baked bread two pieces of sweet pastry.

"I'll be damned. Why didn't you treat me like this all that time I spent here? Why did you keep putting off to the last day?" Horn joked.

Joe placed the tray on a little table next to the door and answered in a shaky voice, "Tom, don't say that. You know I would do anything in the world that I wouldn't have to bring this fancy breakfast today."

"Don't worry. We can still joke a little, can't we? At what time are they coming to get me?"

"Around ten." Joe reached into his pocket and pulled out a watch. Then without looking at Horn he added, "You have still two more hours. Here, if you feel like it, I brought you a cigar." Joe placed an expensive Cuban cigar and a box of matches on the tray next to the breakfast, closed the cell door and disappeared into the dark corridor.

Horn enjoyed the food. The eggs and bacon were first class and the black coffee tasted better than usual. It just occurred to him that even the cook at Coble's ranch could be proud of such breakfast. As soon as he finished, he lit up the cigar and began to think if there was still someone he should write to - to whom to say good-bye and to whom to will some of his possessions. Coble had picked up the braided bridle before that failed attempt to escape and the leather lariat was in Snow's office. He wrote Coble not to forget it there. Joe would get his slippers and sweater and the books he gave to the Irwin brothers from Bosler.

When they told him that he could invite to his execution anybody he wanted to, he didn't think too long. Charles and Frank were his best buddies and in case he would like to listen to a good-bye song, he couldn't find better voices in the whole Laramie County. Then Rick Jackson the journalist from Denver. He read all the stories he had written about his life in Arizona and he did a great job. Rick was the only newspaperman who treated him fairly. Finally Coble and Lacey. However, he was not sure if they both would have nerves strong enough to stay to the end, to the moment when the trap door opened under his feet.

Steps in the corridor again interrupted Horn's thoughts. He could tell that this time two men were coming. He stepped up to the metal bars and spotted Joe and John Coble. Joe unlocked the door, collected the dishes and walked out. Then he stopped, stood next to Coble for a while because he knew he must not leave any visitor alone with the prisoner, but then he waved his hand and walked downstairs. Coble sat down on a bench and without saying word looked at Horn. He was the first to speak out.

"Tom, I came to say good-bye," he said haltingly. "You know I did what I could... but... but fate was against you."

Horn sat on the chair, face covered with his palms and only listened. Coble with a shaking voice continued, "You won't believe it, but after you were found guilty, everybody at the cattle association pretended that they didn't know you. Nobody wanted to have anything to do with you as if you were a mangy dog. They even pressured me. They were afraid that you could get them somehow into trouble."

Horn raised his head and quietly remarked, "Don't worry, John. I won't fail anyone who expects some gain from my death. Couple of hours from now nobody has to fear that I would compromise him."

The gray-haired rancher could not suppress tears. His voice broke. "Tom, die like a man. Like the Tom Horn we all knew. Show them that you are better than they. Tom... I'll never forget you!"

Coble paused, wiped off the tears and then asked Horn to write down briefly everything he knew about that tragic event involving the death of young Nickell and what he really did on that fateful day. Then he could give the letter to Lacey. He was still downstairs in the sheriff's office. Horn nodded that he understood and stepped up to the bars. Joe, as if he sensed this touching moment, appeared in the corridor and without much thinking pulled the key out of his pocket and opened the door. Both grieving men embraced for the last time. Joe then again locked the cell and Coble with tears running down his face left the jail.

Horn in the meantime sat down at the table, pulled a sheet of paper from the drawer and tried to concentrate. After a while he overcame the excitement, organized his thoughts and began to write. Half an hour later he put the pencil aside, folded the paper and called Joe to bring Lacey. The lawyer came right away and when Horn handed over to him the letter addressed to Coble, he asked if he could look at it.

"Of course, but I am afraid that it won't do any good."

Lacey unfolded the letter and began to read:

Dear John,

Following your request, I am writing down everything I know about the murder of William Nickell. On the day when I stopped at the Millers, his neighbor Bill McDonald came. We all three met at the creek behind the house. Bill started the conversation by a statement that he and Miller intended to wipe out the Nickell's ranch and asked me if I wanted to join them. Jordan and Underwood from the cattle association would pay me for this job. I resolutely refused because my job was to catch rustlers and not wiping out ranches. McDonald then told me that there were sheep on the pastures belonging to Coble's ranch. I mounted my horse and rode there to check it out. In the course of the afternoon I found out that it was not true. Miller then insisted that I stay overnight so I obliged him.

McDonald came the next day and asked me if I had changed my mind. I again repeated that I was not interested in such action, to which he responded that it was okay, that he and Miller would do it by themselves. Shortly after breakfast I saddled my horse and rode to Mule Creek where Plaga saw me. On Saturday I returned to your ranch and there I heard about young Nickell. At that time I was convinced that the whole affair did not concern me.

Six or eight weeks later I again visited this area and again talked to McDonald and Miller. They both bragged how they killed all Nickell's sheep. Then they laughed saying that I was suspected of this deed because I was seen in the area. At that time, unfortunately, I did not take this suspicion seriously.

As to Irwin and his claim that he saw me Thursday in town, he just lied. The so-called confession I allegedly made in LeFors' office was also phony. Of course, we talked about Nickell's murder, but I never confessed to it. He talked most of the time and I, unwisely, only allowed LeFors to make allusion to it and myself. Ohnhaus, LeFors and Snow swore to lies to have something on which they could build the charges against me.

This is what truly happened. I am going to die in about an hour, but I'll be dying with a clear conscience. Thanks again for all you have done for me.

Sincerely Yours,
Tom Horn

Lacey finished reading, remarked something in the sense that this was really the last chance and ran downstairs to the sheriff's office. There he stepped up to Snow, shoved the letter in his face and categorically declared, "Based on this document I demand the stay of the execution!"

Snow just condescendingly laughed. "Look, the court set the execution for ten o'clock. Could you kindly explain to me why I should put it off? If you are trying again some of you legalistic tricks, you are wasting time - yours as well as mine."

Just by sheer will power Lacey held back, did not explode, but opened up the letter and read it aloud. Those present in the office listened silently. When he finished he turned to Snow. "Don't you see that this was written by a man who will lose his life in less than half an hour! Don't you think that what he wrote should be taken seriously?"

Snow just shrugged his shoulders, but the other men - Joe, Dick Proctor and both physicians - agreed.

"Alright," answered Snow with poorly hidden aversion. "I'll give you an hour. If the governor does not change his mind, Horn will hang regardless of all your attempts to save him from the just punishment. You can bet your life on it."

Lacey ran upstairs to the courtroom and asked the secretary to retype the letter. Then he was off to the governor's office. Minutes were slowly passing. Horn sat down on the bed, then got up again and began nervously to pace the cell. He was ready to die. Yesterday a Catholic priest came and read him passages from the Bible about the Lord's mercy and then he wanted him to ask the Lord for forgiveness. In that respect, Horn could not oblige him because according to his true conscience he had not done anything for which somebody had to forgive him. If somebody would have to one day ask God for forgiveness, it would be all those who perjured themselves and because of their own gain took his life.

Suddenly, several loud blows a couple of minutes apart interrupted Horn's thoughts. They were coming from outside and after each blow an unpleasant creaking sound followed. Horn looked out of the window and saw a man in black standing on the floor of the scaffolding giving orders to another man bellow. Then he put his foot on both wings of the trapdoor and stepped aside. For a while it was quiet, but then came the blow and the trapdoor accompanied by a creaking sound opened. Horn realized that that guy on the scaffolding was showing to a bunch of curious newsman how the mechanism of the trapdoor worked. Disgusted, he turned away and looked at the clock on a nearby church steeple. It was quarter to ten.

The mood in the sheriff's office was gloomy. No one spoke. Joe, Dick Proctor, Snow and both physicians covered by clouds of cigarette smoke sat at the table and only from time to time one of them would get up to peek out of the window trying to catch a glimpse of Lacey returning from the governor's office. Shortly before ten they were joined by Julian who designed the gallows, and a handful of newspapermen who represented the biggest dailies in the area.

The church bell struck ten. Snow got up, reached for the handcuffs especially modified for the execution which were hanging on the wall and slowly walked toward the staircase. Proctor readily blocked his way.

"Are you crazy? We can't do anything until Lacey comes back!"

Snow angrily threw the handcuffs on the table, stepped up to the phone and asked the operator to connect him with the governor's office at the state capitol. A while later a female voice was announcing that Mr. Lacey had finished his meeting with his Excellency and was on the way back to the jail. The result of the meeting? Unfortunately, she was not privy to it.

Snow hung up and returned to his desk. The sheriff's office fell silent again. About ten minutes later the door opened and Lacey walked in. About fifteen pairs of eyes hung on his mouth. Lacey stooped as if carrying a large invisible weight on his shoulders leaned on the door frame, looked at Snow and quietly said, "The governor did not change his mind. He insists on the execution."

"That's good," responded Snow. Then he mashed the cigarette and signaled Joe and Dick to follow him. Proctor took the handcuffs and with obvious hesitation joined both men.

Horn caught sound of three men walking upstairs. By the way they walked he could reliably tell that it was Joe and Snow. As to the third one he wasn't sure. Probably Lacey, he thought and stepped up closer to the bars. No, it was not him. The third man was Dick Proctor. He walked slowly next to Joe with special handcuffs used for executions over his shoulder.

When Horn saw the steel buckles and leather straps just plain animal fear gripped with icy fingers his stomach. Instinctively, he bent a little bit forward and then took one step back.

Joe opened the door and all three men walked into the cell.

Horn quietly asked, "Where is Lacey?"

"Downstairs in the office. That stuff you wrote didn't help much. The death sentence will be carried out as the Supreme Court decided." Snow paused for a second and then sharply ordered, "Take off the sweater and lower your arms so Dick can secure your hands!"

Horn obeyed. Proctor stepped up to him and using the straps tightened both arms to his torso. Then just remarking, "We'll tie up your legs downstairs," stepped out of the cell.

Suddenly, an incredible calm and peace prevailed in Horn's soul. The gripping, clenching feeling in his abdomen disappeared and the wild whirling of his thoughts stopped. He began to rationalize. After all, he has to die some time. In this way it will at least not last too long. He enjoyed his life as much as he could and his best years were over. Such a great time he had in Arizona he would never have again anyway. To leave this world, a world full of pettiness and hypocrisy where freedom is disappearing like snow in the spring sun is no tragedy. Finally, Coble's words came to his mind: *Tom, die like a man. Like the Tom Horn we all knew. Show them that you are better than they.* Horn straightened up, looked around the cell where he spent almost a year and accompanied by three men stepped into the dark corridor.

When they walked into the office, the conversation stopped and all present men rose, perhaps out of the respect to the condemned prisoner. All newspapermen stepped back to the wall except one younger guy wearing a fur coat. It was Rick Jackson.

He grabbed Horn's hands and said in an uneasy voice, "Tom, this is the last good-bye. I never believed that you were guilty. One day it will be established who the real killer of William Nickell was, and then I'll make sure that the whole world will hear about it. And, above all, about the injustice which is going to happen today."

Horn just smiled mechanically, nodded his head and looked over the room. The priest who was assuring him yesterday about God's grace was crouching in the corner and the Irwin brothers Charles and Frank stood next to the door. He was looking for Lacey, but he was no longer in the office. As he correctly assumed, Lacey did not have nerves and stomach to witness consequences of the case he had lost. Then both brothers stepped up to Horn, embraced him and uttered a few parting words. His two best friends from Coble's ranch decided to stay with him to the end.

Snow watched impatiently this touching scene and as soon as the cowboys stepped aside, he ordered Proctor to shackle Horn's legs. Then he opened the rear door and walked out in the open space in front of the scaffolding. At the same time the commander of the National Guard gave an order and one could hear the clicking sound of bayonets being fixed to the rifles. The guardsmen pushed all onlookers away from the fence and formed an impenetrable cordon around the city hall.

Horn taking little steps walked to the scaffolding and when he reached the upper platform, he looked around. On the balcony reflecting the sun glittered the barrel of a Gatling gun. Then in the window of the second floor he caught the glimpse of two men. No, there could be no mistake. The men standing behind the window pane were LeFors and Stall. *Cowards*, thought Horn. *They don't have enough courage to come down and watch the hanging of an innocent man at a close distance.*

Snow, holding a hemp rope, approached the gallows and attached it to the upper beam. Then he addressed Horn in an official voice.

"Tom, you have one last chance to confess or name people who paid you. Do you want to ease you conscience?"

Horn shook his head and turned toward Joe.

"Joe, forgive me that I tied you up when I tried to escape."

Joe raised his eyes full of tears and just waved his hand.

Then Charles Irwin asked, "Tom, do you want us to sing?"

Horn nodded.

"Which song do you want to hear?"

"Sing the Mountain Railroad."

Two clear tenors filled the area around the scaffolding. Both cowboys sang a song about life which resembled a mountain railroad. It was also full of curves, dangerous spots and obstacles. Just like an engineer who watches closely the tracks in front of the train, a man must also pay attention to every step he takes on the way through his life. If he fully trusts in God's guidance, his train will never derail and he will successfully reach the end station.

The singing stopped. Snow stepped up to Horn and reached for the noose when Horn shook his head.

"Not you, Dick Proctor!"

Snow shrugged his shoulders, stepped back and Proctor carefully placed the noose with thirteen rings on Horn's neck. Then he pulled a black hood over his head and asked Horn to take three steps to the right onto the trapdoor.

A light breeze began to blow. The grave silence was disturbed only by the priest's voice and the rustling of water flowing out of the bucket below the scaffolding. Horn closed his eyes. He imagined the endless Arizona desert covered by blooming sage. Saguaro cacti like giant three-arm candle holders were towering toward the sky and at their tips shone large white and red flowers. A bluish strip of mountains was stretching along the Mexican border and at its foot he saw an Apache village. The warriors whose faces were covered with black and white war paint sang death songs and the squaws brought the weapons of their dead husbands. Horn suddenly felt the thundering of hooves. It was no longer a black hood that was touching his face but a flying mane of a horse racing toward those mountains. The staccato of the hooves was quickening and Horn could not tell whether it was the horse's or his own heart beating stronger and stronger. Then as if from a far distance he heard a loud blow, the horse tripped and...

15

Rick pushed aside a folder full of newspaper clippings, leaned back in the chair and set his eyes on a large cast iron stove.

"It wouldn't hurt to feed the fire a bit," he muttered only for himself because no one else was in the office. He thought for a while whether he should wait for the janitor from the ground floor, but then he got up, grabbed the bucket and emptied the rest of coal into the stove. At the same time, it occurred to him that this was actually the last winter he was spending in this cold room. In the spring the whole newspaper company would move to a brand new building on Broadway. True, he wouldn't have such a nice view of the Capitol, but he would have his own centrally heated office. Pete visited the building site any time he could free himself from his duties and drew plans where to put the telegraph, the telephone switch board and the archive.

Rick stepped up to the window, looked at the Capitol and in his mind he relished the image of a smartly furbished office with a rug and without dusty shelves and filing cabinets. Pete even had mentioned a possibility that he may have his own telephone. Now he would be able to see visitors in the privacy of his office and not in the saloon across the street. Rick complacently smiled and returned to his desk. Three days had passed since the Horn's execution and now it was necessary to sort out all the material he collected from the day he got arrested. When finished, he would have a complete documentation including letters and photographs about the whole case. Particularly the letters and photos would be worth gold one day. For example, right here, Horn is sitting in the sheriff's office, his shirt is open and in his hands he is holding the lariat he made for Coble. Rick couldn't help himself not to smile. When they were taking this picture, neither Snow nor the photographer had any clue for what other purpose this rope could be used. Then this shot. It was taken couple of days before the execution. Horn is standing in the corridor leaning against the cell door.

Rick picked up the photographs and put them in the folder. Then he looked again at the letter Horn wrote just before his death. It was a gift from

Lacey. Coble got the original and Lacey had made two copies - one for himself and one for him. Rick put a fresh sheet of paper into his typewriter to prepare a complete list of all the items when a messenger brought the mail. First, he placed a pile of letters on Pete's desk and then he turned toward Rick.

"Here is something for you from the ad department. It came yesterday and this letter arrived today in the morning."

The messenger handed Rick two envelopes. The white one immediately drew his attention. Below the address of *The Denver Post* was printed with large letters the words: "The Double." Rick held his breath. Without looking at the other letter, he quickly opened the envelope, pulled out a folded sheet of paper and his eyes ran over densely written lines.

New Orleans, December 27, 1902
Dear Sir,

Excuse me please that I am answering your ad a little bit late, but only several days ago a friend of mine mentioned to me that he had seen an ad that could have been meant for me. First, I could not believe it, but after reading the actual ad, I realized that he was right. Because you mentioned Tom Horn and as code word you used the words "The Double", I realized immediately that you were alluding to the conversation in the Scandinavian Saloon during which the alleged Tom Horn bragged about killing William Nickell.

To the best of my knowledge, I have to say that the man in question was not Tom Horn. I knew Tom quite well because he had been visiting the Scandinavian Saloon for almost two years. Tom had a scar on his left arm, a result of a wound he suffered during the Apache wars in Arizona. The fellow who was bragging that he was the best short and detective in the whole West and that that young Nickell was his best shot did not have a scratch on either arm.

I hope this information will help Tom because as I knew him he could not have committed such a crime.

Sincerely George Roberts.

Rick felt that his head would burst. He turned around to see if the messenger was still in his office, but he was already gone. He had to talk to somebody. Somebody had to explain to him why it was possible that the fate was so wicked. The long sought after proof of the conspiracy was now lying on the desk, right in front of him. It was just several days late. Rick tortured himself for a while imagining how long it took before the barkeep's friend finally decided to tell him about the ad. How long did it take for Roberts to sit down and write this letter? Dear God, if they both knew how precious every day was.

Rick reached for the other letter. The address of the newspaper with his name didn't tell him anything. He turned the envelope over and saw the sender's address: Glendolene Kimmell, Kansas City, Missouri. He anxiously opened the envelope and pulled out two sheets of paper. One was a copy of an official typed document and the other was a letter written in minute female handwriting addressed directly to him. He hesitated a second and then began to read the copied document. On the top there was the name of Miss Kimmell and an underlined title "An Affidavit". Down below there was a black stamp of the local notary public.

The affidavit consisted of a detailed summary of all the events before and after the murder of William Nickell. In conclusion, Miss Kimmel stated that she knew who the killer was shortly after this tragic event. She inferred that from a conversation between the father, Jim Miller, and his son, Victor. Several weeks later, Victor tortured by his conscience confessed himself to her that he was the perpetrator of the crime.

The lines started to dance before Rick's eyes and one question after another raced through his mind. Where is the original? Was it submitted to the governor? If the governor saw it, why didn't he order Victor's arrest? Rick glanced at the date next to the notary's signature - December 27th, 1902. Almost two weeks had passed between the day the affidavit was notarized and the day of the execution. Rick put the document aside and began to read Miss Kimmell's letter feverishly hoping to find the explanation of this time gap. The letter was dated January 10th, one day after the trap door opened under Horn's feet.

Miss Kimmell learned about the execution from the newspaper and immediately decided to write him. A man who introduced himself as Timothy Burke, defense lawyer Lacey's assistant, visited her on December 27th. She never saw him before, but she knew his name from the newspaper. The man asked for information which could help convince Governor Chatterton to change Horn's death penalty to life imprisonment. The situation was serious and the governor was Horn's last chance. Then she decided to reveal this horrible secret. To Burke's question why she did not name the murderer during the trial, Miss Kimmell answered that the persons who had been really responsible for this crime were old Nickell and Miller. Eighteen year old Victor grew up in the atmosphere of hatred and violence and due to his youthful imprudence he got carried away and stooped to this ill-conceived act. At that time everything indicated that Horn would be found not guilty and so she decided not to say anything. But when the Supreme Court refused to renew the trial, she realized that there was no use covering up the real murderer and by doing so risking the life of an innocent person. Having the affidavit prepared earlier, she had it notarized and gave Burke the original while keeping one copy for herself.

Rick could not believe his eyes. Was it possible that Lacey purposefully held up the affidavit? Is it possible that during those critical two weeks somebody managed to bribe him? Rick got up and all agitated began to pace around the office. On the other hand it was quite possible that somebody impersonated Burke. Having this thought Rick almost shivered. Miss Kimmel admits in her letter that she never met Burke, she only knew his name. Lacey asked her earlier that he might need some information that would help Tom and she responded that she would provide one which would put away all doubts about his innocence once for all. Then believing Lacey was pressed by time and needed it as soon as possible he sent his assistant. *Oh my God. That's it.* Somebody passed himself as Burke, extracted from her the decisive testimony under the pretext that time was critical and then either held it up or destroyed it. Miss Kimmel in the meantime quite satisfied that she did all she could stayed at home believing that her testimony would have the desirable effect and the Governor would pardon Tom.

Rick felt like screaming. He felt like running from one office to another and then on the sidewalk and tell everybody of what kind of knavery the Cheyenne authorities were guilty. When he calmed down, he sat at his desk and instead of working on the list of items related to Horn's case he slowly tapped in the capital letters a headline for the Sunday issue: **"TOM HORN: JUSTICE OR JUDICIAL MURDER?"**

The Epilogue

Did Tom Horn really kill Willie Nickell? Numerous historians, lawyers and authors of various publications tried to answer this question for many years. The detailed study of the court records and other available materials indicate that the prosecution did not prove his guilt beyond any reasonable doubt and its strongest argument was only the Horn's "confession". From a slew of facts and discrepancies one could conclude that most probably a conspiracy was afoot to "job" as they used to say in the old West, anybody to satisfy the public clamoring for justice. Needless to say that former Deputy U.S. Marshal LeFors played an important role in this scheme. According to many old timers he was not alone and was also aided by some members of the cattle association who were eminently interested in Horn's removal.

There are countless examples confirming this presumption. Just off hand we can list the testimony of George Matlock, shoe store owner in Cheyenne, who claimed that Horn left a package in his store saying that he would pick it up later. Several weeks passed, Horn didn't pick it up, so Matlock opened it and found a blue sweater covered with blood. During the trial all the witnesses testified that they had never seen Horn wearing a blue sweater, particularly at the time of the murder. When asked if he bought shoes at the mentioned store, Horn answered that he bought shoes only at Rauner's.

The Matlock testimony is absurd. Willie Nickell was shot at a distance, so how could the killer stain his clothing by his blood and why would he bring the sweater, which could be used as evidence, to Cheyenne? A rationally thinking person would not do it, much less so an anti-Indian scout and detective trained by the Pinkerton Agency.

In a letter addressed to Lacey Frank A. Mullock who testified during the trial that Horn had bragged about killing young Nickell, wrote that in October 1902 he had met George Roberts, the barkeep in the Scandinavia Saloon, in Kansas City and he had told him that it was Horn's double who made these statements. The testimony of the police physician based on his service diary again confirms this assumption because having broken his jaw at that time Horn could not speak.

Discrepancies in the so-called "confession" concerning the distance and the place from which Willie Nickell was shot, clearly indicate that Horn was not familiar with the spot where the murder took place. The curses which litter the text also make an impression that this document was "doctored" because Horn was known for never cursing. Moreover, there was a statement of Thomas C. Allen who worked for LeFors as an agent saying that LeFors asked his friend W. D. Smith to write the letters in which he was asking for someone who could help him to fight a band of rustlers in Montana. In another words, LeFors' goal was to obtain a record of conversation with Horn which he later could adjust as he needed. Therefore, there is no doubt that a web was woven from the very beginning in which Horn was supposed to get entangled.

LeFors' character had to be taken into consideration also. A number of ranchers from southern Wyoming claimed that he was a corrupt individual who would do anything for money. In addition to the announced reward, his actions were motivated also by a promise made by Frank A. Hadsell, his boss, that in the case that he would find the murderer, he could get any job in the state government. Finally, the fact that LeFors never worried much about the truth can be supported by a chapter of his memoirs in which he claims that as a young boy he used to ride for the Pony Express. Any student of the American history knows that Pony Express existed briefly during 1860-1861, but LeFors was born in 1865.

Then there are many doubts and unanswered questions. Horn had no reason to kill Kels Nickell because he was never suspected of rustling by the cattle association. The notion that Horn wanted revenge for stabbing Coble ten years after the fact is just a speculation. The argument that it was a matter of a mistaken identity is hard to believe. Even though Willie wore his father's rain coat and hat, he was still shorter at least by a foot. At the distance of thirty or forty yards from which Willie was shot, an experienced scout and detective like Horn would have to know that the target in front of him was not an adult person.

Then why did Judge Scott refuse to take into consideration the feud between Miller and Nickell? Why was not Miss Kimmell called to testify in Horn's favor and to reveal the real killer? Why did Miller disappear from his ranch after Horn was found guilty? Why did Coble commit suicide six years later? Did he have only financial and health problems or did he feel that he could have done more for Horn? Why did Jennie Tupper, Lacey's secretary who had access to all materials dealing with the trial, state during a radio broadcast in 1930 that Horn had not shot Willie Nickell? Countless questions, but no answers.

Historical Notes

On July 19, 1901 Freddie Nickell, an eleven year old son of the Wyoming rancher Kels Nickell found his three year older brother William in a pool of blood less than a mile from their home. Two years later Tom Horn, the range detective who in the pay of large cattle companies grappled with cattle rustling in the vicinity of Cheyenne, was convicted and executed as a result of an overheard and under dubious circumstances obtained "confession".

During the inquest which followed immediately after the murder Horn as well as the Millers testified that at the time when the killing took place, they were not near the crime scene. Due to the lack of convincing evidence nobody was arrested, even though Kels Nickell when asked whom he would suspect, readily answered - the Millers.

Since the crime caused a major sensation and the public demanded catching the killer or killers and their punishment, the Cheyenne authorities announced a reward of one thousand dollars to anybody who would either bring in the perpetrators and or provide information leading to their arrest. Shortly thereafter, a certain Joseph S. LeFors, the Deputy U.S. Marshal motivated by this sum resigned from his current office so he could fully occupy himself with this case and also so that as a private person he could claim the reward (as a Deputy U.S. Marshal he would not qualify).

Joe LeFors who won his spurs by combating cattle rustlers in Montana focused his effort on Tom Horn. He claimed in his memoirs that he made this decision after a conversation with George Prentice, the foreman of Coble's' ranch who, when talking about Tom Horn, said among other things that Horn talked too much and if he wouldn't shut up, they would silence him by themselves. Influenced by this information LeFors invited Horn to the Inter-Ocean Hotel in Cheyenne where Horn consumed more alcohol than usual. Then, under the pretext of making final arrangements with regard to a job offer in Montana, he invited Horn to his office. There in the presence of the Deputy Sheriff Leslie Snow and the court stenographer Charles Ohnhaus he extracted the infamous "confession". The next day on January 13th,

1902, Tom Horn was arrested because of a suspicion that he was the killer of William Nickell.

The preparations for the trial took ten months. The prosecution as well as the defense tried to accumulate as many witnesses and other material as possible to secure the jury's decision in their favor. Thanks to the campaign unleashed by the local press, the entire case was highly politicized and under the influence of constant attacks against the defendant. Most of the population was convinced that Horn was guilty. During the trial the preponderance of the testimonies provided by the prosecution's witnesses was refuted or proven quite dubious. The information concerning time, dates and his whereabouts which Horn provided during the trial were, except for a few minor details, identical with those he provided during the inquest shortly after the murder. The only argument prosecutor Stoll could use to "irrefutably" prove the Horn's guilt was not only his "confession", but also the "fact" that he had bragged about this crime. After two weeks (October 10th through the 24th of 1902) of dramatic courtroom battles which drew attention in many western states, Horn was found guilty and condemned to death by hanging.

The defense attorneys asked immediately Judge Scott to announce a new trial, but the judge refused pointing out that Stoll was sick and the county could not afford to pay for another expensive trial like this one. Subsequently, Lacey announced his decision to appeal to the Wyoming Supreme Court justifying this step by pointing out numerous violations of the legal norms by the prosecution and again asked for a new trial, this time in a different county. Due to this request, the execution was postponed until the Supreme Court's decision.

On January 21st, 1903 the Cheyenne newspaper *The Daily Leader* (some sources mention *The Cheyenne Tribune*) caused a major excitement. According to its report Horn's friends were supposed to blow up a part of the prison by dynamite at the time when Horn would be on his daily walk and in this way to help him to freedom. A slip of toilet paper with Horn's handwriting with a message for John Coble just confirmed the plan. Needless to say, the sheriff's office was alarmed, the guards doubled and the plan fizzled. The question is, how did the aforementioned newspaper find out about it?

Hubert Herr, a local cowboy, was entrusted with the task to serve as a communication link between Horn and the outside. The trouble was that upon his release he managed to convince himself that the people who hired him may decide to cover their tracks which would include getting rid of him as well. Having panicked and at the same time being in need of cash he turned to chief editor of the Cheyenne newspaper and for five hundred dollars and, as the lore has it, sold out Horn as well as the conspirators. However, the real attempt to escape actually happened seven months later on Sunday, August 10th of the same year. Horn and his new prison mate James McCloud managed to overpower and tie up the unarmed guard Deputy Sheriff Dick Proctor, open both cells and run downstairs. For some reason they brought the deputy with them. The sheriff's office was empty, the deputy sheriff Snow was outside the building sitting on the steps enjoying the sunny morning. A scuffle took place when the prisoners tried to open the gun cabinet. Horn got hold of an automatic pistol while McCloud grabbed a rifle. Snow hearing noises inside the office decided to check it out. When he saw both prisoners, he didn't want to take any chance, slammed the door shut and ran for help. At that moment Horn and McCloud split. McCloud tried to reach a nearby stable and get a horse, but Horn ran toward the front of the courthouse. By that time a crowd of almost fifty people had gathered, some of them armed, and they confronted Horn. He ran east on Nineteenth Street, but then someone fired at him. The bullet creased his head, Horn fell, partly stunned, and then two men subdued him. McCloud did not fare any better. He ran into Sheriff Ed Smalley when he was trying to lead a horse out of a stall. The sheriff fired at him several times, and the horse reared so McCloud abandoned the horse and fled on foot. Between Twentieth and Twenty-First Streets he hid in a barn, but he was spotted by a girl who worked there. She alarmed police officer John Nolan who armed with a rifle rushed to the barn, aimed it at the building and yelled, "There he is. I can kill him now."

The bluff worked. McCloud stepped out of the barn with his both hands up. One may also add that the excited crowd was about to lynch both prisoners, but Sheriff Smalley gathered twelve additional deputies, so cooler heads eventually prevailed and the crowd dispersed.

On September 30th, 1903 the Wyoming Supreme Court in a statement consisting of eighty-six pages rejected the defense request for a new trial, accepted the defendant's "confession" as sufficient and set the date of the execution for November 20th. Lacey and Burke had only one option left, namely to ask the governor for clemency. During the remaining two months both lawyers feverishly collected material and witnesses who would testify on Horn's behalf. The defense as well the prosecution flooded the governor's office with testimonies dealing either with this case or the character of the individual witnesses. These documents, as expected, kept refuting the position of the opponents and were mutually contradictory. The absurdity of this process climaxed when Stoll claimed that he could bring a witness who actually saw Horn shooting. The governor soon realized the dubiousness of these claims and so decided to act independently. As the political pressure grew, the governor's opposition toward the death penalty and doubts about Horn's guilt began to weaken and eventually his personal interest prevailed. He even decided to ignore the statement of Miss Kimmell, the teacher from Iron Mountain, who named the killer. He argued that she had had an opportunity to testify to this effect during the trial and for some incomprehensible reason she did not do so.

On November 14th, Governor F. Chatterton made a public statement in which he announced that he agreed with the verdict of the District Court in Cheyenne. Six days later, November 20th, the sentence was carried out. According to the witnesses, Horn did not lose his calm; in the morning he had a breakfast, smoked a cigar and said good-bye to John Coble, his only friend who did not desert him. Then, at Coble's request, he wrote a letter in which he summarized all he knew about this crime. Lacey tried once more to convince the governor to change his mind, but in vain. Horn walked up on the scaffolding, listened to the song *Life Is Like a Mountain Railroad* and then signaled that he was ready to die. The last words he uttered with the hood on his head were said to the court official Joe Cahill assisting with the execution. "Joe, they tell me you're married now. I hope you're doing well. Treat her right."

An hour later his body was displayed in the Gleason Funeral Home. Tom's brother Charles picked it up the same day and transported it to Bolder in the neighboring state of Colorado. There, at Coble's expense, Horn was buried at the local cemetery. These days two grave stones mark the last resting place of both brothers.

Now let's look at Tom Horn himself. Let's start with his past. Horn was born in Missouri in 1860 in a farmer's family of German origin. When he was fourteen, he left Missouri and headed West like many young people at that time because due to the discovery of gold many western states offered employment opportunities not only in the mining industry but also in the other professions. Initially, Horn worked at railroad construction, but because he was a country boy he was looking for a job he was familiar with. Working with draft animals he eventually made it all the way to Arizona where he met Al (Albert) Sieber. From that moment on his life changed dramatically. Sieber noticed that Horn learned easily Spanish and so he correctly concluded that he would learn quite as easily another language, namely the language of the Apaches. He placed him as a sixteen year old youngster in an Indian camp in San Carlos Reservation for only one purpose - to learn the language, customs and traditions of the local Indians. Horn fulfilled this task so well that a year later it was hard to tell the difference between him and the other Apache warriors.

Then came the other part of his education. Under the leadership of Sieber himself Horn began to learn the trade of the anti- Indian scouts. He again excelled in this field to the point that when Sieber retired from his job, Horn not only "inherited" his rank of Chief of Scouts, but also was recommended for decoration for bravery. Both Generals George C. Crook and Nelson Miles who knew Horn personally praised his service in the Army during the Chiricahua war in their memoirs.

(However, many of today's historians question the veracity of information Horn provides in his autobiography "Life of Tom Horn, government scout and interpreter". They believe he embellished a great deal a number of facts, particularly those pertaining to his person, and placed himself in the forefront of events which transpired during the war with the Chiricahua. They namely question the stories that he had stayed in an Indian village of Chief Pedro, spoke fluent Apache and consequently was given the title of a Government Interpreter, and finally that Geronimo insisted only on negotiating with him rather than with the military officers. Last, but not least, is his claim that he convinced Geronimo to surrender to General Miles. It is Lieutenant Charles B. Gatewood who has been traditionally credited with this accomplishment.)

In 1886 after the removal of Geronimo and the rest of Chiricahua, the unit of the Indian scouts was disbanded and Horn had to look for another job. He tried silver mining in the local mines, but then he began to look for a job where he could apply his experience from the reservation. In 1888, he became a deputy sheriff in the Gila County and in the same year he became famous for winning first prize in the Phoenix rodeo.

In 1890, he began to work for the Pinkerton Agency in Denver, but attending trials, writing reports and working under a close supervision did not please him. Horn was a man accustomed to making his own decisions and also bearing full responsibility for them. In 1894, he quit the detective agency and offered his service to the cattle company Swan Land and Cattle in southern Wyoming where rustling reached a critical level. The big ranches showed consistent losses while newcomers who arrived with a couple of cows could within a few years claim ownership of pretty sizable herds. They had to be only skillful with a rope, know how to change a brand and not to be afraid. The risk, after all, was not too great. The courts in Cheyenne were controlled by Democrats who sided with small ranchers and any time the foremen of big ranches filed charges against people suspected of rustling, the courts let them go because of "insufficient" evidence. At this time the legend about Tom Horn as an assassin paid by some members of the cattle association, and who kept shooting undesirable settlers and small ranchers, was born. I used the word *legend* because in spite of the firmly rooted beliefs of some old-timers that Horn killed many people, not a single murder was proven to him.

According to the testimony provided by W. C. Irwin, the president of the cattle association, Horn in 1895 offered his services to the Wyoming governor, W. A. Richards, saying that he could get rid of the nuisance once and for all. All he wanted was a down payment of $350 to buy horses and provisions and, in case he succeeded, the balance of $5,000. When asked how he wanted to do it, Horn just remarked that he had a tested "system" which unlike the others was quite reliable. The governor became nervous, and when Horn realized that his offer would not be accepted, he left. However, there were some members of the association who allegedly showed interest in his "system" and invited him to their ranches. According to this legend, his "system" consisted of two or three warning letters and if the particular thief decided to ignore them, then a shot from an ambush would follow.

It is generally believed that shortly thereafter Horn shot certain William Lewis and Fred U. Powell whose ranches were located about forty miles northwest of Cheyenne. There were no doubts that Lewis was a rustler who specialized in butchering the stolen cows and selling their meat in town. Moreover, it was known that he got into arguments with many people who eventually threatened him with death. Actually, somebody fired at him twice but Lewis got away without a scratch.

Then at the beginning of August 1895 he ran out of luck. When a sheriff from Cheyenne arrived to the scene of the crime, he found Lewis' dead body lying next to a wagon loaded with a freshly butchered cow. Lewis was shot three times and all three wounds were mortal. One can also add that it happened four weeks before Lewis was acquitted during a trial in Cheyenne.

Powell, just like Lewis, received three warning letters. According to a Cheyenne newspaper Powell sold all his cattle, but refused to leave the area. Six weeks after Lewis' death he and his help, Andrew Ross, were repairing a fence, when suddenly a shot cracked, Powell collapsed mortally wounded and Ross ran away to the neighboring ranch.

During the inquest which took place in Natrona County the jury confirmed Horn's alibi. Horn could prove that during the time of the Lewis shooting he was visiting a place called Bates Hole. As to the murder of Powell, Horn was not charged with this crime. Moreover, Powell's widow stated several years later that her husband had been shot because of a quarrel with one of their neighbors. Chip Carlson states in his biographic work about Tom Horn that, according to one of the ranchers residing at Horse Creek, Horn's job was to catch the rustlers and not to shoot them. As for Lewis, it was his grandfather who shot him because he was stealing their cows.

In spite of all that, people were convinced that it was Horn's Winchester which fired those deadly shots. Consequently, he got a reputation of being a dangerous killer which resulted in the fact that his mere presence caused fear in anyone whose conscience was not all that clean. After the death of these two rustlers, the cattle stealing came to a sudden halt because the people suspicious of stealing either stopped to steal or left the area.

In this connection one can quote Fergie Mitchell whose ranch was located near Laramie. One of her new neighbors moved in the area in the spring with eleven cows. In the fall of the same year he drove to sale in town forty yearlings. Any attempts to catch the guy red-handed failed and so the other neighbors asked Horn to stop by and find the place where he hid the stolen cows. Horn arrived and quite openly rode on the pastures belonging to the neighboring ranches. Within three weeks three ranchers, including the new one, sold their properties, moved away and since that time not a single cow was missing.

In 1898 shortly after the breakout of the Spanish-American War, General Maus (the same Maus who as a lieutenant took part in the shootout with the Mexicans) received an order to look up Horn and hire him for the Cuban expedition. Horn agreed and was put in charge of all draft animals transported from Florida to Cuba. Then he took part in the battle for San Juan Hill where a quick and reliable ammunition delivery secured the victory of the American troops. While in Cuba, Horn contracted yellow fever and returned to Wyoming before the actual end of the war. There he got acquainted with John Coble, manager of a cattle company owned by Frank Bosler. Coble took a liking to Horn and often invited him to his ranch where he spent many evenings listening to Horn's stories about his adventurous past in Arizona.

As expected, the moment the word got out that Horn was in Cuba, the cattle rustling began to spread again. Particularly in the northwestern part of Colorado called Brown's Park, the thieves operated quite openly and without restrain. It is possible that they would have gotten away with it for a long period of time if one of the ranches had not been owned by Ora Haley. Haley, one of the big ranchers in Wyoming, employed Horn as a detective even before his departure to Cuba. Once Horn recuperated to the point that he could ride a horse, Haley asked him to move to Colorado and get a list of people suspicious of rustling.

Horn arrived in Colorado in the spring of 1900. Using the name of Hicks or Hix he visited various ranches and pretended he was interested in purchasing cattle. During this time he developed friendship with many local ranchers and, drawing on the information they offered, he focused his attention on a certain Madison Rash and Isom Dart. Here it is necessary to say that Rash had a reputation of being an honest citizen who even served as the president of the local cattle association. However, his herd consisting of about seven hundred heads originated under questionable circumstances. Horn changed his role and probably his name as well and got hired as a cook on Rash's ranch.

The overwhelming evidence that both men were without any doubt rustlers surfaced sooner than expected. Eventually, Horn became a witness to a quarrel between Rash and Dart in a ravine where Dart butchered a stolen cow. The reason for having this argument was, as it is quite often among the thieves, that Rash accused Dart of stealing some money from their last theft. Horn resigned, passed the information to Haley and waited for his decision. Everything indicated that it was Haley who gave Horn the go-ahead to apply his "system".

In the early summer Rash found a letter nailed to the door of his cabin in which the author demanded that he and Dart stop rustling and leave the county. Rash, having many friends among the local ranchers who were involved in rustling as well, decided to ignore this warning. That, however, cost him his life. On July 8th in the morning during breakfast, three shots ended his double-faced career.

Isom Dart, a freedman whose original name was Huddleston, specialized in stealing horses. When he met Rash, he extended his "profession" to cattle rustling. After Rash's death it was generally believed that the cattle would stop disappearing, but the foremen of big ranches, including the one owned by Haley, again reported thefts of young calves and heifers. Moreover, the local ranchers began complaining about stolen horses. By the end of September, Horn made a list of people suspected of rustling public. It also contained the name of Dart as a horse thief. Dart felt instinctively that his life was in danger and so he and two other men, Rash's friends, sought refuge in a log cabin located in a sparsely inhabited area of Brown's Park. On October 3rd, early in the morning when all three men stepped out of the cabin to saddle up their horses, a shot rang out and Dart collapsed shot in the head. The other two men rushed into the cabin, barricaded the door and spent there the whole day, but never saw the shooter.

The case of Rash and Dart is the only one in which we can say with considerable certainty that Horn was killing in the pay of big ranchers. This is partly because he mentioned it indirectly in the letter addressed to LeFors dated January 1st, 1902, in which he says that he stopped rustling in Brown's Park during one summer, and partly also because of the statement made by Hi Bernard, the foreman of Haley's ranch, that he paid Horn for this job one thousand dollars.

In order to understand Horn's mentality we have to look at the time he spent in Arizona, the time which formed his character and life philosophy. During the ten years he spent in the San Carlos Indian reservation, out of which six of them were actually war years, he had an opportunity on many occasions to be a witness to violence as a last but effective way to solve the conflict, particularly in those cases when the non-violent ways failed. The regular breakouts of Chiricahua Apaches from the reservation, the bloody attacks on the local and Mexican settlers and then returns to the reservation and promises that it would not happen again very strongly resemble the fruitless effort of the Wyoming ranchers to stop rustling by legal means. On the basis of this experience Horn soon arrived at the conclusion that there were situations when only violent means could solve a particular problem. The use of the Army against the roving Chiricahua and consequently death of many warriors which eventually resulted in their removal to Florida supports this position.

There are two kinds of violence. Violence committed by an individual and violence committed by a society. The use of military force or the carrying out of a death penalty, for example, are only different variants of societal violence. However, there is a certain difference between societal violence and violence committed by an individual. Violence committed on behalf of a society is usually in the interest of the majority and because it is the society which determines against whom the violent means will be used, it gains certain legitimacy. However, Horn by defining the "enemy" and morally justifying his elimination by himself erased this fundamental difference. (See Raskolnikov in Dostojevsky's novel *Crime and Punishment*.)

There were two strong undercurrents conflated in Horn's psyche. On one hand, a strong sense of honesty, justice and honor[1] imbued undoubtedly by Sieber, and on the other, a willingness to put them through even by violent means - a combination of which is not only dangerous but in a modern society unacceptable. However, Horn was firmly convinced that in addition to the financial gain he was acquiring, he was also doing the society a valuable service.

Was Horn a maniac, schizophrenic or a psychopathic killer as he was depicted by many during the trial? According to people who knew him personally - hardly. At the same time, we have to admit that he was no saint. Numerous saloon brawls attest to the fact that when under the influence of alcohol he demonstrated certain propensity for violence. (In the case of the broken jaw in Denver he unfortunately misjudged his opponent who was a Colorado boxing champion.) Horn was definitely a product of a society in which, due to the absence of a functioning legal system, violence was the indispensable component of the everyday life. The West after the Civil War was full of dubious characters, misfits and just criminal elements who surface practically always after any longer warlike conflict. Honest citizens who made their livings under harsh conditions were forced to resort to violence as the last option to protect their modest property.

Horn knew that fear was a strong motivator and so he decided to use it as a central component of his system. He never refuted the wild rumors about his person. On the contrary, he didn't mind embellishing them. As to his reputation,

---

[1] *Horn never mentioned people who paid him even when it might have saved his life.

he used to say that it was "stock of my trade". In another words, the more people are afraid of me, the better.

Here also belongs his quote made when talking to LeFors: "Killing men is my specialty. I look upon it as a business proposition, and I think I have a corner on the market". Obviously, he did not realize that the moment his position would weaken, all his enemies would rush to demand his liquidation.

Horn outlived his time - partly because justice in the hands of a few individuals was an anachronism and partly because the political power of the people whose interests he was defending was waning. The capability to influence public affairs no longer depended on the size of herds of cattle, size of the pasture land or, for that matter, size of the bank account but rather on the amount of votes. The local politicians grasped this very quickly, and the only person who did not was Tom Horn. He hardheadedly stuck to his principles and values. Then beset by melancholy and frustration over the loss of the world he knew and which was to his liking he drowned his feelings in alcohol. Subsequently, the otherwise quiet and reticent man became a rogue and braggart, and that, in words of Miss Kimmell, caused his fall.

Born in Czechoslovakia, Jiri Cernik immigrated to the United States in 1967 where he earned an MA in German language and literature at George Washington University in Washington DC. He has worked at Foreign Service Institute, Educational Bureau of the U.S. Department of State as a Language Training Supervisor developing basic as well advanced curriculum and textbooks. In addition to his work in the field of linguistics and language pedagogy he was interested also in American history, particularly in the settlement of the American West. He has traveled extensively throughout all states west of the Mississippi and wrote several novels, stories and non-fiction works dealing with this area and people who settled it. Two most popular works published in the Czech Republic are The Wild West (Divoký Západ, 2003), dealing with special social groups such as lawmen, men of the cloth, trappers and prospectors, and With a Tomahawk against the Muskets (S tomahawkem proti mušketám, 2011) a two volume detailed history of the Indian Wars covering the period from 1621 to 1890. In 2015 he published his first book in the USA, The Trail of the Silver Horseshoes, a collection of stories about the American West. In addition to his writing, he also conducted lectures at Charles University in Prague and the U.S. Embasy for the general public. He is retired and lives with his wife in Needmore, Pennsylvania where for many years they raised and showed Morgan horses. Jiri Cernik is a member of the Western Writers of America.